What lurks beneath the ice?

Marine biologist Sam Aston is hired to explore a series of subterranean caverns deep beneath the Antarctic. Somewhere within this lost world of magnificent caverns and underground seas lies a source of limitless clean energy, but something guards this treasure. As enemies bent on obtaining this world-changing resource for themselves close in from above, Aston and his team plunge further into the depths, and discover they are not the first to come this way...and they are not alone.

As the death toll continues to mount, Aston and his companions are forced to uncover secrets hidden far beneath the ice. Danger lurks at every turn as they face the deadly threat of the OVERLORD.

Praise for Overlord and the Sam Aston Investigations

"Renegade marine biologist Sam Aston is back for a second outing in what is shaping up to be a must-read aquatic adventure series! Danger and intrigue lurk both above and below in this action-filled, white-knuckle romp with a breathtaking conclusion!" —Rick Chesler, author of *Sawfish*

"Everything you'd want from a monster story – great characters, a remote location and a creature with bite! Mixing history and lore with science and action, David Wood and Alan Baxter have penned a thriller that is hard to put down." — Jeremy Robinson, author of *Island 731*

"Bone-cracking terror from the stygian depths! A creature thriller that is both intelligent and visceral. I could hear the Jaws soundtrack playing on repeat, although ~~th~~ · *might have been my heart poundin*⟨ ⟩ *ito the Mist*

OVERLORD

DAVID WOOD | ALAN BAXTER

Adrenaline Press

OVERLORD

Published by Adrenaline Press
Santa Fe, New Mexico, USA
www.adrenaline.press

PROLOGUE

Wilkes Land Crater, Antarctica, 1911

Michael Thornton questioned again the wisdom of the expedition as he trudged through the featureless white of the Antarctic. He was pretty sure he had frostbite in at least two toes. A permanent layer of ice coated his clothes, the fur lining of his thick hood, even his beard and mustache. His eyelashes waged a constant battle with the ice, and two frozen daggers of snot hung from his nostrils.

A layer of new snow crunched beneath his heavy boots as he winced into the frozen wind, flurries of blizzard regularly reducing visibility to little more than a few yards. Then there would be a momentary break in the weather, he would see across vast vistas of rough white landscape, and hope would briefly kindle, only to be extinguished as the landscape was obscured once more moments later. Despite those flashes of optimism, he wondered if he would ever see the rest of the party again. But at least he wasn't alone.

He would never admit his fears to Gavin Lee, stumbling along beside him. He was grateful for his companion's presence. A better man might wish Gavin the safety of the camp and the company of the rest of the scientific expedition, but Michael was terrified of being lost alone. Perhaps it was a strange way to think about things, but while he was desperate not to die out here, the thought of dying alone was infinitely more terrifying.

Gavin tripped, went down on one knee, his thick gloves sinking into the snow as he caught himself from falling flat on his face. The man stayed down, his back arching and sinking with labored breaths. Michael hauled his friend back to his feet, tried to flash an encouraging smile through the curtain of ice-flecked facial hair. Gavin gave a weak nod of thanks and pushed ahead again. He was stoic, no question about that. The expedition to investigate the possibility of volcanoes, or volcanic vents and potential magma deposits beneath the surface that might support life, had been met with a certain amount of ridicule by the scientific community. Nevertheless, Michael still believed in the project. He was certain the Antarctic held secrets that brave and determined men could reveal. The area of Wilkes Land Crater had seemed the best possibility during his research, and he maintained that conviction. Being caught in a sudden and unexpected blizzard while out on their own hadn't been part of any plan, however. He gritted his teeth and pushed on. He could not die now. He refused to even consider it. There had been too much interest in Antarctica during the early years of the twentieth century and he'd be damned if he'd lose his opportunity after getting this far. All the recent treks to the South Pole looking for possible new sources of natural resources couldn't be ignored. His would be successful. It had to be.

"I'm not sure how long I can go on," Gavin shouted over the wind. "Can't feel anything below the knee."

"Push on, man." Michael clapped him on the back. "We must be getting near to the crater. Don't quit on me! This weather will pass. The others will meet us at the destination. That was the plan if we got separated, remember?"

Gavin nodded. "Bloody ignominious way to die, from bad weather," he said with a wry laugh.

"Well, it's always the biggest danger down here, I suppose. But we won't die. Not today." He hoped he wasn't lying.

"I always thought I'd be more likely to expire from a monster than a blizzard." Gavin grinned, his lips blue beneath a mustache that was as much icicles as hair. "I really wanted to see the pyramids." He leaned forward as they pushed up a steep rise, the edges of the crest glimpsed occasionally through the swirling snow.

Gavin wanted to talk, Michael realized. Probably trying to keep himself distracted from the pain and exhaustion. It was a smart move. "I know you believe all those old legends, Gav, but I really doubt they're true." He would talk, but he wouldn't give any credence to unscientific nonsense.

They reached the top of the rise and the blanket of white swept down from their feet, disappearing into the storm.

"Better watch our step here," Michael said, straining to see the lay of the land.

"They're bloody real," Gavin said, almost too quietly to be heard.

"What's that?"

Gavin pointed, out across the crater. "We're here! This is the Wilkes Land Crater."

Michael looked in the direction Gavin indicated, saw only thick clouds of snowflakes gusting in loops and whorls. "I don't see anything."

"Just watch. Wait for a gap in the blizzard."

Michael strained to see something, anything within the cloud of white. He was about to question the man's sanity when a break opened and he saw clear across the huge expanse. He gasped.

"Do you see it?" Gavin asked, more animated than he had been in hours. "I'm not hallucinating, am I?"

"I saw... something." Michael frowned. Surely they had been mountains. Strangely regular in size and shape, with weirdly straight edges, perhaps. But surely natural.

They had to be.

"I think the storm is passing," Gavin said.

He appeared to be correct. The two men stood at the ridge, patient as the howling wind dropped to patchy gusts over the course of a few minutes, then to little more than an intermittent breeze. The flurries of snow thinned, even occasional shafts of sunshine breaking through brief rents in the thick cloud cover. After a few more minutes, the blizzard had stopped completely and they stood staring across a wide bowl of featureless white.

"They're real," Gavin said again.

Michael couldn't believe he was looking at pyramids, thickly covered in snow, but the shape was unmistakable. "Surely just oddly shaped mountains," he said. "There must be a geological explanation for them."

Gavin shook his head. "They look like pyramids to me. That can't be more than a mile, don't you think? Let's check them out."

Michael could think of no reason not to. The rest of the expedition hadn't yet arrived, but this crater was the meeting point, so they would surely be here soon. Unless they had fared worse than Gavin and himself. He chose not to continue that train of thought for the moment. They could investigate the strange range and keep an eye out for the arrival of their friends at the same time.

With renewed vigor, they crunched across the fresh snow. As they approached the pyramids, looming high above them, Michael still couldn't tell if they were man-made or not. The edges revealed themselves to be less regular under the snow as they neared, the overall shape less defined up close. But was that the natural weathering of a man-made shape over millennia, or had Mother Nature's hand sculpted a natural, vaguely pyramidal shape into something more refined?

"Look there." Gavin pointed.

An opening lay shadowed against the relentless white. It appeared to be a cave of some kind. A fissure in the rock, heading into darkness. Snow whipped up again, the blizzard beginning to gain a second wind.

"It's shelter, at least," Michael said.

The two men headed into the cave, wincing against the renewed gale and blustering snow. Once they entered the blessed safety, still and quiet at last, Michael realized his exhaustion again. His legs ached, his toes burned with possible frostbite, his whole body trembled with fatigue. He sat down to rest, about to call his friend to rest beside him. But Gavin was clearly renewed, fueled by wonder at the bizarre discovery.

"This goes deeper," he said, taking a few steps into the darkness. He pulled out a flashlight, the remarkable portable device invented by David Misell only a dozen or so years previously, and shined it down the length of the shadowed passage. "A long way deeper!"

Sighing, Michael hauled himself back to his feet and followed. The last thing they needed was for the two of them to become separated. "We'll check a little way, but not too far," he said. "We can come back properly equipped once we've rejoined the rest of the team."

They wound deeper into the cave as it gradually sloped downward. As they descended, it grew warmer. At first Michael thought it was simply a matter of getting out of the wind, but the rise in temperature seemed greater than that would account for. Was it too much to hope that the theory about volcanic vents might hold true? That it might be this easy to prove?

"You feel that?" he asked. "The warmth?"

Gavin came to a sudden halt. "Look there."

It took Michael a few seconds to accept what he was seeing. Lines had been carved into the frost-encrusted rock up ahead.

"It looks like cave paintings," Gavin said.

"Pictographs," Michael corrected, not sure he believed it even though he saw quite clearly the distinct designs. "It almost resembles language of some kind."

They moved closer, Gavin playing his flashlight beam slowly left and right. "It's remarkable. But who…?"

With a crack and a sudden, stomach-churning lurch, the floor gave way beneath them. They half-tumbled, half-slid in the darkness, Gavin's flashlight flying free from his grasp and blinking out as it bounced end over end.

In the sudden blackness, Michael lost all sense of time and distance. He wondered briefly if perhaps they'd fall into darkness forever, then he slammed into something unforgiving and everything went black.

As consciousness slowly returned, bringing with it a pounding headache, Michael pulled himself into a sitting position. He swallowed down a wave of nausea. He scanned his surroundings and his eyes fell on Gavin.

His companion spun around, excitement clear in his wide eyes and eager grin. "You're awake! Good to have you back."

They were in a massive cavern, dark gray rock curving up and away from them. Michael realized he was seeing that without the aid of flashlights. "Why can I see?" His voice was a little slurred, as though he were drunk. His words blared in his ears like a trumpet. He pressed his fingers to his temples and let out a low groan. He felt hungover, and wished he were inebriated instead. He probably had a concussion. Not good. Not good at all.

"Yes, it's this odd growth on the walls."

Michael blinked, his vision slowly regaining a sharper focus. Glowing softly green, vein-like striations wound across the cavern like twisting vines. Michael almost imagined the weak light pulsing, as if blood pumped through from some distant, subterranean beating heart.

Deposits of a strange, neon green crystalline substance punctuated the walls between the vines.

Michael pulled himself to his feet, ignoring the headache and nausea, the incredible sights before him taking over his thoughts. He looked closer, and saw the veins appeared to be organic, perhaps some kind of lichen or mold. It was pliant beneath his finger as he pressed it and his glove came away with a pale green luminescence that quickly faded. He broke off a small protuberance of rock containing a similarly-glowing piece of the crystal. It took some little effort, but snapped after he applied strong leverage with his gloved fingers. Using his teeth, he pulled the glove from his other hand and dug into the deep pocket of his jacket for a small sample jar no bigger than a standard test tube. He carried half a dozen, thankfully unbroken from the fall. He put the sliver of rock and crystal inside and screwed the lid back on tightly, then returned the slim jar to his pocket.

As he tugged his glove back on, they began to explore further. The space was huge, stalactites extending down from above, gently dripping, the water echoing quietly as it fell. They made their way around large stalagmites, stepped over small pools of gathered water that was not frozen. Realizing that, Michael checked and discovered no frosty patches on the walls. The temperature in the place obviously remained above freezing, much warmer than the many degrees below zero outside. He paused to take a sample of the water.

As they resumed their trek, a feeling of wrongness crept over him. He felt like an intruder in an alien world. Everything around him was gently lit by the glowing pale green of the viney growths, the shadows where the light didn't reach inky black in contrast.

On the far side of the cavern, they found a strange door. It was a solid slab of shiny black rock, like a kind of obsidian, carved with a strange script unlike anything Michael had ever seen. No, scratch that. Unlike anything he had seen except the markings in the cave before they fell. He'd only had a brief look at the pictographs up above, but he was certain they strongly resembled the marks he now inspected. And it was far too neat to be anything but deliberately fashioned. It had to be language. "This isn't possible," he whispered.

"And yet here we are," Gavin said. His excitement had given way to trepidation, the concern clear in his voice.

Michael was glad to hear the fear there, because he thought they should both be alarmed by these discoveries. As he stared at the door, the sense of wrongness, of alienness, grew stronger.

"How can there be a door down here, far beneath the surface of the Antarctic?" Michael asked. "How far did we fall? It seemed like a long way."

Gavin didn't answer, just ran his gloved fingers over the carved symbols.

"We should go back to where we fell in," Michael said. "Try to climb our way back up and find the others. Then we can return and explore properly."

Again, Gavin said nothing. Then he put both hands to the door and leaned his weight into it.

"What are you doing?"

But Gavin gave no indication he was even aware of Michael's presence. He threw his shoulder against the door. With a loud scraping, it slid open. Gavin headed through. Michael called for him to come back, but was again ignored. Hardly any of the glowing crystal or vines lit the passage beyond, and Gavin slowly vanished into blackness.

Biting down his annoyance, Michael followed. Perhaps it was simple fear, or maybe the recent blow to the head, but the darkness seemed alive, as though it were squeezing him. "Gavin!" Michael called, but felt unable to raise his voice to a shout. He saw movement up ahead. "Gavin," he said again, grabbing at his friend's coat, but Gavin jerked his arm free and kept going.

"What's got into you, man?" Michael said. He took a step to follow, then heard a soft whick. Warm wetness covered his face in a sudden spray and he tasted a metallic flavor that could only be blood. Bladder loosening, spreading warmth down his leg, he stumbled back, patting himself all over to be sure he wasn't injured. As he moved quickly backward, returning to the low light of the glowing cavern, he saw a stone the size of a bowling ball bounding toward him from out of the darkness. As the stone rolled over, he saw it wore Gavin's face. Not a stone at all, but Gavin's head, neatly separated from the rest of him.

Michael cried out, caught a glimpse of Gavin's body being dragged down the tunnel into the dark. In the half-light he saw what had hold of his friend, and he let out a throat-rending scream. Blinded by panic, he turned and ran.

CHAPTER 1

Cape Town, South Africa

Sam Aston swam with his legs only, letting his arms trail as he curved around a rock and over a bed of brightly colored coral. Hundreds of small fish darted past, then shifted direction in that mesmerizing way, as if they each shared a small part of a single brain, able to make a unified decision. Aston enjoyed the embracing silence, but for the bubbles of his respirator rising up, glittering in the light. The cool water calmed him. Here he was at peace.

A sleek gray bull shark moved down from above, heading directly for him. Then another. From his left, two more approached, silent, deadly, relentless. Aston reached into a large net sack at his belt, pulled out a fish, its head removed. He lofted it in the water and into the waiting maw of the nearest shark. As the others drew closer, circling, he took out more fish, feeding casually left and right. He raised one hand, covered in a light chainmail glove, and waved to the gawping crowd in the dim light on the other side of the aquarium glass. Sometimes, if he didn't look in that direction, he could almost believe he was back in the open ocean.

But the illusion was always shattered when he had to leave the huge tank, if not before. The job was good, he got to work with the animals, caring and feeding, even taking part in a little research. But it was a big step down from the career he had left behind after the events at Lake Kaarme. He couldn't use his extensive marine biology qualifications any more than he could use his real name. Not until Chang was paid off, the mobster back in Australia still out for

Aston's blood. On this salary, that wouldn't be any time soon. Maybe one day Sam would save up enough to cover that black market debt and he'd be able to resume some semblance of a normal life.

He finished the feeding show, waved to the tourists and watched them drift away, disappointed. He didn't know what they expected, but they always seemed to think it was somehow an anti-climax. They probably hoped the tank's inhabitants would turn on him, take off limbs in clouds of blood like a scene from Jaws.

He lingered in the water as long as he thought he could get away with, then made his way back to the small ladder leading out of the huge tank, into the area out of bounds to the public. As he stepped into the noise of purifiers and filters, kicking off his fins, he saw Ashley Carter walking toward him. The way she moved her hips was enough to make his knees weak, not to mention everything about the rest of her. He'd asked her out a couple of times, but she'd always made some excuse, even while she gave him a sly smile. He got the feeling she wanted him to work for it, but wasn't going to make it easy for him. He would ask one more time, though he would also be careful not to act like a dick. If she refused him again, he'd back off. Maybe those smiles were just her trying to be polite while she had no intention of ever agreeing to a date. Sometimes it was hard to tell. But maybe now she had found him alone, out of sight of staff and public alike, for a reason. Perhaps she'd decided to take matters into her own hands.

She stopped halfway across the large room. "There you are, Pete. You have a visitor."

Aston did his best to mask his disappointment. What a fool. He really ought to know better. "Who is it?"

"What am I, your secretary? Bob told me to come get you. There's a visitor." Before he could answer, she smiled and walked off.

There it was again, that cheeky grin she always gave him. Surely she was playing games. So be it, he'd play along. But the idea that he had a visitor put him a little on edge. No one knew him here, even under his fake identity, let alone as Sam Aston.

He changed into his aquarium shirt and chinos, stowed his SCUBA gear, and headed out to the staff office. Bob was nowhere in sight, but a man in a tailored suit sat on the faux-leather lounge reserved for visitors. He was tall, and filled the suit with muscle rather than fat, and had a strong, confident face under a close crop of salt and pepper hair. Aston thought the guy had a kind of ex-military vibe about him, and found that unsettling.

He reached out a hand to shake. "I'm Pete Cartwright. You wanted to see me?"

The man stood, smiling warmly. "I'm Solomon Griffin, but everyone calls me Sol. It's nice to meet you, Sam."

Every warning nerve in Aston's body fired at once, adrenaline racing into his system. His hand felt suddenly trapped in the vice of Griffin's giant paw. Was this another of Chang's goons? How had they found him here? He had figured Cape Town was about as far from both Australia and Finland as he could get. His left fist clenched, ready to knock the guy on his ass if need be.

Sol obviously saw the concern in Aston's face. Not releasing the handshake, he gripped Aston's forearm with his other hand, but the touch was comforting rather than aggressive. "Relax. Your secret is safe. Can I buy you a cold one?"

Aston didn't like any of this, but one thing he definitely needed was more information. Even though he had finished for the day, this Solomon Griffin didn't need to know that. "I'm only on a break, but I have time for a cup of coffee. We can go to Café V. It's right here in the aquarium."

Sol flashed his warm smile again. "Sounds good."

They each got a stool at one end of the blue, neon-lit corner bar in Café V and waited in companionable silence while their order was filled. In those few minutes, Aston's mind ran through a hundred different scenarios of what this guy might want. And a hundred ways he might slip quickly and unnoticed from Cape Town at the first opportunity. He hadn't planned on being found, but he did have a bug-out bag in the room he rented not far from the aquarium. He could be on the road in less than an hour if necessary. But he didn't really want the disruption of running. It was a hassle, and it had taken him a while to develop a secret identity here, paying less than savory people for false papers, always at risk of becoming their victim instead of their client. He didn't want to have to go through all that again somewhere else.

Before he wound himself up too tightly about it, Sol turned to face him, still wearing that smile. He seemed so upbeat it almost came across as insincerity. "So! I'm assembling a team for a job that's right up your alley."

"How do you know who I am?"

"There are many ways to find people, Mister Aston, even in this big old world." To his credit, he kept his voice low so that no one else might hear the name Aston. "For now, how about we accept that I'm with people who have extensive resources, and let me tell you about the job."

Aston frowned, but chose to say nothing. He didn't like any of this, but let the guy talk.

Sol nodded. "I'm working for a company called SynGreene." He paused, as if an answer was expected.

"The green energy outfit, right? Solar power, home batteries, all that stuff. What would they want from me?"

"Well, I can't reveal too much due to non-disclosure agreements, which you would need to sign before you get the full story. But in a nutshell, we think we've located a new source of renewable energy. A genuinely world-changing new mineral. However, before we can mine it, we need a full environmental assessment. You know the kind of thing, the geology, flora, fauna, all that stuff. And some other things."

"What other things?"

Sol gave an apologetic shrug. "Things covered by the NDAs."

Aston sighed. "So where do I fit in? Surely there are thousands of other people qualified."

"Well, we need you mostly with regard to the fauna. And we need this on the quiet, so your desire to remain in hiding makes us think you're less likely to risk breaking any secrets. Plus we think some of your unique experiences make you a perfect fit."

Aston sipped coffee, thinking fast. Unique experiences? That just set off more alarm bells for him.

"We're offering decent compensation. Starting with thirty grand, US."

Aston raised his eyebrows. The exact amount required to cover his debt to Chang and give him a chance to restart. How much did these people know? Everything, it seemed. And the temptation was strong, but his instincts told him to turn this guy down with extreme prejudice. Sol presented as friendly enough, but there was clearly something under the surface the man was hiding. His real intent circled down there, like a shark in a shallow bay, awaiting its chance to attack. "Look, that's one hell of a tempting figure," Aston said. "But the last time I received an offer like that, things didn't turn out so well."

Sol nodded, laughed softly. "Yeah, we know all about Lake Kaarme."

"You saw Jo Slater's documentary."

"Of course," Sol said. "Who didn't, right? But we

know it's real even if ninety-nine percent of the population wrote it off as a giant hoax."

"And from what I've seen online, the whole thing seems to have damaged Jo's career more than helped it," Aston said. He winced internally at the mention of Slater, guilt chewing at him. He hated not backing up her story in public, not letting her know he was still alive, especially after the documentary had included an incredibly touching In Memoriam at the end. Her emotion on screen was real, he knew her well enough to see that. He told himself she was better off without him, but the truth was her documentary declaring him dead did more to help him hide from Chang than anything else. He'd stopped reading the online comments about it, even though he knew lots of people, especially the scientific community in Australia, still considered him missing rather than deceased. He wondered how much grief Jo Slater had received from the authorities over it. More guilt for him. But if she genuinely thought him dead, she was safe from his past and his future.

"Regardless of what the rest of the world thinks," Sol said, "we know the documentary was real."

"Just what are you playing at?" Aston's anger was more for himself, he knew, but it was easier to direct it at Solomon.

"I promise, everything with us is above board. We'd be happy to leave you to your exile, but it's not that simple."

"I'm pretty sure it is!"

Solomon paused, lips pursed. "I'm not supposed to tell you this, but we found a door."

"A door? Damn it, Griffin, I'm a marine biologist, not a carpenter."

"An unusual door."

Scenes from Slater's documentary flashed through Aston's mind. Her piece to camera about the mysterious door of carved stone, supposedly an entrance to the Hollow Earth, that had been lost when the explosives took out the beast down there under Lake Kaarme. Slater's film had included sketches drawn from her memory, but no footage was made at the time. They'd had rather more pressing concerns. Regardless, the doorway was real, and it mystified him constantly. But it was lost now. Could there be another? How many more? And where?

Sol nodded again, watching Aston work it out. "It's just like the one beneath Lake Kaarme."

Aston shook his head slowly. He wanted no part of any of this. Did he?

Sol cleared his throat. "The figure I offered, that's only the up-front payment to get you on board. We've been in touch with Mr. Chang in Brisbane, and he will accept it to clear all your debts with him."

"What? How do you know how to–?"

"When the mission is over," Sol interrupted. "We'll pay you that much again as your own salary. It's a lot of money for what will be a couple weeks' work at most."

Aston knew he would regret any agreement to go along with this frankly frightening turn of events, but he was tired of living with a price on his head. He imagined unknown years more swimming in tanks, feeding sharks for gawping tourists who were never satisfied. Last time, the chance to make good money and clear his debts hadn't worked out well at all though. Surely he couldn't be that unlucky twice?

"Rest assured," Sol added, "that our founder and chair, Arthur Greene, is no Ellis Holloway." He paused, watching Aston's face closely. "Admit it. You want to know what's behind that door as much as we do."

Aston swallowed the last of his coffee, then clunked the mug down onto the bar. "I'll take the job," he said resignedly. He raised a hand before Sol could speak. "But I have two conditions. One, I want evidence that Chang is paid and satisfied before I go anywhere. And two, I want full disclosure from day one."

Sol smiled. "You've got it." He reached out a hand to shake and seal the deal.

As Aston returned the handshake, he said, "But if it's anything like Lake Kaarme, I know what's behind the door."

"Really? What?"

Aston grinned at the well-dressed man. "Nothing good."

CHAPTER 2
V&A Marina, Cape Town, South Africa.

Jo Slater walked along the waterfront of the V&A Marina in Cape Town, questioning pretty much everything in her life. The two and three story blue and white port buildings to her left bustled with people as she threaded through the milling crowds heading onto ships going to exotic locations, or disembarking into Cape Town, eyes wide to capture whatever wonders might come their way. The city billed itself as the "Best Destination in Africa" and even without her foul mood, Slater was pretty sure she would scoff at that claim. Sure, it was nice, but better than Morocco? Or the savannahs of Zimbabwe? Kruger National Park? Victoria Falls? Hardly.

Table Mountain stood tall in the background behind the man-made expanse of Cape Town, and that was most definitely a breathtaking sight. She thought maybe she would rather be there right now. But she had a job to do, and a job was important these days after the debacle of the Lake Kaarme film. Of course there would always be a certain percentage of the population who considered anything a hoax. There was huge movement denying the truth of the moon landings, after all. And an equally large contingent convinced the attack on New York on September 11th, 2001 was the work of the government, or aliens, or the Illuminati. One thing for which humanity could always be relied upon was its consistent percentage of absolute idiots.

But the vitriol she had received for her documentary, the solid mockery from all quarters, had been brutal. And the network had told her, enthusiastically, that a bombshell like that was the perfect note to end the series on. Which was just another way of firing her, none too subtly. So she had been left treading water, unsure where to go with her career, the chances of ever being taken seriously as a genuine journalist more damaged than ever.

Then came Solomon "Call me Sol" Griffin, with his wide smile, sharp suit, and irresistible offers. Come and document this expedition, he had said, and SynGreene would fund a full new season of her show in exchange for those services. Similar format, bigger budget, new channel. It all seemed too good to be true. And if Jo Slater had learned anything in television, it was that too good to be true usually was exactly that.

But what choice did she have? There weren't any other offers on any tables. She thought it an odd arrangement, with virtually no information given, but Sol promised it would all make sense once she'd signed her NDA and learned the full story. And he had also pointed out that as her reputation was in tatters, no one would take her seriously if she broke those NDAs. That was a backhanded compliment if ever she'd heard one. Regardless, she needed the work.

So here she was in Cape Town, with a new team. Marla Ward, sound engineer, and Jeff Gray, cameraman, trailed along a few steps behind, smart enough to leave her to her thoughts. She'd been prickly with them both, and had apologized for it, but hadn't been able to shake off the black mood that hung over her. Marla, bless her, had been supportive and was intelligent and fun to have around. Jeff, not so much. As if on cue, the man coughed and laughed. Marla made a sound of disgust. Slater glanced back to see Jeff wiping ice cream from the front of his t-shirt with one palm, the melting cone dripping over the other. His huge backpack of equipment hung off his shoulders, made him stick his rotund gut forward like a ram. His wheeled case stood unattended in the crowd a yard or so from him. There had to be more than five grand's worth of camera gear in there and he acted like he'd forgotten all about it.

Marla shook her head, moved to stand beside the wheeled hard case while Jeff got himself fixed up. Marla was everything Jeff wasn't. Slim, short, mousey in appearance. But Slater had quickly learned not to judge this particular book by its cover. She had a firecracker personality when roused, happy to stand up for herself and anything she believed in. Marla was a competent and confident colleague. At least one of them was.

Slater tapped her foot while Jeff finished cleaning up. She missed Dave, who had been lost, like so many others, at Lake Kaarme. Dave, Carly, Aston, all gone. She swallowed the rising lump in her throat and had a moment of realization. It wasn't just the disruption to her career that was making her melancholy and on edge. It was the start of a new job, so like the last one that had ended in disaster and death. That had begun with a boat, and now she was headed to a ship to meet Sol and the rest of the expedition. To learn exactly what it was she had agreed to. No, she reminded herself. Not agreed to. Only agreed to hear about. She would sign the NDA, find out what the expedition was, and if it all seemed too dangerous or too crazy, she would walk away. The NDAs she, Marla, and Jeff signed would remain in effect. They wouldn't tell anyone anything. Besides, her reputation was in tatters, as Sol had so kindly pointed out. But they were under no obligation to go along if they didn't want to.

They moved on again and Slater saw Sol waving from the gangplank of a huge ship. Bright red, with a sharp, high prow, a crane in front of the bridge and a tall scaffold tower of antennas and satellite dishes above the bridge, it was an impressive sight.

"That's an ice-breaker," Jeff said, appearing beside her.

"Is that what it is?"

"Yeah. And since we're meeting here, I bet the expedition is to Antarctica." He immediately started bouncing in a weak imitation of a hip-hop dance. "Ice, ice baby!"

She rolled her eyes and nodded, figuring he was likely correct. The details of their mysterious invitation had been discussed at length on the flight over from Washington DC. Slater had assumed the expedition would be somewhere in Africa, but if Jeff was right about this vessel being an ice-breaker he was probably right about Antarctica too. Her entire perception of what might lie before them shifted dramatically sideways. She had been picturing heat and wild animals, maybe distant tribes. Now a chill ran down her spine despite the blistering sunshine, the perspiration beaded on her forehead cold, as she imagined nothing but ice and snow in every direction.

Sol walked down the ramp to the cement of the port to greet them, hand outstretched. She shook it, then introduced Jeff and Marla.

"Right on time," Sol said. "So glad you could make it."

"Jeff thinks this ship is an ice-breaker," Slater said.

Sol grinned. "He's right. There's some capacity for research, which we'll use to a certain extent, but mostly it's to transport us to Alpha Base."

"So that must be in Antarctica," Slater said, one eyebrow raised.

Sol's smile didn't change. "Come on up and I'll introduce you to the team. Everyone else is already here."

He turned and strode up the gangplank. With a sigh, Slater followed. A few people milled around on deck, some of them obviously sailors getting the ship ready to depart. But a couple of others looked like soldiers, paramilitary or perhaps private contractors. They were hard-eyed and calm, but seemed somehow coiled, ready for action. They made her immediately nervous.

Sol led her down steel steps and along a narrow corridor into a large cabin. A bar ran along one side, with portholes above it, coffee and cookies at one end, alcohol and glasses at the other. In the middle of the space stood an oval table with a handful of people seated around it. Other than the door they had entered by, one other door stood closed at the far end of the cabin.

"All right," Sol said. "Let me introduce the team. I'm the representative for SynGreene, obviously, but in terms of team skills, I'm your doctor. Officially, expedition physician."

Slater was surprised. The man didn't have the bearing of a medical professional at all. He was large and muscular, disciplined in bearing. She had thought he was almost certainly ex-military. Perhaps he was an Army doctor. He confused her, but people were endlessly surprising.

Sol indicated a large, heavily muscled, dark-haired man in olive green combats. This one definitely had the presence of a military man. "This is Anders Larsen, our geologist."

The man stood to shake hands and Slater chided herself again for being wrong. Had she completely lost her ability to recognize people? She doubted it. Perhaps both Sol and Anders Larsen might be a physician and geologist respectively, but she was convinced they were ex-military too. Why did that bother her? Did it matter?

Next was a fit and strong-looking woman, quite beautiful, Slater thought, with dark olive skin and thick black hair in a loose pony-tail. This one, at least, had the look of a scientist and not a soldier, though Slater had the distinct impression the woman would handle herself well in a fight if necessary. She exuded confidence. "This is Jahara Syed, our biologist," Sol said.

Slater shook the woman's hand, smiling, glad it wasn't a testosterone pool of a team. Always better to have more women around.

The last person at the table was a middle-aged man, maybe early forties, with neat brown hair and a chiseled chin. He wore new and expensive-looking clothes, had the air of money about him. Old family money, Slater guessed. He stood as Sol introduced him as Digby O'Donnell, expedition archaeologist.

"Call me Dig," the man said. "Everyone does. Digby is the name all the oldest males in my family share, and father hates me reducing it to Dig. So of course, that's exactly what I do."

"Nice to meet you," Slater said, suppressing a smile. She felt maybe her people radar was recalibrated now. The man's accent almost had dollar signs falling off it.

"So there's obviously a lot of extra muscle around coming along with us," Sol said. "No doubt you saw some of them on deck, and our expedition head, and provider of all funds of course, is Arthur Greene, head of SynGreene. But he won't be coming along. We'll keep in touch with him and keep him informed as we go. But this is the core group of experts." Sol stopped, frowning. "No, wait a minute, we're missing one."

The sound of a flush came from the closed door at the other end of the cabin, then the door opened and Slater's stomach dropped, her face went cold.

"Here he is!" Sol said. "Of course, you know our diver and demolitions expert, Sam Aston."

Slater's jaw dropped, her hands trembled, as Aston approached, a nervous smile painting his face.

"Hi, Jo."

CHAPTER 3

Alpha Base, Antarctica.

A ston sat in his cabin on the ice-breaker feeling sorry for himself. His jaw still ached from where Slater had punched him. She had a hell of a straight right. When he had first emerged from the bathroom back at Cape Town she'd stared at him for a good ten seconds in utter disbelief, then turned and strode from the room. But she didn't make it more than a yard past the door before she came hurtling back in and surprised him with a sock to the jaw that sent him reeling backward, seeing stars. As his head slowly cleared she had yelled at him, red-faced, something his ringing ears missed, then she stopped and stared again. As he hauled himself groggily to his feet, she said, "You let me think you were dead!" And the genuine hurt in her eyes had undone him.

He couldn't blame her for her fury. He deserved every last atom of it. He had needed to hide, needed to avoid Chang, and get his life together again. He honestly believed she would be safer without him, but he knew, deep in his heart he knew, that he could have trusted Jo Slater. That he should have trusted her. She was honorable. She wouldn't have sold him out. And he owed her better than this.

But at the time, head ringing from her blow, the rest of the team standing around agape, he had only said, "I'm so sorry. I know we need to talk about this, but please don't walk away from this job. I know how much it means to you. To your career. If you can't handle me being here, then I'll walk away."

Sol had tried to intervene and they had both turned on

him, told him to shut up. Aston had warned Sol days ago that there would be fireworks. As soon as he had learned that Jo Slater was coming in, he had told Sol it was a bad idea to have him, Aston, along. In truth, he'd nearly backed out right then. But the knowledge she was coming had unlocked something inside him, releasing a torrent of guilt. He had to face her. It was time to come clean. Perhaps they could repair something of their friendship. If not, at least they knew they could work well together, if she could get past or ignore this betrayal. It was a lot to ask. Back there, in the meeting room, Slater had turned on her heel and stalked out. Aston told Sol to go after her and he had made himself scarce. Sol had convinced her to come back, reconvened the meeting, and collected Aston from the deck, where he sat in the sunshine rubbing his jaw.

Sitting on his bunk now, Aston sighed. What an idiot he had been. There was so much broken between them that he needed to repair, but she wouldn't let him. Back there in the cabin in Cape Town he had seen something harden in her eyes, some shutter of defiance and self-preservation.

Back at the table, she had turned to Sol and said, "So, what's this job?"

Sol smiled. "Each of you needs to sign your NDAs here, then we go to Alpha Base on Antarctica. You get the full story there."

And that's where Aston and Slater had come briefly together, both protesting stridently that being transported to the literal end of the Earth before knowing the job trapped them into doing it.

"You have a choice," Sol had said. "Sign now, come along, and learn what there is to know. If you really want nothing to do with it, the ship will take you back again. But I'm sure you'll want to be involved." Then his face had hardened slightly and he'd added, "Besides, what choice do either of you really have? Your careers, your lives, pretty much depend on this expedition and what it can help you rebuild."

Sol's friendly veneer showed a crack then and Aston saw a hint of malice behind it. He had been affronted by the assessment, but also infuriated at its accuracy. Slater seemed to share his outrage. They looked at each other, him hopeful, her scowling, then both shrugged.

"Fine," Slater said. "Give me the forms."

She signed, had her cameraman and sound assistant sign theirs, then all three had left, Slater demanding to know where their cabins were. For more than a week, the time that it took to reach Antarctica, Slater had managed to prove that a ship could be a wasteland if you wanted to avoid someone. She had taken her meals in her cabin, insisted her crew do the same, and had avoided Aston at every turn. If she saw him coming, she simply turned and went the other way. If he managed to get close enough to talk to her, to apologize, to beg her to have a conversation with him, she blanked him, icy, and left.

She had every right to her anger, and he had no right to force her to talk with him. He supposed she'd have no choice but to interact with him eventually. Or he would get back aboard the ice-breaker and insist they return him to Cape Town. He'd leave her to have the job, the money, the career she deserved. It was the least he could do, but he hoped it wouldn't come to that.

Sol's voice over the PA interrupted his reverie, informing them that they were approaching landfall and Alpha Base. Whatever else, Aston was getting to see Antarctica. A rare experience. He headed up on deck to watch as the ship approached its destination.

Wrapped in a navy blue, fur–lined parka, Aston breathed deeply of the cold, salty air. The ocean all around them was slate gray under an overcast sky that merged seamlessly in the distance with the coast of Antarctica. As his eyes adjusted to the brightness, powerful despite the clouds, he picked out sharp edges of ice and snow, dark rock slicing through it here and there as the land cut into the sea. Then he noticed Slater standing at the rail not ten strides from him, her crew behind. The cameraman was Jeff Gray, Aston had learned, and the sound assistant was named Marla Ward. He got a lump in his throat, remembering Dave and Carly, counterparts to these two who had both died, horribly, at Lake Kaarme. What fate might await these unsuspecting folks? Then again, surely they had seen Slater's Lake Kaarme documentary. Did they consider the whole thing a clever hoax too? Were they along for the money, assuming anything exciting would be added in post-production, which was the prevailing theory on the Kaarme film? He realized they had been filming a sequence, capturing Jo Slater, intrepid reporter, arriving at the Antarctic continent. Slater waved a cut and they hung up their gear. Slater glanced over and saw Aston watching and her jaw hardened.

"Jo, please," he called over, not moving to get any nearer. "Can we talk?"

"What about?" she snapped. "The way you let me think you were dead? The way I tried to convince the world my film wasn't a hoax without any backup from others who were there, because they'd all died? The way my career fell apart while you could have been there to help me? The way I grieved for you, you asshole!"

Aston swallowed, licked his lips, searching for anything to say. At least she was finally talking to him. "I'm sorry," he managed, and it sounded weaker than saying nothing at all.

Slater turned and strode away around the deck, putting the bulk of the bridge tower between them. He wanted to follow, to try to smooth things over, but she was right. He was an asshole. What a total mess.

Jeff Gray approached him, smiling crookedly. The man had a way of being annoying, just by existing. The cameraman took a huge bite from a sandwich he had fished from his pocket and talked around the bulge of food in his cheek. "She'll calm down. Give her time."

Aston tried to ignore the enthusiastic mastication. "I don't know. She's got every right to be angry with me."

Gray shrugged. "She loses her temper with me all the time, but she always comes around."

"You worked with her for long?"

"A few months. I had my own production company but we... had a run of bad luck. The company was highly successful, just not profitable."

Aston frowned. "How is that possible?"

Gray gave him a condescending smile, ruined by the crumbs on his shirt and the speck of mayonnaise clinging to his lower lip. "You'd have to work in television to understand. A producer friend bailed me out and hooked me up with a job on Slater's show, supposedly until I could get a new project up and going. But, you know what happened to her show, right?"

"Yeah. Hopefully it'll get resurrected here. With you on camera, I guess that's a new start."

Gray's laugh was a high-pitched giggle, incongruous with his oversized body. "Talk about back to basics, huh? How the mighty have fallen. Still, I'm not complaining. I'm glad to be working."

Aston wondered what this guy's story really was. It seemed the man had glossed over some significant details. Marla stood back a little, listening in, but saying nothing. She flicked a little smile to Aston when he glanced at her and rolled her eyes. He smiled back. He had decided immediately upon meeting her that he liked her. She seemed like the sort of person he could get along with. He and Marla had enjoyed a few conversations on the voyage, while Slater wasn't around. But the young sound engineer always seemed a little guilty, like she was maybe betraying Slater by talking to Aston at all. Regardless, he liked her. Smart and interesting. Unlike the generally unpleasant Jeff Gray. "Well," he said. "I guess we're all lucky to be working."

"Was it all a bunch of crap?" Gray asked suddenly.

Aston raised his eyebrows, surprised the man would question him about that. "Kaarme?"

Gray nodded.

"No, it wasn't. It was all true.There were no special effects in Jo's film. We lost a lot of good people."

"Whoa," Marla whispered. In all their conversations over the past week, she had never brought it up. Gray just stared, momentarily motionless. Aston wondered if the man was trying to decide whether to believe him or not.

"Anyway," Aston said. "When we get back from this trip, I plan to go public and make sure everyone knows that. If Jo will let me."

"I think that ship may have sailed," Marla said, coming to join them at last. "People pretty much have their minds made up. And you coming back, after all that stuff about you dying there? It'll only make people more certain that Jo made everything up."

Aston hadn't thought of that and it annoyed him. She was dead right. It had been an olive branch he intended to offer Slater, to try to make things better. But maybe it would do more harm than good. What a mess. The phrase kept rolling around in his mind like a mantra.

"Oh well," he said. "I guess I'll ask Jo what she'd prefer I do. If she ever talks to me again."

Marla laughed. "She'd like you to jump overboard into the freezing ocean, I think. Preferably with something heavy tied to your ankles."

Aston smiled, infected by Marla's easy confidence.

"Yeah, I reckon you're right."

"I love your accent."

Aston looked down at Marla, a good foot shorter than him, looking up through her sandy fringe. "Really?" She hadn't mentioned it before.

"That wasn't a come on, by the way. I just really dig it."

Aston was slightly disappointed by that comment, but did his best to hide it.

"Australian, right?" Jeff Gray said, clearly trying to re-insert himself into the conversation.

"No, you damn Martian!" Marla said. She rolled her eyes again, grinning, and strolled off in the direction Slater had gone.

"I knew it was Australian or some other kind of British. You can't really tell the difference between your accent, and South Africa or Scotland. All the same." Gray made a single, sage nod.

Aston stood uncomfortably with Gray, a smile tugging his lips. Gray made to say something else, but was cut off when Sol's voice came over the PA. "Team, gather your things, please. Meet by the forward starboard ramp in ten minutes."

"Here we go then," Aston said, and headed back below decks, glad to be away from Jeff.

They disembarked a little while later to meet a snowcat waiting for them. Like a large bus on four huge tracks that left ladder patterns in the snow. Aston was struck again by just how white everything was. Though he wore sunglasses to cut the glare, the uniformity of the landscape was disturbing.

"All aboard," Sol said. "This is our ride to Alpha Base. It'll take a little while."

The journey was rough, and noisy with the engine roaring and the tracks crunching the ice and snow. They plowed through the seemingly endless, unchanging landscape and Aston felt a sense of isolation settle over him. The idea that the ship would take him back if he changed his mind shrank the further from the ocean they got. After an hour they rose over a low ridge and saw a much higher range of mountains in front of them, still a long way out. Some peaks seemed edged, almost geometrically regular.

Jeff Gray leaned over the seat from behind and slapped Aston's shoulder. "Pyramids!" he declared, wide-eyed, his voice loud over the background noise. "Giant ones!"

Aston knew the legends. Only a year or two before, a screenshot from Google Earth had shown a set of near-perfect pyramids, partially covered by snow, and the internet went into meltdown. It turned out the "pyramids" had been discovered over a hundred years before and geologists hadn't made much of it, kind of an open secret. But then Google sent the internet truthers into a new frenzy. But they were just mountains. Aston even remembered the type, because he thought it was a cool word. A nunatak was a peak of rock sticking out above a glacier or ice sheet. And the shape was apparently pretty common. Even the Matterhorn in the Alps, one of the most famous mountains in the world, bore the same geometry. But the internet's gonna internet, Aston thought with a smile.

"What do you think?" Gray asked. "Aliens or ancient races?"

And Jeff Gray is gonna Jeff Gray, Aston thought. He shook his head. "Just mountains, buddy. Just rock."

Gray laughed, slapped Aston's shoulder again. "Suuuuure! And the Lake Kaarme monster was just a floating log." He dropped heavily back into his seat, still chuckling.

Aston wondered if these were the same peaks that had

caused the internet stir, or new ones. It was entirely possible there were a number of similar formations to be discovered. He supposed it didn't matter. After another hour, dark marks against the snow became visible, beneath the shadows of the peaks. Soon enough the base was right in front of them, and it turned out to be far more impressive than Aston had anticipated.

He had expected wooden buildings and corrugated iron huts, maybe something like the set from that Carpenter movie, *The Thing*. Instead he saw sleek, aerodynamically designed buildings on crisscrossed stilts. Single story, olive green wedges with narrow vertical windows splashing warm orange light onto the snow outside. Solar panels adorned the roofs, wind turbines stood in ranks on low ridges behind, turning in the stiff breeze. Surrounding the modern buildings were the tin sheds he had expected, and ranks of gas bottles and oil barrels in cages, wooden shacks with Ski-doos and all-terrain vehicles parked inside. The whole place was ordered and well-kept, and he presumed it was newly set up. Had SynGreene financed all this? They must be pretty confident about their discovery, and about getting permission to mine it, if they had.

Sol led the team up steel steps into the largest of the dark, futuristic buildings and Aston was even more impressed with the interior. Everything was modern, new-looking. Modular lounges and glass-topped tables, sleek marble bars and chrome-legged chairs. Obviously SynGreene had poured a lot of money into the place and Aston wondered just what they hoped to get back. Their expected return on investment must be huge to justify this level of commitment and expense. A few armed men wandered here and there, calm but serious, all casually carrying weapons, sidearms at the hips. Other staff moved busily around, presumably there to cook, clean, and maintain the base.

"What's with the security?" he asked Sol. "The polar bears particularly aggressive near here?"

"No polar bears here, Sam. Just birds and seals. You're thinking of the Arctic."

Aston rolled his eyes. "I know that. I was being facetious. But it's more than just birds and seals." Sol frowned and Aston was pleased to have turned the tables. He was the biologist, after all. He wouldn't be condescended to by this guy. "Yeah," he said. "You can't forget the ATIs."

Sol quirked an eyebrow. "What's an ATI?"

Aston grinned. "Antarctic Terrestrial Invertebrate."

"You're kidding me. What even is that?"

"Nope, not kidding. Nematode worms, mites, tardigrades, springtails, stuff like that."

Others in the group had gathered to listen and Jahara Syed took up the point. "He's right, it's pretty fascinating. There are sixty-seven species of insects recorded here, which is nothing compared to the millions on all other continents, but significant for a place where until very recently people thought nothing could live."

"They respond to temperature," Aston said. "They might be awake for a few hours, or even less, then dormant, sometimes actually frozen, for days or weeks or even months, before they thaw out and go about their business again."

"Well, that's just creepy as can be," Marla said quietly.

Aston was pleased to see that even Slater was paying attention, her fury momentarily forgotten.

"But we're talking microscopic, right?" Jeff Gray asked.

"Like his package," Marla whispered, just loud enough for Aston to hear.

"Not entirely," Syed said. "But the biggest of them is a wingless midge that reaches a maximum of about thirteen millimeters in length."

"So not likely to eat us in bed," Jeff said.

"Nor is anyone else," Marla said. "God, the jokes write themselves with this tool."

"Well, if they did eat you, it would happen incredibly slowly," Aston said with a grin, trying not to let Marla distract him too much. "Even so, they're among the toughest creatures on the planet."

Marla shook herself. "Bugs. I can't believe that even down here we have to deal with damned bugs."

"Bugs own the planet, really, but that's a long series of lectures we don't have time for," Aston said. He turned back to Sol. "So, back to my original point. Why all the armed guards?"

Sol laughed. "Just company policy. Besides, it's never a bad thing to have a few peacemakers around, don't you think?"

To make peace between which people, Aston wondered, but kept the thought to himself. Slater glanced back at him, caught his eye. He gave a little shrug, but her expression remained neutral. She had been checking though, looking for his reaction to Sol's casual dismissal of the armed guards. It made him happy that she was paying attention to what he thought of things. It boded well for a possible thawing of their own relationship. Or maybe that was just wishful thinking on his part.

Sol led them into a large conference room, those tall narrow windows all along one side looking out over the frozen expanse of Antarctica, away from the sea, invisible some two hours away in the other direction. Slater wouldn't meet Aston's eye again and took a seat at the far end of the oval table, as far from him as she could get. To his annoyance, Jeff Gray sat right beside him. Did the man think they were friends now?

Aston looked around the table once everyone was

seated, trying to guess what was happening here. Apart from himself, and Slater with her crew of Jeff and Marla, there was Sol Griffin, supposedly a physician, but obviously much more. To Aston's left sat Anders Larsen the geologist, then Jahara Syed, the biologist. Next to her was Dig O'Donnell, an archeologist. And that gave him pause. He hadn't thought about it before, but archeologists were experts in ancient civilizations. What use was there for that knowledge down here? The door, he presumed, which he still had trouble accepting as real. Still, if he put that concern aside, it was a pretty standard scientific crew, he supposed.

"Sorry, I'm late. Getting the squad to bunks."

Aston turned at the voice, a strong Boston accent. The man who entered was African-American, a beast of a guy, well over six feet tall, muscles stretching his arctic camo outfit, bald head shining under the fluorescent lights. Clearly ex-military of some sort. He had a pistol holstered at his hip.

Sol smiled. "Just in time, Terry." He raised a hand to introduce the man to the rest of the team already seated. "Ladies and gents, this is Terence Reid, head of security both here at the base and for the expedition in general.

"Good to meet you all," Terry said. "No need to introduce yourselves, I know you all from your files."

His grin was wide and friendly, but Aston thought it slightly disturbing the man had files on them all. He supposed some standard procedure was at play there, but he found it discomforting nonetheless. He watched Slater down the length of the table. She scrutinized Reid for several seconds, then looked at Aston. He raised an eyebrow, but she winced, seemingly annoyed that he'd seen her look his way. With a sigh, he turned his attention back to Sol.

Sol Griffin fired up a screen, but it remained blank as

he addressed the gathering. "Well, you've all signed your NDAs, so now you get the full story. Any guesses?"

Aston wasn't surprised when Jeff spoke up beside him. "I've been giving that a lot of thought. I doubt it's just new energy sources. Especially given the team here. So here are some ideas." He glanced around the table, oblivious to the frowns and impatient stares. They would all rather Sol got on with it, but it seemed Jeff was determined to answer the man's obviously rhetorical question. "So much weird and unexplainable stuff has been found down here," Jeff went on. "The blood falls, you heard about that one? From a lake under the ice that won't freeze, but leaks blood red water out into the sea. Or the Antarctic pyramids, that are supposedly just mountains, but they're so regular, I find that hard to believe. A lot of people are thinking aliens, or Atlantis, or Russian space experiments. For that matter, we know there was once a secret Nazi base here."

Aston winced at the mention of Nazis, remembering the disturbing cave under Lake Kaarme. Then again, it had saved their bacon more than once. "Just let Sol talk, Jeff," he said.

"What? You don't think that stuff is fascinating?"

Aston sighed. "I'm a marine biologist, Jeff. I know the science of this stuff, not the nonsense. The blood falls, for example. It's not weird and unexplained at all, some people just like to pretend it is. It's actually the outflow of an iron oxide-tainted plume of saltwater. You know what that is? Iron-rich, hypersaline water intermittently emerges from small fissures in the ice from a subglacial pool under about 1,300 feet of ice. It was discovered over a hundred years ago, by an Australian geologist, as it happens. We're good at discovering stuff. His name was Griffith Taylor, and the valley still bears his name. He thought it was caused by red algae, but it was later proven to be due to iron oxides. Science!" His hard stare dared Jeff to challenge him.

The cameraman shifted uncomfortably, clearly annoyed at being schooled in front of everyone. "What about the other stuff?"

"Equally bullshit, Jeff! I don't have time to debunk every conspiracy theory you've ever read about. That's the trouble with bullshit. You ever heard of Brandolini's Law? It states the simple truth that the amount of energy needed to refute bullshit is an order of magnitude bigger than to produce it. Which is why it's so hard to make people see truth when the nonsense is so easy. You need more critical thinking, mate."

Sol laughed. "Well, enthusiasm is good. But let's not get carried away. I'll begin with some history. In the early twentieth century, an expedition set out in this region. Two men got lost, separated from their fellows in a sudden blizzard, and found their way into an underground cavern. Only one survived, but what he saw down there was remarkable." Sol passed out manila folders, one to each team member. Inside was a text summary followed by lots of color photos. "Read the details later, but for now just have a look at the pictures," Sol said.

The shots showed a massive cavern, an underground lake, lots of odd, glowing fungi, strange rock formations.

While the team thumbed through their folders, Sol set a slideshow going on the screen of the same photos. "There's a lot of underground volcanic activity in the area," he said. "Geothermal vents, rising spring water, stuff like that. It creates a warm, comfortable environment down below, which gets warmer the deeper you go. We're not looking for uranium or anything like that, but an element previously unknown to humankind."

Aston looked up. "Wait. For one, where is this place you're talking about? And how do you know about it now if it's previously unknown?"

"Remember the old expedition I mentioned? Well, the

explorer who escaped had a chunk of it on him. It was lost to science for decades, but SynGreene recently acquired it. Its properties are amazing and our top scientists are convinced it can be a powerful new source of clean energy."

"Does this stuff have a name?" Syed asked.

Sol gave her an apologetic smile. "Not officially, but SynGreen refers to is as greenium."

"Are you serious?" Syed asked, eyes wide.

Mirth rippled around the table and Sol shrugged. "I'm afraid so. It's a kind of working title, because its properties are still being explored. But Arthur Greene of SynGreene is no stranger to celebrating himself in his work."

"Quite the case of nominative determinism," Aston said.

"Indeed."

"You didn't answer the other question," Aston said. "Where is this place?"

Sol pointed at his feet. "We're right on top of it. Well, not quite." He gestured to the windows. "It's about a hundred yards that way and extends away from the base."

"Under the mountains?" Digby O'Donnell asked.

"I guess so. That direction, certainly."

Dig nodded, smiling.

"So where does this team fit in?" Slater asked. "If you've got a sample and you've found the location, what are we for?"

Sol grinned. "Good question. We'll need a complete survey first. Flora, fauna, geology, anything that needs to be studied and preserved or protected. We have to put together all kinds of dossiers for all kinds of government agencies. And we're thinking the whole thing needs to be documented well anyway, because if we have discovered a new energy source here, your documentary on its emergence will be invaluable in educating the world. That's why you, specifically, are here."

Slater's eyes narrowed, but she said no more.

"What if we find something?" Jahara Syed asked. Aston was glad the biologist had raised the question, because it had been his first thought, too. He had a feeling SynGreene had invested too much money already to let an environmental protection order get in their way.

Sol raised his palms. "Who knows what we'll find. But make no mistake, we will extract the resources one way or the other. We simply want..."

"Deniability," Aston said, anger beginning to boil low in his gut.

"We want to be able to demonstrate that we made every effort to do things the right way," Sol finished.

Slater laughed. "Still sounds like we're to be your cover story."

"If you wish to see it that way, but I assure you, we intend to do the right thing here. By everyone. It is possible, if we're all honest and diligent." Sol's face remained friendly and open, as it always seemed to be, but his eyes had hardened. Aston didn't trust the man as far as he could throw him.

"Some of us don't seem to have skills that fit the purpose of your expedition," Aston said.

Sol hesitated for a fraction of a second before he spoke. Aston wondered if anyone else had noticed it. "Let's just say we want to be prepared for any contingency," Sol said.

CHAPTER 4

Slater woke the next morning and looked about the stark, white room she had been assigned. It was comfortable and functional, but no more than that. She couldn't complain. It was actually refreshing in its own way. Immediately her thoughts returned to Sam Aston. Rage still boiled in her gut that he had let her think he was dead for all that time. But despite her hurt and fury, a great relief lurked somewhere under the surface. She had enjoyed the time they spent together, despite the horrors. And of course, they had shared the experience of those horrors, so perhaps Aston was the only person in the world she could ever talk to about that stuff. Maybe the relief lived there, in the knowledge there was someone still alive who got it, who believed her because he'd been there too. And then the rage came again. He was the only one who could have made any of it easier for her, and he'd hidden for months, like some cowardly whipped dog, refusing to come out from under the house.

Was she being unfair to him? She made a noise of disgust. Screw him! He'd left her to suffer. Maybe he had his reasons, but she didn't care. Perhaps one day the relief that he lived would take over the anger at his hiding, but she didn't think it would be any time soon. In some ways it felt petty to ensure he suffered before she even thought about forgiving him, but that was exactly what she intended to do.

"Asshole," she muttered to herself, and went into the cramped en-suite to shower.

When she headed into the canteen half an hour later,

the entire team was present. She winced at Jeff Gray funneling scrambled eggs into his face like a factory machine, half of it already down his sweater. Aston caught her eye, started to smile. That twisted combination of anger and relief flooded through her again and she looked away.

Once she had eaten and gulped down two mugs of coffee, she began to feel a little more balanced. The coffee, she noticed, was pretty good, so that was something positive about this whole debacle of an expedition.

Sol Griffin stood and called out for their attention. "We're heading down this morning, so get wrapped up for the short trip to the elevator, but you won't need to overdo it. A jacket and regular clothing will be fine once we go down. Be sure to bring all the gear you want with you, as it's a long ride back if you forget anything. Our first foray will be relatively brief, though."

Wrapped in parkas and lugging gear, the team soon found themselves crunching over fresh snowfall from the warm comforts of the base. Despite the bright sunshine, the impact of the cold on Slater's face made her catch her breath as they stepped out. The landscape was awe-inspiring, undulating white, occasional ridges of gray stone, then the huge peaks of the mountains rising over them, almost close enough to touch. The morning sun struck the north faces of the strangely geometric range, making bright white and dark shadow stand out in stark contrast. Sol led them about fifty yards from the main base building, past two large garages and a stack of oil barrels, to a fenced off area with a bright yellow sign above the gate. The sign read AUTHORIZED PERSONNEL ONLY and an armed guard stood by the gate, his breath clouding in the cold air.

"Good morning," Sol said.

"Sir." The guard opened the gate and stepped aside to let them through. Beyond was a metal hut about five yards square and inside what looked like a huge freight elevator.

Slater was reminded of the elevator in the movie *Aliens*, where Ripley, flamethrower in hand, descends to save Newt while the entire complex explodes and falls down around her. While the elevator looked just like that, Slater hoped she would never be using it under anything like those circumstances.

Come on, she told herself. We're here for a damned rock of some kind. Calm down. But memories of Lake Kaarme and how that job had gone still regularly gave her nightmares. She would wake in terror, images of deep underwater caverns and that huge maw full of teeth snapping at her, fresh in her mind. She drew a deep breath and steeled herself. This place couldn't be more different.

The elevator was more than big enough to comfortably carry all eight team members, plus Terence Reid, the muscled security guy, and two of his subordinates. They came in last and as Reid slid the large gate closed, he said, "This is Mike Gates and Ronda Tate." The two nodded, their faces serious, weapons at their sides. "The three of us will always go where you go, so get used to us hanging around, but feel free to ignore us."

"I'm still not sure why you feel there's such a need for so much... muscle," Aston said.

Despite her annoyance with him, Slater agreed with that assessment.

"Like I said," Sol interjected before Terry could answer. "Just company policy. Take the man at his word, just ignore them."

Sol reached for a large control hanging from a thick cable at the front of the elevator. It only had two large buttons, one above the other. Up and down, Slater presumed. Sol pressed the lower one and the elevator jerked once, then began to smoothly descend.

The shaft was dimly lit, a black cable hanging down

along one wall with small, oblong halogen lights every so often. The car rattled softly, steel cables hissed through the mechanisms above. They passed rhythmically through bright patches, then dimness, then light again for what seemed entirely too long to Slater. Just how deep were they going? Her ears popped once, then again. As she began to feel an irrational fear that they would never reach the bottom, the elevator slowed, then bumped to a stop.

"Holy cow," Jeff said. "Journey to the center of the earth, am I right?" He looked around, grinning, but no one else shared his humor.

Slater saw the same trepidation in all the other faces, except Jeff's, that she was certain was mirrored on her own features. Being this deep underground was uncomfortably claustrophobic despite the fact that ahead of them was a large and well lit cavern.

Reid slid the gate open and stood back to let everyone get off the elevator. As Slater stepped out, she stopped dead and gasped. The cavern wasn't large, it was huge, arcing up above them into a dome of rock high above. Stalactites pointed down, stalagmites beneath them, some taller even than Terry Reid, the biggest of their group. Warm air tickled her face, the temperature higher than she had expected, and almost humid. Striations of the glowing green fungi covered the walls like veins, spread out mostly, but occasionally in a thick patch. Spotlights on the ground provided the light, pointing up into the dome, creating areas of light and shade.

"Stand still one moment," Sol said, his hand resting on a control box near the elevator. "I'm going to turn out the lights. Give your eyes a moment to adjust."

Once everyone had stopped moving, he flicked a switch and darkness fell like a lid had been closed. Almost immediately, the glowing fungi stood out, a network all over the walls. Slater's sense of wonder increased as her eyes grew accustomed to the dark and the whole cavern took on an otherworldly glow, more and more features standing out in the soft green illumination.

"That's some of the most bioluminescent fungi I've ever seen," Jahara Syed whispered, eyes wide as she scanned left and right. "Is it a fungus?"

"That's partly what we're here to find out," Sol said. "Beautiful, isn't it? Okay, watch out, lights coming back." The cavern burst into life again, orange and suddenly artificial. "Take a look around, everyone."

"Jeff, get footage of everything," Slater said. "Start with a close-up of the elevator and controls, pan around for wide shots of the cavern, then start gathering all the details you can."

"Yes, boss." Jeff gave a crooked grin, waited as if expecting some response, then shrugged and turned away when Slater just stared at him.

She turned to Marla. "That guy, honestly."

Marla laughed. "He's an idiot, but he's harmless enough. I'm going to try to be more forgiving of him."

"You're a better person than I am, then! We need to pick a spot where I can do a piece to camera. Somewhere that looks good, but the sound won't be lost."

Marla's eyes widened as she turned away from looking up at the vaulted ceiling high above. "Oh yeah, work. This place is amazing."

But Slater wasn't really listening. She watched as Aston and O'Donnell were led away from the group by Sol, over to a distant part of the cavern. Suspicious, she called Jeff back and had Marla fire up the mic and set her levels. Once they were ready, camera and audio running, she said, "Follow me.":

Sticking to the shadows, she led them around one side to slowly creep up on the three men. Aston and O'Donnell were examining a strange-looking, smooth black door while Sol and another man, clearly a guard, watched over them. The guard wasn't one of the two who had come down with Reid, so Slater assumed he must be stationed down here, guarding the door. She wondered if that was really necessary. He stood by, looking bored, absently balancing a metallic blue fidget spinner on one finger as it spun silently. His other hand rested on his holstered pistol.

Slater turned her attention to the door. Large blocks of gray stone, neatly carved and fitted together, made the frame, the door itself a single slab of smooth black rock. It had a kind of recurring pattern lightly carved into the surface. Immediately, cold settled into her gut. From an interesting cavern with strange fungal growth, the place suddenly had something to be scared of, front and center. She remembered the door deep under Lake Kaarme, the mystery of its presence that they had never been able to ascertain, now lost forever. What was this door doing here? It certainly wasn't new, but how long had it been there? Did that early twentieth century expedition Sol had mentioned put it in? For what? Where did it go? And even as she thought these things, she knew it had to be far older than that.

None of the men were talking as they looked over the door, Aston running his fingertips over its surface. Eventually he said, "I can't say for certain that it's the same, but it looks similar."

Similar to what? Slater thought, but deep down she knew, thinking of Lake Kaarme again.

"I'll need to do some checking," O'Donnell said. "But I feel like I've seen photos, or maybe drawings, of doors like this before. There's a lot of conflicting stuff out there, a lot of made-up nonsense. But I'll take photos and cross-check this."

"You'll be able to get online when we return to base," Sol said. "You can do all the checking you need."

They turned away from the door and were all clearly surprised to see Slater and her team, filming them. Sol's face darkened with annoyance.

"Just documenting everything," Slater said, before Sol could speak.

She strode toward them, making a beeline for Aston, forcing the others to step out of the way or be run over. She knew the action was partly irrational, but her anger at Aston seemed to override every other thought. She shouldered past the men and approached the door, catching Aston's arm as she went to stop him from moving away. The guard quickly pocketed his fidget spinner and made a move to stop her, but Sol raised a hand to stay him. "It's all right."

Slater took a long look at the door, enjoying Aston's discomfort as he stood beside her, too scared to move away after she had stopped him. But the door held her attention. It felt somehow alien to her but she had no rational way to explain why. Discomforted herself now, she drove away the eerie feeling by focusing on a more powerful emotion: her desire to punch Aston in the throat. She took his elbow and yanked him back toward the door, then took up position next to him, and turned toward the camera.

He started to protest and she gave him a hard stare and held her index finger in front of his face. He shut up like a told off school boy. She turned back to the camera, caught Marla's nod that she was ready, and said, "Three... two... one...," then paused a moment before her television face fell down like a mask. With a soft smile, she said, "Believe it or not, this is Sam Afton..."

"Aston," he said meekly, his expression annoyed and cowed at the same time.

"My apologies, Mister Aston." She turned back to the camera. "Sam Aston is a member of the team," she said, enjoying the juvenile pleasure of intentionally omitting any credentials. "Mister Aston, what can you tell us about this door, on the far side of a huge cavern, hundreds of feet beneath the Antarctic surface?"

He frowned, swallowed, shook his head. "I'm really not sure. It's not necessarily my area of expertise."

"Is it proof of life beneath Antarctica?"

From the corner of her eye she watched Sol and Dig smirking, enjoying her putting of Aston on the spot almost as much as she was. She remembered how resistant he was at Kaarme too, never even suggesting a theory he couldn't prove. And how uncomfortable he was in front of the camera every time she had it pointed at him. And now he almost squirmed under the eye of the lens, and the others grinning at him.

"Maybe you should ask Dig," he tried. "It's probably more his…"

"What do you think could have made the door, Mister Aston? From among known Antarctic life, I mean?"

"I'm really not sure…"

"Do you believe subterranean penguins did it? Or Antarctic Terrestrial Invertebrates?" While she was enjoying her mockery of him, she realized it was also a cover for how much the presence of the door had disturbed her. She found herself perturbed by everything since the elevator had gone so deep, and was using her anger at Aston to deal with it.

"Penguins?" Aston said, forcing a smile. "What?"

"You said the door looks similar. Similar to what?"

Aston's forced smile melted into a frown. "I know you're not happy with me right now, but you know what? We're done here." He turned and stormed away.

Slater watched him go, then turned her attention to Sol, who startled slightly to find himself suddenly under her scrutiny, the grin sliding off his face.

"Sol Griffin, expedition leader," she said. "What do

you know about the door?"

"Not much," he replied, rallying as the camera turned to pin him in its gaze. "The survivor of the twentieth-century expedition reported seeing it. Otherwise, we haven't studied it yet."

"And what's on the other side?" Slater asked.

Sol smiled. "You're going to find out very soon."

CHAPTER 5

Halvdan Landvik sat pensively in his office on London's Threadneedle Street, one finger stroking his neatly trimmed salt and pepper beard as he looked at a painting on the wall opposite. It was large, dark tones of old oil paint in browns, reds, yellows, by Mårten Eskil Winge from 1872, depicting Thor's Fight with the Giants. Landvik stared at the hammer Thor held high, yellow lightning arcing around it. He shook his head, thinking of what was lost. Of what might have been. He supposed he should be grateful to be alive, but sometimes that seemed like small consolation. The anger that boiled in his gut at those events would likely never go away. No matter, he could use that as fuel for future endeavors. A knock at the door interrupted his thoughts.

"Come."

Two nervous-looking employees, Cooper and Waite, entered. Cooper was tall and thin, completely bald. Waite was of a bigger build, but shorter, his hair dark and curly. Both of them largely useless. Genuinely good quality help was almost impossible to find. Landvik watched them, his mood soured further by their obvious weakness. Where were the strong any more? Where were the heroes in this age of digital excess and human frailty? They were clearly waiting for permission to speak.

"Well?" he snapped. "What do you have to report?"

"Our man is successfully embedded with the team," Cooper said.

Landvik nodded approvingly. At least his underlings could do one thing right. "What else?"

"Our operatives are on their way. They'll be ready to strike at the appropriate time."

"Good. I'm pleased that something is going to plan."

"Should we not simply go ahead and take the base?" Waite asked.

"No. Let SynGreen's team do all the hard work for us, then we'll strike. No point making unnecessary work for our lot. The scientists will work harder if they believe they're doing it for a financial reward, and not under duress. The carrot is more effective than the stick." They both nodded, but made no move to leave. "I sense you have more questions," Landvik said, his voice tired. "Reservations, perhaps?"

"Honestly, sir," Cooper said. "We're a little confused at your interest in this project. It all seems a bit sketchy, not to mention nearly impossible to believe."

"Really? Why don't you let me worry about that?"

"Can it be true though, sir?" Waite pressed. "A new source of energy?"

Landvik took out a folder from his desk drawer, opened it and thumbed through the several sheets inside. He had no intention of letting these two fools actually study the material, but often seeing some physical evidence helped people accept a truth. "I found confirmation of a sort in the form of this record. It's from a pre-WWII Russian expedition to the very place SynGreene have set up their base. The Russians were in search of a powerful energy source, one they thought could make them the greatest superpower in the world. They ran into problems, unexplained in these documents. But of course, survival in the Antarctic that long ago was fraught with danger." The two men still appeared puzzled. "What don't you understand?" Landvik asked, losing patience.

"Well, this company isn't exactly an energy corporation," Cooper said, raising his palms.

Landvik smiled. "I'm not interested in the energy potential. That is for others to consider. I am interested in the military potential. Trust me, this is going to change the world."

CHAPTER 6

A ston loitered near the back of the cavern by the elevator, stung by Slater's verbal assault. He knew he deserved her anger, but that little ambush had been downright juvenile. At the thought, he couldn't help a smile tugging his lips. In a way, he had to respect her for it. Maybe it was one step nearer to them having an actual conversation. At least public mockery was a level up from icy snubbing.

He watched as Slater did a piece to camera beside the stone door. She was a professional, and she deserved so much better than this. There was no reason she couldn't front a serious show on the major networks. She had the looks, the presence, the eloquence. Sometimes, the world threw the strangest curveballs at people. The same could be said for himself, he supposed, staring past Slater at the mysterious markings on the smooth door. The door that filled him with a kind of dread. It marked a point where everything about this trip changed. Where he could no longer pretend things weren't awry here. But, he had to remind himself, the presence of a door like the one under Lake Kaarme didn't mean a prehistoric monster like the one they had encountered there also lurked here. Though that beast had been a guardian, if the local legends were to be believed. So maybe there wasn't a cretaceous throwback here, but could there be a different type of guardian? Was it possible, or was he projecting his own fear? But his fear was well-founded. The temperate conditions, the strangely glowing fungus, the obviously man-made door. Or something-made, anyway. It all pointed to problems Aston didn't want to run into. But what choice did he have now?

He was committed to the job, even though Sol had said he could leave at any time. He questioned the truth of that, though he wasn't committed to Sol, but to his own curiosity.

Slater finished her piece and looked up past the camera. She saw him watching and held his eye for a moment, her expression neutral. He stared back, gave a small, non-committal smile that he hoped conveyed a *No hard feelings* vibe. She didn't respond, but didn't immediately look away either. That was something.

"Can I talk to you a moment?"

Aston turned to see Jahara Syed approach him. He glanced back, but Slater was already back in conversation with Jeff and Marla. He sighed. "Sure," he said to Jahara. "What's up?"

"You're a marine biologist, I know, but that's a specialty, right? I mean, you're a biologist first and foremost?" She looked frightened of something.

"Sure, I guess so."

Syed pointed to a patch of wall nearby, bright with the glowing fungus the grew on it, spreading out in a web. "Have you ever seen anything like this before?"

"Honestly, I hadn't had a close look yet. I've been distracted."

"Yeah, but even from a distance, this isn't normal, right? It's so bright, so virulent."

Aston looked at her face for a moment and realized what he had at first taken for fear was actually excitement. "There are kinds of photonic plankton that are really bright..." he started.

"I know, I know, but this is plant life!"

"Well, it's fungus, isn't it? I know that's a gray area, but we have to be careful how we classify this stuff."

Syed nodded, moving to look intently at the nearest growth. "I need better equipment. Sol said there's a lab up top I can use."

Aston went to say something else, but Syed plowed on. "And, dude, what in the name of Allah and all his angels is that?" She pointed to the stone door. "It was made by that expedition a hundred years ago, I'm guessing? Please say that's what it is. But why go to such extravagant lengths?"

Aston drew a deep breath. "I wish I could tell you they built it. Truth is, I don't really know."

Syed's neatly shaped, dark eyebrows drew together in a frown. She opened her mouth to say more, but Sol's voice overrode her.

"Everyone ready to move on? As the old saying goes, you ain't seen nothing yet!"

Aston and Syed exchanged a glance, then headed over to join Sol and the team at the stone door. Slater, Jeff and Marla stood off to one side to record things as Sol addressed the rest of the group.

"We're going through here now. It's the only exit from the cavern, other than the elevator shaft, of course. We've only gone as far as the next cavern before organizing this expedition, so after this next place, we're all on new ground."

Without waiting for any further conversation, he pushed against the stone door and it slid back and to the left, opening a wide gap to reveal a dark tunnel beyond. The guard with the fidget spinner stood to one side and let the team file through, but didn't follow.

The tunnel beyond was short, surprisingly warm even after the temperate feel of the previous cavern. The ground sloped down quite steeply, the only sounds the scuffing of their feet and the occasional drip of water. They walked in darkness, the only light from the beams of flashlights playing over the walls. It grew warmer as they went, occasionally narrowing so they needed to move in single file, then opening out again so they could easily walk three abreast. Sometimes the ground sloped up briefly, but the overall trajectory was down, deeper and deeper. Aston resisted the urge to turn around and run back for the elevator, claustrophobia clawing at his hindbrain, some inbuilt, instinctive survival mechanism adding to his overall trepidation. Occasional patches of the glowing growths appeared, casting wan green light, but they were small and infrequent.

Aston glanced back, saw Slater and her crew filming from behind, then Terry Reid and his two subordinates following the party. Sol Griffin led the way forward. How far had they gone? It seemed as though they'd been trudging along for quite a while.

"How much further?" Digby O'Donnell called out, clearly sharing Aston's concerns.

"It'll take a while," Sol said back over his shoulder.

"How much of a while?" Anders Larsen asked.

Sol paused, turned back to them. "Don't worry. We're nearly there. Maybe another ten minutes." He turned and carried on, unaware or uncaring of the rest of the group exchanging concerned glances.

Eventually, another source of light began to show from in front. The now familiar green glow painted the walls and floor weakly, then brightened as they rounded a slight curve in the passage. They emerged into another cavern, similar to the first, only smaller, perhaps a little over half as big. Several passages led off in a variety of directions, more veins of fungus glowed softly from the walls, in far greater profusion than the previous cavern, though that one had been much bigger.

Jahara Syed made a noise of excitement and hurried across to one side of the cave. Slater jabbed Jeff in the ribs, and the man hurried to film the biologist. Aston went to join her, ignoring the camera but infected by her delight.

She crouched beside a small clump of fern-like plants. Some leaves were open, others still curled, ready to unfurl. The leaves were tiny, no more than a couple of millimeters across, and oval-shaped. Each stem of leaves that had extended was only a few inches long, but stem and leaves alike were a deep jade green, shiny and waxy-looking.

Syed glanced up at Aston as he joined her. "Have you seen anything like this before?"

"I don't know. I don't think so. They're vascular, certainly, so not related to the fungi or a simple lichen. They're an actual plant, all the way down here." He leaned closer. "Is it glowing too?"

Syed grinned. "I think it is, very subtly. Nothing like the fungus, but it appears to be at least mildly bioluminescent. It's definitely some kind of leptosporangiate fern."

"A true fern, you mean?"

"Yes, not a horsetail or rush or anything like that. An actual fern, but growing deep underground without sunlight for photosynthesis. How is that possible?"

Aston shook his head. "I don't think it is possible. It can't be a true fern, it must just resemble them in form. Unless the bioluminescent glow from the fungus is enough for it?"

"Then it's an entirely new species!" She rubbed her hands together, eagerness shining in her eyes.

Aston smiled, further infected by Syed's excitement. "It might be. You ever get to name a new discovery before?"

She grinned. "Polypodiopsida Syedii," she said, trying a name on for size. "I like it! But I may have the class entirely wrong there. I need to study more."

"Take a sample back up top."

"I will!"

He left the biologist to gather her sample and strolled

slowly around the rest of the cave. Anders Larsen, the geologist, ran his large hands over the rock at one side. He seemed to be lost in thought, as though he were trying to commune with the stone itself. Digby O'Donnell stood in the middle of the cave, hands on hips, looking up at the stalactites pointing down from above. The archeologist kept glancing back up the tunnel, then looking up again. Aston assumed the man was preoccupied with the door, but wondered what fascination the cave's natural formation held for him.

Sol remained by the tunnel where they had entered. Terry Reid and his two fellow guards, Ronda Tate and Mike Gates, stood nearby. It seemed as though they were all waiting for something. Maybe they were simply anticipating the findings of the team. Aston himself felt like a spare wheel. Syed was the biologist, and there was no marine life for him to investigate using his specialty expertise. So he'd seen a weird door under Lake Kaarme. So had Jo Slater. He was superfluous to this group in every way.

Several small side passages led off from the cavern, radiating out away from the one they had entered through. Aston began exploring them, ducking to fit without banging his head. The first few were dead ends, and Aston couldn't suppress his discomfort. He remained unnerved by the place. He could see no reason to believe they were anything but naturally-formed, yet the place had what he could only describe as an alien vibe. As he headed for the fourth passage, exploring clockwise, Sol called out.

"Okay, team. Once you've got what you want from here, shall we call it a day there? I know Syed wants to use the lab up top and I'm sure Larsen has some following up to do."

"We haven't been down here long," Aston said. "Don't you want to go on further?"

"Of course, but I want to do it well-equipped. You've all got an idea of what we're facing here now, so when we come back tomorrow I want us to be ready for a long haul. We'll bring supplies and aim to explore further, maybe spend the equivalent of a couple of days or more down here, yes? We'll head back up now, you can make your notes, think about all the stuff you want to bring down, whatever else you may need. Feel free to leave anything here that you won't need until next time. It's about lunchtime, so by the time we get back up you'll all be ready for a meal, I think. We'll go eat and you can rest and plan for tomorrow."

He gestured to the tunnel behind him and the team slowly made their way back to the elevator.

CHAPTER 7

Aston was happy to be back in the world of light and sky, even if it was the wild expanse of Antarctica. The caverns had been amazing but oppressive, and he was pleased to get back to the base. He also had to admit the catering at the place was impressive. SynGreene clearly had money to burn on this expedition. Once everyone had helped themselves from the varied buffet and sat to eat, Sol Griffin tapped a glass for their attention.

"We're on our own recognizance for the rest of today, so feel free to rest, work, whatever suits you. There are lab facilities for any who want them, and WiFi for your devices or a computer lab with desktops you can use. After lunch, come and see me and I'll show you all where to find those things. You've had a glimpse of what's before us, so think about what else you might want to take down tomorrow and that's when we'll get into it properly."

Sol sat back down and tucked into his lunch. Aston ate slowly, savoring the delicately seasoned shrimp and crunchy snow peas, trying to process all he'd seen. And trying to think why he was there. The thought of his debts finally being cleared was good, but he wondered what other price he might pay for this endeavor.

Syed moved over to him, her face dark. "Can you believe I didn't think to take a sample of the damned fungus?"

"Really?"

"Yes! I was so pre-occupied by the new fern we found, I forgot to get the fungus or whatever it is. I might try to go back down this afternoon."

Aston shrugged. "I wouldn't worry about it. That fern will keep you busy. Get the other stuff when we go back tomorrow. It's not going anywhere." He glanced over at Sol, eating happily, but altogether too comfortable in his command. "Besides," Aston said. "I don't think he'll let you go back on your own, or without the full party. I think he's going to insist we all stay together."

Syed frowned. "Maybe you're right. Honestly, what kind of biologist am I, not collecting samples?"

"Better than me!" Aston laughed. "I didn't take anything, or do anything." His feeling of uselessness persisted. But if SynGreene wanted to pay him a ridiculous amount of money for little to no work, so be it.

Syed smiled and patted his shoulder. "I'm going to ask Sol anyway." She moved away, but Aston didn't fancy her chances.

"What did you mean when you said, 'It's similar'?"

Aston startled, looking up from the food he was pushing around his plate. Slater had moved into the seat beside him and he hadn't even noticed.

"So, you're talking to me now?"

Slater smirked. "I talked to you earlier."

Aston huffed a laugh. "You made a bloody fool out of me in from of Sol and the others, if that's what you mean."

She raised an eyebrow at him. "You don't think you deserve it?"

Aston's dark mood grew darker still. "Whatever I might deserve, it's not that kind of juvenile display."

She folded her arms across her chest. "Is that right?"

Before he could say anything he might later regret, Aston chose to remove himself from the conversation altogether. It was ironic, after days of trying to get Slater to talk to him that he walked away now, when she finally offered him some words. He wasn't even certain he was in the right, only that he was pissed off at her. What a mess the whole thing was. He felt her eyes on his back as he scraped his unfinished lunch into a composting bin and put the plates in the dirty dishes tub for the base staff to collect later.

Sol put out one hand, touching Aston's arm to stop him as he went to leave. "Sam, make sure to bring along some basic gear tomorrow, all right?"

"Basic gear?" He glanced over and saw Syed's dark expression. Clearly Sol had refused her request to go back this afternoon.

"Sure. There's probably no need for full SCUBA at this point, but we might come across underground lakes or something. So pack a wetsuit and mask or something in case there is deep water to investigate."

Aston narrowed his eyes, wondering what the man might know that he wasn't letting on. Maybe he'd penetrated deeper into the caverns than he cared to admit. "Is that likely?"

Sol laughed. "Who knows what's likely down there? Is anything you've seen so far even remotely expected?"

"No, I suppose not."

Sol gave a curt nod, flashed an insincere smile, and returned to his seat, giving his full attention once more to his food.

Aston left the canteen and strolled aimlessly around the base, thinking through all he'd learned so far. Sol's suggestion that he pack basic dive gear, while suspicious, actually gave him a sense of purpose. At least if there were aquatic areas to investigate he wouldn't feel like such a spare wheel around the place. And Slater had talked to him, so that was something too. She only wanted to know about the door, of course, but the Lake Kaarme door was an experience only they had shared. He probably should talk to her about it. Maybe when he felt less annoyed.

The corridor he followed led to the northern end of the

base, a large recreational room. Several bookshelves lined one wall, comfortable lounges were scattered around the space, a big-screen TV and DVD player in one corner. Aston spotted a PS4 tucked into the TV cabinet too and smiled. Maybe shooting the hell out of some zombies or something would help him relax.

He saw two feet sticking over the end of one sofa and moved around to discover Dig O'Donnell laying back, reading a paperback. The man looked up as Aston appeared.

"Samuel! How are things?"

Aston nodded. "Just Sam thanks, Dig. I only get called Samuel when I'm in trouble."

"You're not in trouble now?"

"I'll take the fifth on that question, if it's all the same to you."

O'Donnell laughed. "Fair enough."

"You researched anything about that door in the cavern yet?" Aston asked.

Dig sat up, put the book down on his knee. "Not really. I thought I might let my lunch go down first, then hit the books. It's a weird thing, though, don't you think?"

"It is." Aston was reluctant to offer too much. He wondered how much Dig might know.

Dig pursed his lips for a moment, then, "You saw one before."

"Who told you that?"

"Sol Griffin. He only mentioned it in passing, but I've seen Slater's film about Kaarme, so I know all the broad details. It's not a hoax, is it? Her film, I mean."

Aston sighed. "No, it's not. It's all real, but no one seems to want to accept that."

"People are experts at refusing to accept things that challenge their sure knowledge of the world. Then there are others who will believe just about anything, no matter how ludicrous."

"And where on that scale do you fall?"

Dig grinned. "Maybe somewhere in the middle."

Aston looked down at the book on O'Donnell's lap. H. P. Lovecraft's short novel, *At The Mountains of Madness*. "Is that the best book to read given where we are?" he asked.

Dig barked a short laugh. "Can't think of anything better!"

Aston frowned. "If I remember correctly, it's the story of an Antarctic expedition that goes horribly wrong when they discover mysterious ruins and inexplicable creatures in a huge range of mountains?"

Dig nodded. "Pretty much. The whole yarn is related by a geologist, William Dyer, who's a professor at Miskatonic University in Arkham. He's telling the story in the hope that it will prevent anyone else from going back there."

"And yet here we are," Aston said.

"Yes. And we found an inexplicable door."

"I think the door was put in there by the expedition back near the turn of the twentieth century," Aston said. He was almost certain that he in fact did not believe that, but he wanted to test the theory on O'Donnell.

"No," Dig said. "I'm sure it wasn't."

"Why so sure?"

"The rock. It's not mined from those mountains. Or at least, not nearby. Why and how would those explorers have mined rock from so far away and taken it there in these conditions?" He gestured out the window at the seemingly endless snow. "I'd postulate these weren't the conditions when that door was built. Perhaps all of Antarctica was more temperate then, yes? And why would that expedition construct such an elaborate door anyway? If they wanted to shore up the entrance to that passageway, they would have used the nearby rock and made a much more utilitarian, less aesthetic, framework. Don't you think?"

"Yes, I do," Aston said honestly. "It's exactly what I thought, to be honest." His eyes fell to Dig's book again.

Dig tapped the cover with one forefinger. "This is all incredibly fanciful, of course. In the story, Professor Dyer and a graduate student named Danforth fly over the mountains and see a vast abandoned stone-city, one that is alien to any human architecture. We know from Google Earth that doesn't exist."

"But doesn't the bulk of the story happen in subterranean tunnels and caves?" Aston asked. "It was years ago that I read this, but I remember giant blind penguins and formless, multi-eyed blobs."

"Shoggoths," Dig said.

"That's right. We wouldn't see those from satellite imagery."

O'Donnell laughed. "Nor the intricate hieroglyphics the characters found, telling the story of interstellar Elder Gods and their fighting. But let's assume that's as fanciful as the giant alien city, shall we?"

Aston paused, lost in thought.

"Thinking about that door again?" Dig asked.

Aston nodded. "You have to wonder just how fanciful that stuff is," he said, gesturing to the Lovecraft book.

"Well, there are a number of weird conspiracy theories about Antarctica, aside from this rather far-fetched story. *At The Mountains of Madness* was written in the 1930s, after all. But there are a number of suggestions that there could be living beings of some description, even ancient aliens, living beneath the Antarctic."

"You think that's likely?"

Dig shrugged. "Do you?"

"I'm not sure what to think. Recent experience has taught me that I know next to nothing in the grand scheme of things."

"Spoken like a true scientist!" Dig said.

"But it is interesting, don't you think," Aston said. "You being here."

"Is it?"

"Well, sure. An archeologist in the most uninhabited place on Earth."

Dig raised his hands, palms up. "Uninhabited now. Perhaps it was inhabited once before. I guess maybe they brought me along just in case we do encounter a vast alien city under the ice." He laughed, gesturing with the tatty paperback, one eyebrow raised.

Aston laughed too, but couldn't help but feel uneasy about the strange door so far beneath their feet.

CHAPTER 8

Aaron Steele, privately contracted security guard, leaned against the cool stone of the strange door, metallic blue fidget spinner whirring almost silently on the tip of his finger. Almost silent, but the huge empty cavern was so quiet he could have heard a mouse fart. But for the scattered and muffled drips of falling water and the smooth bearings of his spinner, the space was devoid of all sound. He didn't understand why the company wouldn't let him bring ear buds down, listen to music. But they wouldn't even allow him to bring his phone. He could play tunes, tap away at a handful of cool mobile games he had downloaded, even read an ebook. Anything would be better than the mind-numbing boredom of standing around all day. But company policy was company policy, and the pay was pretty great. It was easy money in that respect, though he looked forward to eventually returning to civilization. And his fiancée. He missed those pleasures far more than he missed his phone.

Aaron glanced at his watch, sighed. Another hour until shift change. Almost time to go back topside. Downtime would be good. Hopefully no one would be hogging the PS4 up there.

Something scraped behind him. Frowning, he turned to look at the closed door. He must have imagined it. Or maybe it was his own utility belt rubbing against the stone as he moved. But he didn't remember moving. The sound came again, quiet, followed by a rapid series of taps, almost a ticking, beyond the door.

Had some of those geeks been left down there from

earlier? No, that was ridiculous. He'd have noticed, or at the least he would have been told. Maybe one of the other security crew had been posted inside. He shook his head. He would know that too if it were the case, and the three armed goons with the scientists had all come back too. You couldn't miss those guys.

He stilled the fidget spinner, gripped it lightly between thumb and forefinger, and turned to face the door, listening hard. He heard no more noise, save for the softly echoing drips for so long he had just about given up and decided he was imagining things when it came again.

scraaaape-tic-tic-tic

Then once more after only a couple of seconds. Something was definitely moving around back there. Suddenly Aaron wished for boredom and long, empty shifts on his own. He would have to investigate. It was his job, after all. Besides, it might turn out to be the only useful thing he'd done since he got here. But he didn't like it. Not one bit.

He opened the door, flicked on the bright LED light he wore on a band about his forehead, and played the white beam around the walls of the dark tunnel beyond. Nothing but smooth, slick, slightly damp stone. He knew another cavern lay beyond the long passage, but he hadn't been there. He just needed to watch the elevator and the door, he was told. He looked into the dark, saw only the faint glow of a tiny patch of the of the strangely luminescent fungus and his light making stark shadows. He moved and his headlight cut through the shadows like a sword blade.

scraaaape-tic-tic-tic

He jumped, turned to the right where the sound had come from, but nothing was there. Weird echoes in the limited space, maybe. Did the sound emanate from up ahead? He crept forward, moving the beam of light slowly left and right, left and right. The shadows seemed to press forward, like the darkness itself tried to embrace him.

scraaaape-tic-tic-tic

Quieter this time, further away. He stalked on, the thick soles of his boots quiet as he stepped as lightly as possible. He reached a slow bend in the passage and began to move around it, wondering how far he should go. There was a radio set back by the elevator, linked by cables to the base, as no signal from a transmitter could penetrate this much rock. He should go back and report.

scraaaape-tic-tic-tic

Forward and to his left. His light showed nothing but rock. Hair-thin veins of soft green striped the walls. He moved forward again, just a pace or two.

scraaaape-tic-tic-tic

scraaaape-tic-tic-tic

He stopped, heart hammering. The sounds had come almost simultaneously, from either side. An echo, or were there two now? Two what? He stood motionless, holding even his breath, ears straining to hear anything but the gentle drips of ancient water. Nothing. He allowed himself a small, silent breath. For more than a minute he stood frozen, listening hard. No more sound, nothing moved. He took longer, deeper breaths, determined to calm himself. He slowly moved his head, let his light play over the walls, up to the curving ceiling of the large passage. Nothing to see but gray stone, shadows, patches of soft green fungus like lightning in freeze-frame here and there.

Two more minutes and not another sound except the pulse in his ears. Whatever it might have been, it was gone. Or perhaps there hadn't been anything and he'd imagined the whole thing. Echoes of his own restless feet perhaps. He turned back to the mouth of the passage leading to the door and screamed. His bladder emptied at the sight before him, his groin quickly warm and wet.

The last image in his mind before pain flooded his

nerves was his fiancée waving, a tear in her eye at the airport when he'd left for Cape Town.

CHAPTER 9

Slater entered the large elevator leading to the caverns with a weight of foreboding in her gut. She had slept fitfully, bugged by any number of anxieties. Worry about Aston and the complicated feelings that circled her mind like vultures. Worry about the job itself, what it might mean, where it might lead. Worry also about the key players. Not just people like Sol Griffin, who was in charge on the ground. He seemed unrealistically upbeat all the time and that discomforted her. But the others, out of sight. Arthur Greene chief among them, the man behind all of this. What did he really want? A new source of green energy was an admirable goal, but was that all of it? And why not be here to see it happen? Perhaps he was old, infirm, agoraphobic. Although being claustrophobic would be more likely to keep him away from this gig. Being down in those caverns and tunnels was oppressive. Anyway, there could be a hundred different explanations. But no matter how she thought about it, she had a bad feeling about the whole endeavor.

Then over breakfast this morning, she had spotted another thing. The entire team acted excited, keen to get to work, all eating fast and talking faster. Except for Sam Aston. He looked pensive, troubled. He watched the rest of the team with a suspicious eye, like he tried to fathom something just beyond his grasp. Like he felt exactly as she did. On a couple of occasions they caught each other's eye and while there was still ice between them, a new kind of knowing existed too. She still retained a fury at the asshole for what he'd done, but she realized as well that perhaps he was the only genuine ally she could rely on. And it seemed he recognized that about her, too.

They stood near each other in the elevator as it rattled its seemingly endless descent, but they didn't speak. Aston had a large canvas kit bag over one shoulder, packed full. She had some extra handheld lighting to set up clearer shots, but nothing else. The scientists all carried all kinds of extra kit, and Sol and the security detail carried supplies for a potentially long stint. Though she couldn't imagine staying under for more than twenty or thirty hours, there seemed to be no reason not to return to the surface regularly. How far did Sol think they might travel underground?

Chatter on the way down was muted, but the excitement remained. When they reached the first cavern, that had been so mind-blowing on the first encounter, they all streamed directly through without a second glance, heading for the impossible door. Dig O'Donnell stood to one side, taking close looks at the stones of its frame, taking more photographs of the carvings on them, double-checking in a notebook and a couple of textbooks he had in his pack. Meanwhile, the others waited restlessly for the guard to push the door open and let them through.

It was a different guard to the day before, Slater noted. Besides Terry Reid and his two henchfolk, Gates and Tate, Slater had seen at least a dozen other base security and hospitality staff around, so she assumed the guard posts changed often. A person would want to be rotated out of standing in a cave all day on their own, after all.

Slater held back Jeff and Marla, set them to recording as the team milled by the door. "Stay by the door here, get everyone passing through, then tail them. Try to get the scale of the place, yeah?"

Jeff nodded. "You got it." He shifted to one side, Marla moving on his back left like a shadow. For all his infuriating habits, Slater had to admit that Jeff was good at his job. He had an eye for direction, and producer's knack for the best attention-grab.

The crew all moved along the passageway, leaving only Dig still examining the door and Reid and Tate waiting to bring up the rear. Reid gave a curt smile, gestured Slater forward. She figured the guy had decided to always be at the back, but then again, perhaps that was exactly his job. Although she couldn't help feeling like a cow being herded to the slaughter. She needed to shake off the black mood that hung on her like a heavy cloak.

A short way along the passage to the next cavern, a discoloration on the smooth wall caught her eye. She moved closer, crouched to see better. Along with regular flashlights, they'd all been issued LED lamps mounted on headbands and she wasn't wearing hers yet. But she pulled it from her jacket pocket and flicked it on. The patch on the wall was exactly what she'd thought it was. Red. She touched a shaking finger to it, and her fingertip came away wet with blood. It had to be blood. And why was it still wet? She assumed the temperature, humidity, and generally slick surface would have something to do with that, but even so, it had to be fairly fresh. Her mind flickered back to the change of security guard by the door, suddenly now a potentially far more sinister turn of events.

She glanced back. Dig was still examining the door, and Reid and Tate stood back, patient. The other guard, Gates, with his dull eyes, broad stubbled jaw, and generic football jock body shape, had gone ahead with Sol Griffin, leading the party onwards. Aston, leaning into the weight of the bag on his shoulder, had paused and stood looking back at her.

"Sam!" Slater's voice was a hiss, a forced whisper. She gestured for him to come over. He frowned, clearly wondering what she was up to, but apparently saw the urgency in her eyes and his expression changed. Immediately she saw the friend from Lake Kaarme, and something in her was beyond grateful for that.

He came to crouch beside her and she showed him the smear. "It's blood, right?"

Sam put a fingertip to it as she had, examined the mark in the light of her headlamp. "Yeah. Gotta be." He looked around the passage, presumably for any other signs of injury. Then he leaned back, turned slightly. "See how it kind of smears across like that?"

"Like someone was bleeding and they fell against the wall?"

"Or were dragged along it."

Slater sucked in a breath. "Jesus, Sam."

"Let's not jump to any conclusions, okay? We haven't seen other drops of blood or stains. I can't see any now." He gestured to the floor right below the mark on the wall.

"Don't you think that's odd?" Slater asked.

"Yeah. Maybe it is. What's this?"

He reached down, fingers probing into a small crevice where the tunnel wall curved into the floor. He pulled out a metallic blue fidget spinner. "What the hell is this doing here?"

A thrill of shock made Slater's heart rate speed up. "Remember the guard on the door yesterday?"

Aston's brow creased as he thought back, then his eyebrows rose and he nodded. "Yeah, of course. This was his."

"So where is he?"

Sol Griffin appeared beside them, silent as if he'd materialized from the air. "You two okay?"

Without a word, Aston held up the spinner. Slater noticed that he didn't mention or even indicate the blood stain.

Sol took the spinner, turned it over on his palm.

"That's Aaron's, he was on duty last night. Must have dropped it. Thanks." Griffin dropped the spinner into a jacket pocket and strolled away, heading back along the passageway.

Slater frowned, looked at Aston. "Did we just get the brush-off?"

Aston nodded, his eyes troubled.

As they stood to move on, Dig closed up his books and came along, Reid and Tate following.

"Everything okay?" Reid asked, his deep voice echoing off the stone.

"Yeah. All good, mate," Aston said quickly, flicking a glance at Slater.

She read his intent immediately, *Let's keep this to ourselves for now.* She nodded subtly and they all started marching on the long walk through to the next cave. Slater realized that she and Sam had fallen naturally into stride with each other, hanging out together with unspoken ease. She wasn't sure how good she felt about that, but given the blood on the wall, she could put aside any other hurt and be glad of an ally right now.

Eventually they arrived back in the next cavern and the team slowly investigated, paying more attention than Sol had allowed them time for before. Moving clockwise around the roughly circular space, checking each small tunnel leading away, they discovered the first three only went a few dozen yards before tapering off into dead ends or tiny crevices too small for even a child to get through. The fifth and sixth tunnels were the same. But the fourth one around seemed to go further, and deeper. The floor of it slowly angled into a descent.

"There's a brighter glow this way," Jahara Syed called back from some twenty yards down the passage. "I think we should follow it."

With unspoken agreement, they all filed into the

tunnel. Slater checked for Jeff, but he was already on it, filming them pass then falling in behind, only Reid and Tate behind him. She and Aston stayed just ahead of the camera. The tunnel went on, and down, for some time, the only light their headlamps playing hectically as they all looked in different directions. But Syed was right, there seemed to be a greener glow emanating from somewhere ahead. After perhaps a hundred yards of dark tunnel, they emerged into a new chamber.

Slater's breath caught in her throat. "Oh my God!"

CHAPTER 10

Two Hägglunds tracked transports drove in convoy at speed across the Antarctic ice and snow. In the lead vehicle, crammed with operatives, Jasper Olsen ran a hand over his close-cropped iron gray hair and sighed. He felt as though he were getting too old for these kinds of missions. Surely, at nearly fifty-five, he should be at a comfortable warm desk rather than having his insides shaken loose in the middle of nowhere. But who was he kidding? He'd be bored and restless in less than a week if he was tied to an office. He shifted the assault rifle on his knees and stared out at the endless white expanse. Seemingly endless, but interrupted by the huge range of pyramid-shaped mountains not all that far away.

Olsen's breath steamed. Even in the heated Hägglunds it was much too damned cold for comfort. Halvdan Landvik paid well, but maybe not well enough for such conditions. Olsen smiled to himself. He was getting old. Ten years ago he wouldn't have even entertained these thoughts.

"This is far enough," he shouted to the driver ahead of him.

The man nodded and slowed the vehicle, coming gradually to a halt. The relief at the cessation of jouncing and noise made the whole squad sigh with relief. Eight men in this vehicle, another six in the one behind, plus extra gear. It wouldn't take long to set up their camp.

"Everybody out," Olsen said. "Let's get our shelters up and some food on the go."

"How far from the base are we?" someone asked.

"Far enough to not be seen yet." And that was, after all, the plan.

"Why don't we just go right in there, seize the base? It has great facilities and we don't have to camp out here and freeze our asses off."

General murmurs of assent rippled through the group, reluctant to leave even the dubious comforts of the Hägglunds.

"We're to take shelter and wait until we hear from our operative on the inside," Olsen said. He looked around at the frowns of his men. They were feeling the sting of the cold and the nagging voice of impatience just as much as he. "I know you'd like to enjoy the comforts of the base. So would I! But we need to let the team do their jobs first. Once we've heard back from our person on the inside that they've found what they're looking for, then we make our move."

"With respect, sir, why don't we simply make the captives do what we want?"

Olsen laughed. "Because the easy way is rarely the smart way, son. We'll get better results if the team continues about their work thinking they're getting paid. We need their excitement and enthusiasm to work in our favor, no? Besides, if we take the base now, there's no telling what might happen. Essential team members might be killed accidentally, or they'll resent being taken captive and try to sabotage efforts. It's better if we let them find what we want unharried."

"What is it, exactly, that we want?"

Olsen realized his own concerns with the isolated terrain, the entirely alien landscape and unknown factors of the mission, were concerning the men as well. He couldn't blame them for their questions, but didn't have any answers.

"That's one of the things our person on the inside will

tell us when the time comes," he said. "Now get to it. I want a camp established here in less than thirty minutes. Go!"

CHAPTER 11

The next cavern they entered blew every memory of the previous ones from Aston's mind. The entire subterranean system was like a Russian Matryoshka doll of wonders, but instead of each being smaller than the last, each was more incredible. A similar size to the previous cavern, this one also had patches of the vein-like fungus on the walls and small clumps of the glossy green ferns in crevices and cracks. But the glow came from entirely bigger and more prominent growths that twisted up the walls and across the high ceiling. Aston could best compare them to meandering vines, like a thick-stemmed ivy but without the leaves, the branches themselves emitting the luminescence. Some no thicker than butcher's string, right up to some broader than his thumb, they snaked and wove around each other, intertwining, filling the cavern with a soft light. It felt like being underwater.

And there was water. A light tinkling came from a stream running across one side of the cavern, emerging from an overhang of rock back and to the right, then disappearing again into a small crevasse on the other side. Just over the stream on that side, another tunnel appeared to lead away and down, but all around the space were caves and indentations, disappearing into shadow.

Syed made a noise of barely contained excitement and ran to the nearest outcrop of vines. Aston, his inner biologist almost as excited as hers, went with her. Syed carefully tapped a finger to one, brow scrunched in concentration. Aston noticed Jeff sidle up just behind them, filming, so he kept to Syed's other side.

"It feels like stone," Jahara said, barely above a whisper. She touched again, squeezed between forefinger and thumb. "They're hard and crystalline, but there is some give in them. I've never felt anything like this. But it looks more like a plant growth than a fungal spread, no?"

"But it's leafless," Aston said. "So maybe some new life form, one that shares the properties of both?"

"You want to name this one?" Syed said with a laugh. She looked up, scanned around until she spotted Sol Griffin. The man stood in the center of the cavern, staring around himself in wonder.

"Sol, is this the stuff? The greenium?"

He shook himself, tore his attention away from the walls. "No. No, the sample is definitely a kind of crystal structure, not like this. I've only seen photographs, but it's embedded in the rock, not growing from it like this stuff." He smiled, incredulous. "What is this stuff, Jahara? Sam?"

Both biologists shook their heads. "No idea," Syed said.

She pulled a field microscope from her bag and lined it up with one of the thicker sections of glowing vine. She stared into it for several moments, adjusting focus, moving slightly left and right like a jeweler appraising a fine gem.

"They're definitely organic but..." Her voice trailed off.

"But what?" Slater asked from behind Jeff.

"I'm not sure. Something isn't right. Let me study them some more. I'll need to take a sample back topside as well, of course."

Aston keenly wanted a look with her instruments, but knew better than to disturb a scientist at work. His expertise lay elsewhere anyway. As Slater and her crew got footage of the others, chatting briefly with each member of the team, he explored. Firstly he went to the stream, drawn to water as his own natural element. It was icy cold, fast flowing, and clear as glass. He used a sample cup and caught some, held it up in the glow of his headlamp. He saw some particulate matter, but it looked mineral. Nothing else of much interest. Even so, he sealed the cup and marked it with a Sharpie, then tucked it into his satchel. His large bag with his wetsuit and other gear sat off to one side and he left it there while he went to investigate the shadowed caves around the edge of the larger cavern.

Along the left side from where they had entered, opposite the stream, five similarly sized caves went back into the rock. Aston entered the first one and found Dig O'Donnell inside, shining his light onto what appeared to be a bench carved out of the bedrock. There were alcoves in the walls that might have been used for storage of some kind. The space was almost certainly a deliberate dwelling.

"This is man-made," Aston said, his stomach light with trepidation. "It has to be, right?"

"I don't know," Dig said quietly, clearly uncomfortable with the whole situation. He crouched, ran his hand along the edge of the bench.

"Looking for marks of tool use?" Aston asked.

Dig nodded. "It's almost impossible to accurately judge the age of stuff like this, but if it is deliberately made, then some considerable effort has been put into it."

"Especially without the aid of machine tools, which we can safely say weren't around when these caves were occupied."

Dig stood, took a deep breath. "Not human machine tools anyway."

"You think…"

Dig turned to leave. "I don't know what I think."

Aston followed him into the next cave along and it had a similar layout, similar constructions. And the next. All five openings along that side of the larger cavern were undoubtedly deliberately made dwellings, though none contained any other signs of habitation.

Standing in the fifth one, Aston asked, "Did they take everything with them when they left?"

Dig shrugged. "You're assuming they left."

"Well, they're not here now."

"No, but perhaps they died."

"Wouldn't there be bones? Lost possessions?"

Dig nodded. "I suppose so. You know, I mentioned it before when we spoke, but it's worth remembering there is a theory that Antarctica was once a far more temperate continent. Ancient climate change froze the polar caps of our planet, and that's what created Antarctica as we know it today. It's entirely possible we're looking at the remains of an ancient civilization. Their bones may have long since turned to dust, leaving only the rock to mark their existence. Rock is, after all, about the only thing that lasts pretty much forever."

Aston was about to question the truth of that when Slater spoke up from behind them. Jeff had the camera trained on them, capturing all the speculation. "How well backed by science is this ancient civilization theory?" Slater asked.

Dig laughed. "Well, there's been precious little exploration here in our modern age. We're no doubt the first to explore these caves since whoever carved them out, which could have been thousands of years ago, or tens of thousands, or even more. So there really isn't any hard science, it's all speculation."

"Otherwise known as conspiracy theory?" Slater pressed.

"Of course. But you of all people should know that sometimes the legends are true."

Before Slater could reply, a sharp crack and a cry of pain echoed to them from the main chamber. They ran together to see what had happened and found Jahara Syed sitting on the ground by one wall, rubbing her eyes. Terry

Reid was standing over her, his muscle, Ronda Tate, crouched beside the fallen biologist.

Sol Griffin hurried over. "I'm the physician here, let me through." He pulled a pack from his shoulder that Aston realized was a medical kit, and dropped it to the ground beside them as he crouched. He put a hand under Syed's chin, tipping her face up into the light of his headlamp. "Are you okay? What happened?"

Syed looked at her hands, rubbed her fingers against each other in confusion, then shook her hands out. She took a deep shuddering breath. "I'm okay. I'm pretty sure I'm okay, anyway. I wanted a sample of the vine, so I tried to break a piece off, but it was far too tough. It kind of flexed and moved, but there was no way I could break it. So I tried a knife, taking a scalpel to it, but it didn't even mark the surface. It's like the stuff has an outer skin that's... I don't know, kind of glassy of something, but flexible. So I decided to try to chip a section away. I put a chisel to it, right where some seemed attached to the cave wall. As soon as I cut through it, it sort of... not exactly exploded, but then something flashed, and I felt something like an electric shock shoot through me. It sat me right on my ass." She grinned sheepishly. "It hurt, but I think I was more surprised than injured. My hands are fine." She turned them palm out for everyone to see. They appeared unmarked.

"I think I want to give you a check over anyway," Sol said. "We need to be certain. I'll just run a few tests, okay?"

"Sure."

The rest of the team drifted away, muttering to each other. Aston moved to the wall behind Syed, looking for where she had received her shock. A small section of vine lay on the floor, where she had successfully chipped it free. He touched it tentatively, but it was cool and inert, so he dropped it into a sample bag and handed it to the biologist.

She smiled her thanks.

Turning back to the wall, Aston could see where she had chipped the small section free. The remaining end of the vine, standing a little free from the stone now, glowed with a hint of red. He frowned, trying to figure out what phenomena of natural plant activity might cause a reaction like that.

"Hey, you guys!" Slater called out. "I've found something."

CHAPTER 12

Alex Wong called a meeting of all Base Camp staff, because it was part of the job, not because he wanted to. These staff meetings were interminable, but they were required in his contract, so he did his job. What the hell he had done in some past life to deserve a job like this, he was at a loss to imagine. But, it paid the bills back home in Sydney, so he couldn't complain. He preferred his post at the Sydney offices of SynGreene, but this temporary assignment and the associated salary boost was too good to ignore. Though it turned out that eight months was a lot longer in reality than it looked on the calendar. And he was only halfway through.

"So no one has seen Aaron Steele?" he asked the gathered staff. The whereabouts of the member of the security team was the number one topic of conversation around the base. Where had the idiot gotten off to?

"I checked his bed in the staff dorm and it hasn't been slept in." Mitchell Boggs, a fairly recent hire, was nosy as hell. No doubt he took pleasure in checking up on Steele.

Wong frowned. "He didn't come back from guard duty yesterday?"

"I don't think so," Boggs said. "At least, he didn't report back. His card still marks him as on duty."

Wong heaved a tired sigh. "So we know he went to his post, underneath, on time. But that's it?"

"Yep. Is there any way he could have left? You know, quite a few people have complained about the isolation here and I know he really missed Crystal."

"Crystal?"

"His fiancée." Boggs' leer undermined his tone of concern.

Wong nodded. "Right. But it's not like there's a bus service back to Cape Town for him to catch. So no, I'm pretty sure he hasn't left. Did he seem especially, you know, depressed about it?"

"You mean suicidal?" The speaker was a woman whose name he couldn't quite remember. He thought she hailed from somewhere in the southern United States.

"Exactly."

"Nah, he was just bored, like the rest of us."

A small man at the back, Timmy something or other, raised his hand. "Do you think he might have shared the fate of the last team?"

A flash of anger surged through Wong and he shot one finger up to forestall any more talk. "We don't talk about that, even with each other. That's not our job, remember? We guard and take care of stuff up here and have one person on rotation to the stone door down there. That's it."

This did not satisfy Timmy. "What'll we do if the new team–"

Wong cut him off. "We do nothing. Not. Our. Job. That's what that big unit Terry Reid and his guys are for. They're the para-military people. We're just a security firm. I mean, half of you were walking office blocks at night four months ago. SynGreene headquarters is almost literally a world away from this place. Most of this is entirely out of our jurisdiction."

"Still, I wish we had a few of the military types up here, just in case." Timmy shifted uncomfortably in his seat. He met Wong's gaze only for a moment before lowering his eyes to the carpet.

Wong couldn't be bothered to carry on the pretense of a staff meeting. Aaron Steele going missing, after everything that had happened before, had him entirely on edge. "A bunch of us are armed and trained in the use of our sidearms. But we won't need them. Get back to work, everyone. At least look busy, if you can."

As his staff filed out, he poured himself a cup of coffee and wondered what might have happened to the other team. He knew more about the situation than most of the staff under him, but still precious little. He knew the team currently down below probably had no better chance of coming back up than the last one and it made him feel like a double-agent or a traitor of some kind. That didn't sit well with him. His nerves couldn't take these kinds of stresses. He was a corporate security guard exactly because he was about as likely to run into trouble in that job as he was in a supermarket checkout role. Actual threats made him antsy.

He jumped when the phone rang on the desk beside him, and he snatched it up. "Alex Wong."

"Alex, Arthur Greene. How goes everything?"

Wong swallowed. The big boss calling like the man could read his treacherous thoughts from afar. "It's all good," he lied.

"How are our scientists doing?" If Greene had any suspicions about the state of affairs at Alpha Base, his tone, courteous if not friendly, belied them.

"They're all down below, sir. On their second day of exploration. So far, no reports of any problems." He didn't need to mention Aaron Steele's disappearance if the boss only asked about the science team.

"That's good to hear," Greene said. "Now, have you seen the latest weather report?"

Wong had, and that only contributed to his anxieties. "Yes, sir, I'm keeping abreast of everything. We're ready for it."

"Excellent. I'll check in again soon, but you let me know if anything comes up that I should know about."

"Absolutely, Mr. Greene."

Wong returned the phone to its cradle, privately hoping he was ready.

CHAPTER 13

Aston had been developing a bad feeling about this whole expedition since Griffin had found him at the aquarium, and nothing that had happened so far had eased the feeling. In fact, everything only made him more uneasy. Syed's shock from a tough vine-like plant should really have been the peak of weirdness for the day, but he would never be that lucky. Of course Slater had found a dead body.

At first, Aston had expected it to be the missing guard, the one whose fidget spinner they'd found. But that disappearance and the associated blood smear remained a mystery. Slater crouched beside the remains, Jeff spotlighting the camera over her shoulder to capture it all. Aston hurried to be the first there, and squatted beside Slater in the gloom of the small side cave.

The corpse was a man, slumped back against the far wall like he'd slid down into a sitting position, as if exhausted. His legs were stuck out straight, arms resting limply on his thighs, head tilted to one side like he had passed out. His mouth hung open, the blackness beyond his teeth absolute in the contrasting shadows. What little remained of his flesh was yellowed like old leather, sucked tight to the bones of his face and hands, split and flaking like old scales. He had simply wasted away, it seemed, nothing in the caves to consume him. Perhaps not even the bugs one might find topside, Aston presumed.

"Judging by his clothes, I'd guess an early twentieth-century explorer," he said.

Sol Griffin stood behind, palms on his knees as he

leaned in to look. "Have we perhaps found the other member of the missing party? The partner of the man who originally brought that tiny sample of greenium out of here so long ago?"

Aston shrugged. It was as good a guess as any, but still, only a guess. His scientific mind wanted evidence.

"I see no injuries. Looks like he simply collapsed here," Dig O'Donnell said. "You think he got lost and starved?"

"Seems entirely possible," Sol mused.

Aston noticed something hanging around the man's neck and reached out a finger to lift it from inside the ancient jacket. A small, black Bakelite cylinder on a thick string emerged, with a silvery lens on one side. A small ring stuck out from the underside.

"What is that?" Slater asked.

"It's an old explorer's light from the days before batteries," Aston said. He pulled the ring at the bottom firmly and a chain came with it. The unit made a soft whirring sound and a light glowed into flickering life, then dimmed again. "Still kinda works! The chain winds an interior mechanism, creating an electric current that lights the bulb."

"A Dynamo lamp," Dig said. "That is a real treasure! May I?" He reached out a hand.

Aston carefully lifted the device over the corpse's fragile head and handed it over. As he did, he noticed the dead man's jacket had a cut right through in the center of the chest, which had gone unnoticed at first glance.He gently lifted the side of the jacket open and saw a glint of black. Using just his thumb and forefinger, he delicately tugged on it, removing the item from between the man's ribs. It was cool to the touch. But it was the artifact's strange appearance that chilled him to the bone.

"It's a knife," he said, voice low with concern. "Looks like flint, but blood red, almost black." He held it up for the others to see.

The Dynamo lamp forgotten in his other hand, Dig reached out to take the knife. "Primitive design, stone age method of construction by the looks of it. See how the edges have been worked?" He held it out so they could get a better look. "How could something like that be down here?"

"Perhaps another member of his team carried it here," Anders Larsen suggested. "And I guess they had a disagreement."

"Now we know he didn't starve to death," Terry Reid said, his voice echoing from the mouth of the small cave.

"Seems unlikely that a twentieth-century explorer would carry such an anachronistic weapon," Sol said.

"Yet here it is," Larsen said quietly.

"But I'm not sure it is the partner of the guy who got out with the greenium," Dig said. "We'd have to study his possessions more, but it's entirely possible this guy is from another expedition altogether. There had been a lot of activity in Antarctica back in those days, and lots of folk didn't make it back. If they got lost down here, I can see why they never returned."

"What about the color?" Reid asked. "Blood red flint. You ever seen anything like that?"

Dig nodded. "Yes, but only in one place, a long damn way from here." He turned the blade over in his hands, his eyes taking it in. "Heligoland, an island in the North Sea. Red flint was so coveted that people risked their lives to recover it."

"Why?" Sol asked. "Is it superior to regular flint?"

"No. Some think it was treasured for its rarity. Others believe it was valued because people believed it come from Doggerland."

"Doggy who?" Reid asked.

"Doggerland," Aston said. "It was a land mass that

connected Britain to the rest of Europe. It flooded about eight thousand years ago."

"Some call it 'Britain's Atlantis," Dig said. Aston rolled his eyes but Dig didn't notice. '

"Was it real?" Reid pressed.

"Oh, it was definitely real. Fossils and artifacts have been dragged up from the seabed. Mammoths, prehistoric tools and weapons. There are plenty of legends surrounding it too. The Nazis and even some factions within Russia shared some far-fetched legends about it."

"Far-fetched being the operative phrase," Aston said, momentarily discomfited by mention of the Nazis. He remembered all too well what had happened the last time he crossed paths with a Nazi legend.

"Do you think this stone is the same stuff as the red flint?" Sol asked.

"I can't say for certain," Dig said. "Perhaps, but this has a different...feel to it. Almost as if it's made of blood, the red is so deep." He barked a laugh. "Don't listen to me. My imagination runs wild sometimes."

Aston half listened as he continued to examine the body, gently probing through the jacket pockets. He found a small notebook, a journal of some kind. He glanced up and saw the rest of the party looking at the strange stone knife, so he slipped the journal into his own pocket for later examination. He wasn't sure what made him keep the discovery from the others, but he felt a need to take some kind of control of events as they unfolded in ever more confusing and concerning directions. He certainly didn't buy the theory that one of this poor bastard's friends carried a Stone Age knife and had used it to murderous effect. But he had no better theory at this stage that wasn't entirely fanciful, and that made him decidedly uneasy.

He took the Dynamo lamp back from Dig and put that in his pocket too. They could perhaps date this guy with an internet search of that item when they got back topside. Slater waved Jeff aside, nodding towards the group still discussing the knife. As the cameraman moved to get footage of their conversation, she pulled Aston out of the cave and past the burly Reid and his two associates.

With some privacy afforded by distance from the others, she whispered, "Have you had any sort of... weird feeling?"

Aston suppressed a humorless laugh. "I haven't not had a weird feeling since all this nonsense began."

Slater smiled wryly. "Yeah, I hear that. But that's not what I mean. I don't mean in general, but right now. I just had a sense of being watched or followed or something."

"You think we're not alone down here?"

"I get that distinct impression," she said.

The skin prickled on the back of Aston's neck. "Is it because we found that fidget spinner thing, and the blood?" he asked.

Slater shrugged. "Maybe. I don't know. But we need to be careful. I'm convinced we haven't been told everything about this place, maybe about stuff that happened here before. And Sol didn't seem too bothered about what we found."

"Maybe he thinks the guy just dropped it. And maybe he did. Perhaps we're being paranoid."

"It's not paranoia when they're really out to get you," Slater said.

"Or when someone really is watching you?" Aston asked.

"Exactly."

"Okay," Sol said loudly, making them jump. The rest of the team had emerged from the side cave. "We need to keep exploring, as we can't spend too much time distracted from the main purpose of our expedition."

"What about that guy?" Dig asked.

Sol raised his hands. "I think it's entirely possible several explorers got lost down here over the years, just like you said, Dig. We may well come across more unfortunate souls as we move on. Just like the frozen bodies on Everest, there's not really much we can do about them."

Syed still sat across the cave, recovering from her unexpected shock. "You can't just leave him now we know he's there," she said.

"Well, we could. But we won't," Sol said. "I'll have a couple of the security staff from Base come down here at some point and recover the remains. Or at least document them and try to inform any ancestors. And if we can recover him, we'll keep him in safe storage and hand everything over to the right authorities." He paused, thinking. Then, "I guess we'll make sure we photograph the scene before we move him, too. But that's not your concern, ladies and gents. We need to focus on our mission. If you've seen all you need to in here, we should press on. We need to find those crystalline greenium deposits and concentrate our efforts there."

As people gathered their gear together, preparing to move on, Slater looked left and right, her brows knitted together. "Where is that idiot, Jeff?"

CHAPTER 14

Jeff Gray stalked along the dark tunnel, all the while questioning his sanity. There couldn't possibly be something down here. They were god knew how deep beneath Antarctica. It was just his imagination. Had to be. But what if it wasn't?

Then he heard the sound again, that soft scuffing and subtle ticking that had caught his ear back in the previous cavern. But no matter how fast he moved, he couldn't seem to catch up with whatever it was, always seemingly just ahead of him in the blackness. He had all his own lights off, moving by the glow from the cave behind, deeper in the dark. But now there was precious little light from his back, the murk almost palpable. He wanted to prove himself. Imagine if he filmed something else in these caves, then showed the footage to Jo Slater. Maybe she'd stop treating him with such disdain. He used to be a boss, for God's sake. This job of running around like a lackey made him grind his teeth.

He paused to catch his breath, thinking about the wisdom of his love of burgers and ice creams. He had certainly grown in girth over the last couple of years, and was far from fit. There had been a time when he could have run five miles without thinking about it. Now he was lucky to walk five hundred yards without panting.

How far had he come? Too far to be safe on his own, that was almost certain. He wanted to turn on his camera light, bathe the passage in brightness, but also didn't want to scare off whatever he had heard. He was torn between excitement to find something and fear of what it might be.

Though he was out of shape, he was no coward. The discovery of the previous cavern, the remains of the explorer, and the blood red knife, had got him revved up for even greater discoveries. There was definitely more to the story here than a simple exploration in search of an energy source, he was certain of that. There were secrets to be revealed, and he had a feeling he might be able to cash in on a few of them if he played things right, as well as earn that respect from Slater that he was due.

When everyone had started organizing their gear, and Slater had been deep in quiet discussion with Aston, Jeff had felt superfluous. A pang of jealousy struck deep in his gut. He knew he stood little chance with a woman like her. Even though he was a bit out of shape and heavier than he would like, he was still a smart and good-looking guy. But he'd seen the way the others looked at him, like he was some bumbling fool. He had proved people wrong before and he would again. But over all of that, for some reason Slater's closeness with Aston really stuck in his craw. He had tried to be friendly to Aston, tell him that Jo would forgive him, even though he hadn't believed that for a moment. Aston had been a complete ass to Jo. And yet, there she was, touching his arm and confiding in him, thick as thieves. Maybe she had forgiven him after all, and that sucked.

Well, let it not be said that Jeff Gray would take that kind of ostracization lying down. While they were quietly sharing secrets, he had heard a sound and was certain he had caught a glimpse of movement in the main passageway leading off the glowing cavern. He had only intended to be a minute, not go far at all, but the sound remained so tantalizingly close. He would follow it a little more before he went back. It sounded small, not something to be too scared of, maybe a creature previously undiscovered that he could claim credit for. Maybe even name. He took a deep breath, his equilibrium regained, and moved on slowly. The silence seemed heavy, even the murmurs of conversation from behind lost to the distance now.

He strained his ears, desperate to hear whatever it was again, and had about given up, cursing his need to rest, when it came once more. A slow scrape, a drag of tail or foot maybe? And then that rapid, soft ticking, like a clock in the distance counting off seconds way too fast. He started forward again, then stopped, looked around, blind in the darkness. He realized the sound had come from behind him that time. Surely that was a trick of the close tunnel, a strange echo.

His heart rate increased, this time with nerves rather than exertion. He lifted the camera, his fingers feeling for the light mounted on top, then hovering over the button to switch it on. He turned a slow circle, listening hard. Then he remembered the camera had a night vision setting. If there was even a tiny amount of light here, it could make use of that, give him a view without needing his bright lamp. His fingers crept over the controls, familiar without needing to see them, and he slowly raised the camera to look through the viewfinder. The tunnel resolved in deep shades of green and black, barely better than blindness, but he picked out a few tiny details. He panned the lens slowly to the right. A soft blur of movement whipped past.

He gasped, moved the camera back again, but nothing was there. Then that soft scraping again, this time to his left. As he turned that way it came again, from his right. He stepped back, moved around, heard it on both sides at once. And then behind him. The dim view through the camera showed him nothing except a few stark edges of rock and occasional blurs of swift movement. Was he surrounded? And by what?

His stomach churned with fear, all thoughts of bravery and discovery fled. Suddenly wanting to see everything clearly, but terrified to look, he gave up all hope of having something to himself and turned tail for the cavern and the rest of the team. His feet slapped the rock, echoing loudly after the stillness of his slow search, every step a gunshot of noise. And the scuffling and ticking seemed to trail along behind him, always right on his tail, never quite catching up. A wail of fear escaped his lips as he gasped for breath and increased his pace. He hurtled headlong through the tunnel, running one hand along the rock beside him so he didn't run right into it. Surely he should be back by now, or at least see the glow from the cavern of luminescent vines. A new panic gripped him. Had he turned himself around? Was he running away from his friends, further into subterranean depths and who knew what monstrous creatures?

If he stopped now, whatever pursued him would be on him in an instant. But he was slowing anyway, lungs burning, feeling like his heart was about to burst, and they hadn't caught him yet. Were the things herding him? Were they deliberately holding back, driving him further into the darkness with some malevolent purpose?

"Oh my god, no!"

Jeff gave in to his fear, screamed out in desperation, calling for help. Unable to bear the darkness any longer, he slid the switch on the light above his camera. The tunnel leaped into view in stark contrasting tones of gray rock and black shadow. His legs, jelly from lack of oxygen and over-exertion, failed beneath him and he tripped and fell. He hit the rock on his knees and one palm, the other hand holding the camera high to protect it. The palm he had landed on flared into pain as the skin was scraped off by the rough ground, pain blossomed in his knees from the impact. He fell onto one side, rolled onto his butt, and swung the camera around to shine his light on whatever pursued him.

He screamed as his beam reflected back off shining,

armor-like surfaces swarming up the tunnel. He saw an array of multi-faceted eyes, snapping mandibles like curved swords. For a moment, whatever the things were arched back, screeching shrilly as his light seemed to assault them, then one struck out, smashing the camera from his grasp. It hit the rock with a crack of glass and plastic, and the light broke. Everything fell into darkness once more. Jeff Gray felt his bladder release, had a moment to contemplate the horror of what he'd seen, then all thought fled as his body was shredded by dozens of tiny striking slashes, and sharp pain sliced through his flesh.

CHAPTER 15

"**H**as anyone seen Jeff?" Aston scanned the cavern, trying to catch sight of the annoying cameraman. Funny, when you didn't want him around he was omnipresent. But now he seemed to have vanished.

People stopped packing, looked around themselves.

"The cameraman?" Dig asked.

"Yeah," Slater said. "Anyone see where he went?" She put her hands on her hips and let out an annoyed huff of breath.

"He was right beside me in the cave there, when we were looking at the body," Marla said. "I didn't see where he went when we came out."

There was a general shaking of heads and murmuring, people looking to one another to confirm no one was wise to the man's whereabouts.

"Well, he couldn't have gone far," Slater said. "It's not like there's far to go."

"Plenty of caves and tunnels down here," Larsen said.

"That way."

Several heads turned to see who had spoken. Ronda Tate pointed to the dark tunnel mouth on the other side of the small stream.

"You're sure?" Aston asked. She nodded. "Why didn't you say something before?"

Tate shrugged. "I assumed he knew what he was doing." The woman's eyes were hard, her expression stark beneath brown hair so short it was almost a crew cut.

"You didn't think to stop him? Or tell any of us?"

Tate smiled like she thought Aston was asking her to

sprout wings and fly. "We're here to protect you, not babysit you."

Aston smirked. "But it was definitely that tunnel?"

"Yes. It's the only one you haven't checked yet anyway, and as he hasn't come out I'm guessing it's not another cave. Looks like it goes a fair way." Tate looked down the tunnel, then back at the group. "He only kinda stuck his head in anyway, it didn't look like he planned to leave. I didn't realize until you brought it up that he wasn't here. But he definitely didn't come back past me."

"Tate, we need to be more vigilant," Reid said, giving his subordinate a hard look. "As it happens, we are here to babysit these people. From now on, I want everyone to stay together. Tate, Gates, if either of you sees anyone going off on their own, you call them back."

Tate pressed her lips together, clearly embarrassed to have been so publicly scolded. She nodded sharply.

"Yes, sir," Gates said, throwing a grimace of commiseration in Tate's direction.

"You better go ahead and check," Reid told Tate. "See if you can catch up to him."

"Wait a minute," Sol said. "It's the direction I was going to suggest we go next anyway. Let's all move on together and we can probably catch him up."

Slater frowned, shook her head. "Why did he go off on his own? That idiot." She looked over to Marla. "Did he seem okay to you?"

Marla shook her head. "As okay as you could expect, I guess. He's a bit weird, after all."

"Everyone ready?" Aston asked, trying to keep the annoyance from his voice. "We'd better find him before he gets in trouble."

Packs and bags were hoisted into place and the group gathered near the stream. Reid sent Tate out in front, the rest of the group to follow, and he and Gates brought up the rear. They lit their head-mounted torches and entered the dark mouth of the tunnel.

The walls were rounded, the floor mostly flat and smooth. The ceiling of the passage arced above them, just beyond Aston's reach. Even a little more than an arm's length above his head, the place felt claustrophobic. They traveled a long way, several hundred yards by Aston's estimation, and eventually came to a fork. The larger passage led off to the left, a smaller one to the right.

"I'm going to fire that idiot," Slater said, for only Aston to hear. "I wanted to replace him before this job but there wasn't time."

"Hardly worth it at this stage. Not like you can hire a new cameraman right now. Just put up with him. He's annoying, but he's good at the job, right?"

"I suppose so, if I give him constant nudges to keep working."

"I could do his job and mine just as well," Marla said, with a cheeky grin. "For what it's worth. Of course, I'd need the camera."

Slater returned the young woman's smile, but Aston saw the concern in her eyes.

"Which way?" Sol asked.

Aston shone his torch into the left-hand tunnel, then the right. Down the right side he saw something wet on the ground and took one step forward. He glanced back and saw Slater, Marla, and Dig side by side just behind him, also looking at the wet patch. By Slater's expression and Dig's suddenly pale face and tight lips, he figured that they shared his opinion that it was blood. More from the same source as before, just beyond the door? The blood there that may or may not have belonged to the fidget spinner guard? This could be more of his. Or it could be new, maybe Jeff's. Or it could have come from someone or something else entirely. Terry Reid moved up beside Aston, saw the blood on the floor, and gently pushed Aston's hand aside, moving the beam of light away from it.

Aston frowned at him and the big man said, "Let's not panic everyone."

"Panic them? That was blood, right? You think it might be Jeff's?"

"I don't know what to think. It had to come from somewhere, but if that's your cameraman's blood, why isn't there a trail?"

Slater frowned. "Maybe we'd find one if we went looking that way?"

"I didn't see one leading away, did you?"

"I guess not."

Sol, Larsen, and Syed had moved a little further down the left-hand tunnel and Sol called back to them. "More green glow this way."

Aston and Reid shared a long look. Eventually Reid said, "Let's just keep our eyes and ears open, okay?"

"Maybe you and your pals could go all up front now? You know, as you've got the guns."

Terry grinned. "Sure."

Slater looked from Aston to Reid and back again. She cupped her hands around her mouth and shouted, "Jeff! You up there?"

They all paused, listening hard as her voice echoed away. There was no reply.

"We should go look," Slater said. "I know Jeff is an idiot, but we can't ignore that blood or the fact that he may be up there. Maybe hurt."

Reid nodded. "Gates, Tate." The other two mercs came over. "I want you two to go up this passage, lights on, stay alert. The cameraman may have gone this way. Give it a few hundred yards, see what you find. If the way splits, you come back and tell me. If you find anything, you come back and tell me."

"And if we find nothing after a few hundred yards?" Gates asked.

"Guess."

"We come back and tell you?"

"Right."

With a nod, the two moved off, shining their lights left and right. "Come on," Reid said, and led Aston and Slater back around to the other tunnel. The rest of the team waited a few paces along.

"Anything?" Sol asked.

"No." Slater's face was dark. "Reid sent his two to have a look."

"Okay. Meanwhile, let's go this way. We might find Jeff up here."

Slater didn't reply, but exchanged a knowing look with Aston and Reid. They clearly didn't expect to find Jeff any more than she did. They moved ahead, towards the next gentle green glow.

CHAPTER 16

The downward-sloping path wound deeper into the bowels of the earth. Aston couldn't shake the feeling they were descending into the maw of a waiting beast. After several minutes' more walking, Reid led the team into a magnificent chamber. The group stood dumbfounded for several long moments, staring around themselves in wonder. The space was huge, stretching a good fifty yards or more across and almost as high. It was long, more than a hundred yards from left to right. The tunnel they had emerged from stood about one-third of the way along one long side. Across the other side, two more tunnels led away into darkness. The walls were largely smooth, crenelated in places, with stalactites and stalagmites bigger than two men, one standing atop the other, making a forest of upthrusting and down-hanging spikes. In the center-right of the enormous cavern a huge lake shimmered in the green glow. And that glow grew brighter as they stood there. More of the luminescent vines and fungus striped the walls, more small curling ferns filled the crevices. But more than that, sparkling flecks of bright, almost neon green glittered from every part of the cave, even the ground. The crystals seemed to absorb the light of their flashlights and grow brighter with it, as though they drank the brightness in and exulted in it.

"This is remarkable," Larsen said, voice low with astonishment. "These crystals, they could be the..." He grimaced. "The greenium."

"You think so?" Aston asked.

The geologist gestured weakly around them. "Look at

it. What other explanation is there? It matches the profile. And the deposits are numerous."

"Is this it?" Sol asked. "Is this the greenium?"

Larsen winced again at the word and Aston couldn't blame him. But given the stuff was green, and the whole venture financed by Arthur Greene of SynGreene, it seemed unlikely the name would change. He felt that it had already stuck, however cringe-worthy it might be.

"I'll start some tests," Larsen said, setting down his bag.

Aston moved immediately to the large pool. The cavern floor sloped down towards it, the water filling a natural depression in the cave's formation. He dipped his fingers in at the edge and smiled. It was warm, like a welcoming bath. He sensed a presence beside him and looked up. Slater stood there, filming with her smartphone.

"See what I've been reduced to?" she said, but her smile was weak. Aston saw some measure of fear in it.

Marla stood beside her, sound gear packed away in the bag over her shoulder. "At least you're doing something," she said. "I'm kinda redundant all of a sudden."

"Kids are making entire movies on iPhones these days," Aston said. "You're hip, that's all."

"Hip?" She flashed a peace sign. "Far out, man! Peace, love, dope!"

He laughed, embarrassed. "Whatever. This is warm, almost hot. Must be fed by a geothermal spring."

Terry Reid had been helping Sol set up some halogen lights and the cavern burst into brighter relief. Immediately the green crystals responded, brightening too, giving everything an alien vibe. But the light penetrated the water more and Aston felt a surge of joy.

"Look!" He pointed down into the water.

Schools of small fish darted back and forth in the deeper part of the pool, a few feet out from the edge. Jahara

Syed came to squat beside him, Slater moving to the side to quietly film.

"You feeling better?" Aston asked.

Syed nodded. "A little shaky, but I'm fine. Look, see that plant life along the edge where the water gets really deep?"

"Almost the same bright green as the light from the crystals," Aston said. "They almost look more like tentacles than leaves. Like some kind of giant anemone rather than a plant, you think?"

Syed scooted along on hands and knees to get closer and leaned over the water to look. "Could be. Hard to tell, they're too deep to see properly."

"And the fish!" Aston's excitement had driven away all other concerns for the time being. This was his natural element. "I wonder if they're a unique species or a strain evolved from a known species?"

"Do they have eyes?" Syed asked. "Or blind, like the cave fish we know?"

"Again, hard to tell from here. But they have bioluminescence, you can see the glow of it along their lateral lines, and around the face. Makes me think they have at least a rudimentary eye."

"Do you think they eat this plant or anemone or whatever it is?"

Aston pursed his lips. "Maybe. There some particulate matter in the water too. We need a closer look at all of this, and samples." He dragged his bag over with a grin. "I'm going in."

Syed watched him for a moment, a small smile playing at the corners of her mouth, then she pulled over her own bag. "I'll collect water samples and whatever else I can reach from the edge. Let me know if you need help."

"Sure."

Aston pulled off his shoes and clothes, keeping on only

his underwear, and put his things in a small pile beside the large pool. Appearing unmindful of the stares from Slater and Syed, though secretly enjoying the fact that both were taking a good, long look, he pulled on his wetsuit and fins, then pulled a mask and snorkel from the bag. He strapped a dive light to his wrist and turned it on, then turned to sit on the edge of the pool and hung his legs into the water. The wetsuit seemed superfluous, the water was so warm, but it added the comfort of protection beyond simple temperature. He'd worn chainmail underwater before, against sharks, though doubted he'd need anything like that in this circumstance. Then flashes in his mind of blood on the rock, the missing cameraman, the metallic blue fidget spinner. Could there be danger down there? He pushed the concerns aside and slipped into the water. He'd go slowly and stay alert.

The warmth of the pool enveloped him. Knotted muscles began to loosen. He was at home here beneath the surface.

He swam across toward the far side, looking down into the shimmering, clear pool. The green glow in the cavern was so bright now that it illuminated the water to considerable depths, assisted by his dive light. He saw more tiny signs of life, crustaceans glowing the same ubiquitous green, curling and twisting in the beam from his wrist. The plant or anemone thing he and Syed had seen from the edge grew everywhere, deep past where shadow obscured his vision. He still couldn't decide if it were vegetable or animal. He'd dive for a sample on the way back. Then something else caught his eye.

He turned in the water, shifted to better shine his light. Down deep he saw a distinct right angle of dark stone. Drawing a breath, he dived and kicked down. A small dome of rock, like a miniature hill, rose from the murky depths of the pool, and set into one side of it was a doorway. The frame was dark like the one they had encountered before, and carved with similar disquieting designs. But while it was similar to the one in the first cavern, this doorway looked exactly like the one he and Slater had seen under Lake Kaarme. A perfect rectangle, made from carved blocks of stone set into the rock. Around three meters high, nearly two wide, a man-made piece of engineering, leading away into pitch blackness, no actual door filling it. He had the same thought he had entertained back in Finland, a seeming lifetime ago. Man-made or something-made. Something with the intelligence and skills and tools to construct a portal like this, deep beneath the water in the middle of the most isolated place on Earth. His lungs burned and he kicked back up to the surface, blew the water from his snorkel and sucked in fresh air.

He floated on the surface for a while, breathing deeply, staring down at the impossible rectangle. He had to know more. Drawing and holding a deep breath, he kicked down again. His ears popped as he went, reaching for the top of the huge doorway. He could hold his breath a long time, having had a lot of practice in his chosen career, but he wished he had a SCUBA tank and plenty of time to explore. He would have a quick look, then insist on returning for a tank once he'd learned a little more.

He pulled himself down and into the stygian passageway beyond the doorframe. His dive light showed him a rocky tunnel going a few yards forward then curving up. He estimated he had about a minute to explore before the need for air became desperate, and pushed on. He swam a short way and saw the unmistakable rippling of light on the water's surface. He frowned. There was no way he could be back at the surface now, he had to be a good twenty feet under at least, probably more. But he pushed up and his head broke through into fresh, cool air. Around him was another cavern, much smaller than the one he had dived from, but large nonetheless. More of the glowing vines and crystal lit the space, making dark shadows where the rock creased away. Stalagmites and stalactites filled the cave, making a strange forest, reflecting the light of the greenium.

Aston stared around himself, stunned and confused. He looked back over his shoulder and the rippling surface of the pool he had emerged into. Every sense of direction he possessed insisted the level of this pool had to be well below the surface of the large pool in the huge cavern above. Why didn't this pool and cave flood, draining the one in the cavern he had come from? It had to be some strange property of trapped air or pressure. Or something.

"Who are you kidding, Sam," he said quietly to himself. There was nothing natural about any of this. The others needed to know.

He sucked in a deep breath and dived back, through the short passage and out the large doorway, then kicked up to the surface shimmering with green light above. He burst up and shook water from his hair and face, about to call out to the team and tell them the impossible news, but the words died in his throat. Everyone was gathered on the far side of the huge cavern and they were all clearly upset.

CHAPTER 17

Aston peeled off the wetsuit, gave himself a quick once-over with a towel, then pulled on his jeans and sweater again. The far end of the cavern had several tall outcrops, almost like the folds in a giant curtain. The team had gathered around one, shining their lights into its shadows. The green crystals all around glowed twice as brightly as they had when Aston had entered the water. It seemed they continued to draw energy from the torchlight and the halogens Sol had set up again. There wouldn't be shadows in this place for much longer.

"What is it?" Aston called out.

Slater spun on the spot, face relieved. "There you are! Where the hell did you go?"

"I'll explain later. What have you found?"

Her face soured. "More dead bodies."

Aston pushed through to take a better look. A corpse lay in the depths of the indentation in the rock, propped against the wall in a slumped sitting position.

"The clothes are modern," Aston said.

"And she's not really decomposed at all," Slater said. "Hard to guess how long she's been here, but not long, I'd say."

"What do you think, Doc?" Aston asked Sol, not caring that his sarcastic emphasis raised a couple of eyebrows.

"Honestly, I'm not sure what to think," Sol Griffin said. "I've made a cursory examination and there are no obvious signs of injury or sickness. I agree, she can't have been here long, but beyond that I'm at a loss."

Aston frowned. He couldn't put his finger on why, but

he didn't trust Sol at all. Right now, he was convinced the man was lying about something.

"Speaking of injury," Slater said. "Wait until you see the next one."

"There's another?"

Slater led him around to the next recess of stone, holding her flashlight ahead of her. She stopped and gestured him forward, clearly reluctant to get too close to whatever lay in the shadows. Marla, Aston noticed, stood off to one side, her face dark.

Aston blew out a long breath. He was so over all this already, but they were in too deep now. He moved past Slater to see a body that had been horribly abused. Its head was missing, nowhere to be seen. The torso, arms and legs had been shredded, as though someone in a furious rage had taken to it with a machete. Or something with long, sharp claws and teeth, Aston mused, a tickle of fear at the base of his spine.

"What the hell do you make of that?" Slater asked.

"I wouldn't think an animal would do this. The body hasn't been consumed at all, just ripped up. Animals don't tend to kill for fun."

"So what then, if not an animal? A tribe of headhunters?"

Aston turned away from the atrocity, happy to look at Slater's beautiful, living face instead, even if it was blanched with horror. He shrugged.

"Hey, come here," Sol called out from a little further around the cavern. "We've found another and she's alive."

Anders Larsen sat back, smiling at the samples of green crystals in the jars in front of him. While the rest of the team were distracted with what appeared to be some rather gruesome discoveries, he'd had an opportunity to quietly complete an array of field tests. His geologist's soul was buzzing with what he'd found. The sparkling stuff teemed with energy, off the chart for their size. It was like nothing else he had ever heard of, let alone seen for himself. It had to be greenium, however much he hated that name.

He couldn't even begin to wrap his head around the how and why of it all. His mind spun with theory after theory, trying to make some sense of it. But nothing in his extensive professional bank of knowledge offered up any answers. It was almost as if the cave were seeded by aliens or something. He chuckled to himself. Why the hell not? After everything else they'd seen thus far, it was no more outrageous a suggestion than any other. But it didn't matter. What he was certain about was that this miraculous stuff was exactly what Halvdan Landvik was looking for. While the others remained distracted, he hastily packed up his gear. Right now was the perfect time to slip away unnoticed.

"This is all too much!"

He startled, turned quickly to see Jahara Syed standing behind him. The biologist hadn't noticed his guilty jump as she stared across the cavern at the rest of the team.

"Too much?" he asked.

She looked down at him, offered an uncomfortable half-smile. "Everything is so weird, and I can't look at any more dead bodies."

Larsen frowned. "You're a biologist. You're disturbed by bodies?"

"Human bodies, yes! I study animal and plant life. I'm not a damn medical examiner."

"No, I guess not. Me either."

She crouched beside him. "Have you found anything interesting?"

"Yes. The crystals have unusual properties, lots of energy."

Syed looked nervous. "Radioactive?"

He laughed. "No, thankfully. But I can't tell much down here. I'm limited as to the kind of analysis I can perform without decent equipment. I can't wait to get back to base camp and investigate properly."

"Me too," Syed said. "I'm facing the same limitations. But even with the basic equipment I have here, these tough vines are bizarre."

Larsen clenched his jaw, desperate to be away, but he couldn't raise suspicion. "Bizarre how? I mean, apart from the obvious."

"Well, the obvious weirdness is the fact that they're even here at all. Then there's the shock the thing gave me. I'm still tingling from that. But beyond all that, the structure itself is weird."

"Cellular, you mean?"

Syed nodded eagerly. "Exactly. Based on what I can see with the portable microscope, the cellular structure is wrong."

Larsen found himself fascinated despite his need to get back topside. "Wrong? What do you mean?"

Syed licked her lips, shook her head. "It looks crystalline. But it's living, organic. If I didn't know better, I'd say it was from an alien planet or something."

Larsen suppressed a physical reaction to her voicing exactly his own thoughts of only moments before. Thoughts that were frivolous at best, but echoed now by the biologist, they scared him. Before he could say more, Slater stepped out of the folded rock across the cavern and called Syed's name.

"Jahara, we need your help here."

Syed nodded and stood. She glanced down at Larsen, brows creased. "What do you think is happening?" she asked.

Larsen raised his hands. "I have no idea. But let's stick

to science, yeah? It's always best to let emotion take a back seat and just study the facts."

"Maybe that's good advice." She trotted away towards Slater and the rest of the team.

Larsen watched her go, relieved that Slater had done him an inadvertent favor, and then grabbed his bag and slipped quietly out of the cavern. Landvik's men would be in place somewhere nearby, assuming everyone had played their part correctly. As soon as he could get a signal, he'd call them in. He smiled as he hurried back through the tunnels and caves, heading for the freight elevator.

CHAPTER 18

Slater watched as Syed jogged over to her and then said, "We've found someone alive. Sol is taking a look, but she says she's a biologist, so I figured you'd be interested."

Syed gaped. "Someone is alive down here?"

Slater saw her own incredulity reflected in Syed's eyes. And the realization as the woman quickly put together exactly what Slater herself had immediately thought: that there had been another party down here very recently. Slater thought perhaps Sol Griffin knew all about it. Her paranoid thoughts were becoming reality quicker than she liked. "Yeah," she said. "Seems like none of us had a full story before, huh?"

Sol crouched by the woman, tucked back into the deepest of the tall alcoves in the rock wall. She was short, with dark hair, and large brown eyes that blinked slowly in the greenish light. She took quick, shallow breaths. Her skin was pale, tight over her cheekbones, her lips dry and cracked.

Slater frowned. How long had the poor woman been down here? When asked her name, the woman had simply blinked, confused, and whispered, "The biologist," in a weak, cracked voice. Now Sol had mixed a cup of water with protein powder and glucose, and held the back of the woman's head as she sipped at it. She winced every time she swallowed.

"Take it slow," Sol said. "Tiny sips, just two or three. You can have some more after a few minutes."

He took the cup away and the woman managed a

weak smile of thanks. "I can't believe someone came," she said, her voice slightly less rasping than before. She was Latina, but her accent was American.

"What's your name?" Slater asked.

"Genesis Galicia, but everyone calls me Jen."

"And what are you doing down here?" Slater ignored Sol's annoyed glance.

"I'm a biologist, part of the SynGreene team."

Confused looks flicked back and forth among the team members.

"What are you talking about?" Slater said, though she thought she knew full well. "We're the SynGreene team."

Aston made a noise of disgust. "Obviously, we aren't the first."

Sol stayed crouched beside Jen, refusing to look up again, to meet anyone else's eye. Slater had a lot of questions for the expedition physician.

"Tell us what happened," Sol said.

He gave her more to drink, which she took gratefully. After more painful-looking swallows, she took a long shuddering breath. "I was part of a research team, hired by SynGreene. We were to investigate a possible new energy source found down here decades ago. Honestly, we all thought it was a joke, but the money was good." She looked around at the faces above her, nodded softly. "I guess you guys thought the same, eh?"

Slater laughed. "Yeah, you've got our numbers."

"So you know, we started to find things that made no sense. Impossible things. Then we were…" She stopped, swallowed, tears standing suddenly in her eyes.

"It's okay," Sol said. "Take your time."

"We were attacked."

"By who?" Terry Reid said, his voice hard.

Jen shook her head. "Not who. What. Some kind of creatures."

"What sort of creatures? Aston asked.

Slater glanced at him and he caught her eye, silent communication quickly passing between them. She knew he was thinking about the missing guard, the fidget spinner, the blood on the walls. That idiot cameraman, Jeff. And the desecrated body in the next alcove. But she saw a faint glimmer of excitement in his eyes too, and realized he was probably considering the possibility of a new species. Though it pained her, the biologist was programmed into him, so she supposed he couldn't help it.

Jen shook her head slowly. "It was dark, everything happened so fast. Three of us escaped the attack and managed to hide in here. But we were too weak and exhausted to carry on, we just stayed put, hoping a rescue would come. We didn't know what to do."

Slater saw Sol Griffin and Terry Reid exchange a knowing look and knew immediately that they expected this, but they'd hid it from the team. She turned to Aston and saw he had noticed the same thing. He met her eyes and nodded, clearly reading her thoughts.

"Tell me everything about what attacked you," Reid demanded. "Every detail you can, however small."

Jen shrugged. "There's not much to tell. They move fast. Sometimes they drop down from above, so I guess they can climb the tunnel walls or they're dropping from holes in the ceiling." She stopped, tears on her lashes again as she relived the horrible memories.

"You said only three of the team made it back here," Reid said. "Did the creatures kill the rest?"

Jen nodded. "I think so. We stayed here, hiding in the shadows, for hours. Finally Thomson crept out, heading towards the tunnel over there." She pointed towards the tunnel Slater and her crew had entered by. "I didn't watch, I couldn't move, but I heard them attack him. His screams were..." She finally broke down in dry sobs, face buried in her hands. "They ripped him apart and just left him. Except…"

"Except his head?" Slater asked.

Jen nodded into her hands.

"You dragged him into the shadows over there?" Slater pointed toward the violated body she had shown Aston.

"No. I didn't dare to move. But eventually Spedding said she was going to drink. We had some rations, but not much. We waited for help to come, but no one did. We stayed hiding for what felt like days, and our rations of food and water quickly ran out. Then more days, starving, so thirsty. Eventually, Spedding slipped from cover here, and I heard her dragging the body out of sight. That's when she told me they'd taken his head, and she couldn't bear to look at him."

"Is Spedding the woman who died over there?" Slater asked, pointing back towards the first body they'd found.

"Yes. She went to the lake there and drank the water, said she couldn't stand the thirst any longer. We were so weak, but no way in hell was I going to drink that water. There is nothing safe or natural anywhere down here. But then, I don't think it was the water that killed her. She came back, tried to get me to drink, but I refused. Then Spedding started talking about hunger. She said she saw a brightly glowing plant in the pool, that it looked like a sea anemone or something, only much bigger."

"It's growing all over the sides of the pool," Aston said. "But I don't know that it's edible."

"That's what I told her," Jen said. "And I told her to wait, surely someone would come. She said no way, that we had to find our own way out, but we were too weak. She said we had to eat, get the energy to save ourselves. I was afraid to even touch the stuff, let alone eat it. But she did."

"You think it poisoned her?" Sol asked.

"Oh, it did. She got so sick. But not her body." Jen absently rubbed her abdomen. "She was sick in the head. Within maybe an hour or so of eating the stuff, she started raving, saying there was somewhere she had to go, that she was being called to."

"Did she say where she was being called?" Slater asked.

"It was nonsense. Madness. She said she was being called 'down, down to the Jade Sea.' She kept repeating that over and over again. I tried to talk to her, to ask her to explain, but her eyes were wild. Her mind was gone. And she was too weak to go anywhere anyway. Eventually she started convulsing, moaning and still talking that horrible, senseless madness. I crawled away, around here to be away from her and she eventually became quieter and quieter and then stopped. I assumed she had died. And by then I was too weak, too scared, too depressed, to do anything. I lay down here and decided I would rather starve to death than go nuts or be torn apart by those monsters. And then you came after all." She looked up suddenly, her eyes haunted. "Why did you take so long?"

"We need to talk more about the creatures," Reid said. "Can they be killed?"

Jen took another shuddering breath, sipped more of the drink Sol had made. A little color returned to her cheeks. "I can't say for sure. We only had one member of the crew who was armed. After the first attack, he hung back and tried to hold them in hopes that we could escape. We heard lots of gunfire, and finally screaming. Then nothing."

"Did you get even a glimpse of these things?" Aston asked.

"Just a few flickers of movement in the flashes of our lights. It was mayhem. They were dark, shiny, no fur or feathers. What I saw looked almost like armor."

Aston nodded, brow creased in thought.

Sol gestured for the team to move back. "We need to let her rest, regain her strength."

"I'll secure this area for now," Reid said, and hurried away, barking orders to Tate and Gates, who had returned from checking the other tunnel.

As the others moved, Aston grabbed Sol's sleeve and dragged him to one side. Slater went with them as Aston said, "How about you tell us exactly what the fuck is going on here?"

Sol's face darkened. "You need to calm down, Aston."

"Oh, I haven't even started to get angry yet, mate. Why the hell weren't we told about a previous team? A team that went missing!"

"We thought they'd simply got lost. We hoped to find them. We didn't know anyone was attacked or killed."

"That's bullshit!" Aston pushed Sol back against the wall of the cavern. Slater was impressed with his fury, especially as Sol was close to double Sam's size. "You must have known there were exotic creatures here, else you wouldn't have included me on the team."

"Not true! We didn't know anything for sure. Including you was a matter of covering all possible bases."

"SynGreene had an obligation to tell us about the previous team," Slater said, enjoying the fact that Aston was putting Griffin on the spot. "They should have warned us of the potential danger."

Sol shrugged. "Maybe that's true. But it makes no difference to our current situation."

"That's not good enough!" Aston yelled.

Sol sneered, grabbed him by the front of his sweater. Aston's face twisted in outrage. He reacted immediately, turning and ducking his body to hip toss the large man, planting Sol heavily on his back on the hard ground. Sol barked a noise of surprise as much as pain as the air rushed from his lungs. Aston leaned down, one fist balled up ready to slam into Sol's face, but Reid was suddenly there. He grabbed Aston and dragged him away before he could pummel Griffin.

"I get that you're pissed off," the big security guard said. "But this isn't going to help."

"Really?" Aston spat. "It's helping me feel a lot better!"

Reid grinned in spite of himself. "I don't doubt it. But save it for later."

Sol sat up against the cave wall, dragging air back into his lungs. He looked like he wanted to kill Aston. Slater couldn't entirely blame the man. She felt like planting a boot in Aston's face herself. After a moment, Sol's expression smoothed, and he let out a deep breath.

"Listen," Sol said, voice tight with pain. "I understand this is a tense situation. It is for all of us. But we're a team. We're all going to have to work together if we want to get out of here safely. Let Reid and his team stand watch until Jen is strong enough to move, then we all get back topside together, okay? We've found the crystals, we know better what's happening. We'll come back better prepared, with an army if necessary."

"We could leave you here with Jen and get out now," Aston said.

"You could, but I think it's best if we all travel together and with an armed escort, no?"

Aston ground his teeth, but Slater saw the sense in what Sol suggested. "He's right, Sam," she said. "We need to stay together. Let's wait until Jen can travel."

"And how long might that be?" Dig asked. The archeologist's face was pale, his eyes a little wild.

Sol shook his head, standing up again, albeit a little shakily. "Let's all eat, get some proper food into Ms. Galicia. We'll rest up here for a few hours. I hate the delay but we've been at work all day. Maybe after some food and a little sleep, we'll be in a better position to get back. We've come a long way, we'll need our strength and our focus to get back safely."

"What if Jen is still too weak to walk?" Syed asked.

"We'll carry her if we have to," Sol said resignedly. "Regardless, eat, rest. Try to sleep. Okay?"

"Hey, where's Larsens?" Dig said, looking around the cavern.

Silence fell as everyone stopped, looking about themselves. Slater's nerves wound another notch tighter. First Jeff, and now Larsen. How did these people vanish without anyone noticing?

"Dammit," Sol barked. "We need his confirmation that these crystals are what we're looking for down here."

Aston rounded on Griffin and Slater was certain he was about to lay into the man again. "You're really concerned about that right now?" Aston said. "Everything that's happening here, and you're still thinking of the damned crystals?"

"We've lost two men now," Sol spat back. "I don't want it all to be for nothing!"

"You need to straighten up your damned priorities, mate!"

Reid stepped in again. "All right, everyone calm down. Maybe he ran when we found more bodies. He could be back at base camp already."

"Hardly," Aston said. "It's a bloody long way back."

"Maybe. But we can't afford to split up and look for him. We need to stay together." Reid shook his head at Sol in disgust. "If we find him on the way back, you can ask him about your precious crystals then."

"I talked to him," Syed said. "He said the crystals here were bursting with energy. I think he was pretty certain this stuff is the greenium."

Sol sighed. "Well, at least we have that. When we get out of here, we tell SynGreene we've found what they wanted. This won't have all been in vain."

"For what it's worth," Aston said, almost reluctantly, "there's a hell of a lot else besides the greenium that's worth investigating down here. But we should concentrate on getting out alive and worry about all that later."

Sol lifted his hands in silent agreement, conceding the point.

Slater fumed. She saw the light of satisfaction in the man's eyes. She couldn't help thinking he would sacrifice all of them if necessary. She wondered how he thought he might survive without them. Was there even more he knew that he wasn't letting on?

"Maybe whatever got Jen's team got Larsen too," Dig said. His voice trembled with ill-concealed fear. He turned to Slater. "And maybe your cameraman as well."

Sol stepped forward, catching Dig's attention. "Do me a favor. Collect some samples of the crystals from here, okay? In case we don't find Larsen."

Dig's eyebrows rose. "Seriously?"

"Sure. Make yourself useful, then eat and rest. Okay?"

Dig shrugged and turned away, rummaging in one of the bags for sample jars.

Reid, Gates, and Tate took up positions guarding the three passageways leading out of the cavern, the one they had entered by and the two on the far side of the pool they had yet to investigate. Slater would be happy to never know what lay down them.

Aston stood still for several moments, his fists clenched at his sides. Slater couldn't blame him for his anger. She shared it. Eventually he stalked off to one shadowed corner, sat down and pulled a small book from his jacket. He flicked on his headlight and started to read. Slater frowned. What the hell could he be reading down here? Why did he even bring a book? She smiled at Marla, still keeping to herself, away from the others. "Get something to eat and have a rest."

The young woman nodded, her face hard. Slater respected her bravery in the face of all this. She had a survivor's streak, was clearly someone to be relied upon. She went over, put a hand on Marla's arms as the woman began to turn away. "Screw all the rest. We'll look out for each other, okay?"

Marla grinned. "You got that right."

Slater watched her go to find food, then went to Aston. He looked up, nodded once. She put her back against the wall and slid down to sit beside him. "What are you reading?"

"That first body we found? When everyone was distracted I found this journal."

"Why didn't you say anything?"

He gave a small, humorless laugh. "Because for some reason I didn't quite trust anyone."

"How prescient of you."

"Right?"

She smiled. It was good to be talking like friends again. Her rage at him, she realized, had softened in the face of very real, new threats. And she had missed him so much. "So what is it?"

He showed her the front page, a neat script of fountain pen inscribing it as belonging to Dr. Murray Lee. "Seems Lee was an American professor of geology. I've been skimming this first part of the journal. Typical fare. He talks about general life events, research findings, day-to-day highlights of his lab experiments and so on. Then it gets interesting."

"How so?"

Aston tapped the page he had reached. "Turns out Lee joined an expedition in 1928, led by one Admiral Adam

Greer. They were searching for the Arctic Pyramids when their party was set upon by armed men speaking Russian."

CHAPTER 19

A ston was pleased Slater was talking to him like a friend again, but he didn't want to jeopardize it by bringing attention to it. He would simply enjoy it for however long it lasted.

"Does it say why the Russians attacked?" Slater asked. She leaned in close, a loose strand of hair brushing his arm and sending a shiver through him.

"No." Aston turned the page, eyes scanning. "But Professor Murray Lee got separated from his group and became lost. Seems he found his way down here."

"To hide?"

"I'll read it to you."

Aston glanced quickly around the cavern to check no one was listening. He couldn't articulate why, but he wanted to keep this knowledge between himself and Slater now. She was the only one here he trusted. Most of the others sat quietly, eating and drinking or resting. Dig had already curled up, head on his bag, eyes closed in sleep. Sol sat with Jen, helping her to eat small bites of rations. They talked in low voices. Reid, Gates, and Tate each stood at the entrance to one of the three tunnels leading from the cave, relaxed but alert. Aston couldn't help feeling like they were sitting in the calm before the storm. He began to read.

"Once separated from my colleagues, lost in the swirling blizzard, and frightened I might run into the Russians once more, I decided the best course of action was inaction. At least until the weather cleared and, hopefully, the Russians moved on. I found a cave at the base of one of the strangely regular mountains (could these be the very pyramids we sought?) and I tucked myself into

its safe depths. But the wind still whistled in and here's where I made a mistake. Rather than winding up my dynamo lamp and checking carefully, I simply pushed deeper into the darkness, seeking shelter. The floor dipped suddenly downward and I had no purchase on the icy rock. I slipped and fell, hurtling down a steep incline, then dropping through open space. For an awful moment I thought I would surely be dashed to a premature death on sharp rocks below, but I hit a second incline that broke my fall, slid further, then crashed into a cavern floor. A jarring pain shot up my left leg (I believe I've torn ligaments in my knee there) but I was otherwise unharmed but for scrapes and bruises. Lucky, or so I thought, other than the obvious misfortune of falling through some natural fissure in the rocks. But there was no way I could scale the slopes that had led me in, so I needed to find another way out.

"I began following passageways, marking the walls periodically so I would know where I'd been, in hopes of finding an exit. Better, I thought, to take my chances with the Russians and the weather than to become lost and starve in subterranean darkness. And dark it was, pitch like the depths of hell. I would wind my lamp to check, then feel my way in blackness, then wind the lamp again. I went some way like this, beginning to despair of ever finding the outside world again, when a new wonder distracted me entirely. I began to realize that I could see, dimly, by a faint green illumination. Then I emerged into a cavern softly lit by its own radiant glow, emitted by sparkling veins of strange plants and minerals."

"I guess he found this place," Slater said.

Aston shrugged. "Or one like it. I wonder how far these caverns and the vines and crystals spread. It's possible this stuff goes on for miles under the ice."

"I hadn't thought of that. This mountain range is massive, after all."

"Exactly. But he must have been somewhere near here, as we found his body. So wherever he was in this account, he made it as far as us."

Slater shivered, nodded. "Read more."

"I limped on, the pain in my knee excruciating, but my determination to escape outweighed the inertia of agony. I found more caverns, lit by strange glowing tendrils of vegetation, and by glittering crystal deposits. I found streams of water, which slaked my grateful thirst, and underground lakes and pools. I began to wonder how extensive the network of caves and tunnels, and their indigenous life, could be. The water contained my thirst, but my hunger grew. Separated from the team, I had no pack, no supplies. Eventually I devised a way to use my clothing to net some of the small, slow-moving fish that inhabit the larger pools. Lacking any other means, I ate them raw, swallowing them down, cold and writhing. At first I felt my strength returning thanks to the fuel they gave my body, and despite the pain in my knee, I pushed on. But I began to hear things. Surely they could only be auditory hallucinations, but it was like the sibilant voice of something bodiless whispering to me. I assumed it was simply ravenous hunger, despite the small amounts of fish I had consumed, and general stress, of course, but now I'm not so sure. The voice cajoles me still."

"That sounds a bit like what Jen told us about her friend," Slater said.

Aston nodded. "Spedding. Jen said Spedding thought she was being called 'down, down to the Jade Sea'."

"Down to a sunless sea," Slater whispered.

Aston cocked his head. "What was that?"

"Just a flashback to high school English." She drew a deep breath, then blew it out slowly. "This journal creeps me out. What do you think it means?"

"I don't know."

"But Spedding ate the glowing plant stuff from the water, not the fish."

"That's true," Aston said. "But I got a close look at the fish when I dived the pool over there. They share the same bright green bioluminescence. It stands to reason that whatever makes the plants glow, makes the fish glow too."

Slater quirked an eyebrow."You think the fish eat the plants?"

"It's definitely possible. And honestly, I'm not certain they are plants. I think they might be some simple form of animal life, like anemones. And perhaps they all eat the same particulate matter. Or the water itself causes the glow. We just don't know enough."

Slater pursed her lips. "Well, I'll be glad when we get out of here, because I don't want us to run out of food. Seems like nothing is safe to eat or drink here."

Aston pointed at the book. "That entry ends there, but then there are a couple of pages of drawings. It's headed here 'Observations' and then lots of these pictographs." He turned the book so Slater could see.

"They look a bit like Egyptian hieroglyphics," she said.

"A little. But I've never seen any like this."

"Do you have wide experience with ancient Egyptian?" Slater asked with a grin.

Aston laughed. "Not really. But don't you think they look different somehow?"

"There is a unique quality to them."

"And look here," Aston said, turning to the next page. More sketches, little people with large heads bowing down before a roiling pool of water, steam rising in thick tendrils. The style was simple, like cave paintings. "You think he's done his best to copy what he saw on cavern walls?"

"What other source?" Slater asked.

"Maybe this is how he draws and he's recording something he saw happening down here."

Slater looked up sharply. "I'm not sure I want to consider that."

Aston shrugged. "Let's assume he copied carvings he saw." He turned the page. Another scene depicted two groups of the odd little people. One group carried fish, arms outstretched toward the same pool of water as if the fish were an offering. The other group, bearing spears, faced the opposite direction, poised to battle an unseen enemy.

"Surely he's copied scenes from markings on the walls," Slater said. "Like he copied the pictographs."

"I don't know. We haven't seen pictographs like those or drawings like these. We've seen the strange designs on the doors, but not this."

Slater frowned. "Doors? There's only been one door."

"Oh yeah. In all the excitement of finding Jen and everything else, I forgot to tell you something. Let's concentrate on this first, then I'll explain."

"Okay." Slater said, a note of reluctance creeping into her voice. She flashed him a skeptical glance, then returned her attention to the book. She pointed to the sketch of people offering fish to the pool. "So assuming Lee has copied things he saw on cave walls, rather than things he personally witnessed, who or what made those drawings?"

Aston shook his head. "I think we have to assume that at some point, an ancient race of some description lived down here. Perhaps in a previous era, before the Antarctic was all ice?"

"That's buying into a lot of conspiracy theory crap."

Aston thought that comment a bit rich, given the woman had built her career spreading conspiracy theories.

"No use getting annoyed about that," Aston said. "The evidence for it is building up."

Slater's frown returned. "Read more."

Aston turned the page to find more neat, tight handwriting, and read on. "I needed to rest, my knee had blown up to twice its size and throbbed with my pulse. I cursed the crooked landing I had made, wondering if I would ever find a way out. And, if I did, whether this ruined knee would allow me to climb should I need to. I distracted myself with ruminations on the strange designs I had seen.

"A rudimentary study of these unusual hieroglyphs, about which I feel I have some inexplicable intrinsic knowledge, has given me a starting point to understanding. Making inferences based on this knowledge and the pairings of glyphs and scenes, I believe I have translated some of it." Aston pointed at the page. "He's drawn a kind of key here. It's all a bit out of context, but he's sketched some glyphs and what he thinks they mean. Fish. Fight. Worship. Stuff like that." Then Aston indicated an odd glyph at the base of the page, like a stylized squid. Next to it were several words, each a question.

Master? Ruler? Leader? Overlord?

"What do you make of that?" Aston asked.

Slater shook her head. "I don't know what to make of any of this, Sam."

"In your work have you seen anything like this?"

"Not really. I mean, I've seen pictographs and hieroglyphics, but this…" She finished with a palms-up gesture.

Aston turned the page. "The handwriting is worse here, look. Shaking as if he's shivering or weak." He read on.

"I rested as best I could, even slept a little, I think. But hunger and a desire to escape drove me on again. But I'm sure I'm followed."

"The things that Jen described?" Slater asked.

Aston kept reading. "I don't mind admitting that I began to panic. The pain in my knee, the hunger, the incessant voice in my head beckoning me on. It all began to drive me mad. The voice told me which way to go, every time a choice appeared in the form of a fork, or alternate passages, the voice guided me. But every time I listened to its instruction, I found my path blocked. So I did my best to ignore it and forge my own way, fighting against all instincts while simultaneously trying to trust my gut. And the hunger chewed at me, and my knee has become so painful I can barely take weight on it at all. My staggering, limping gait is exhausting. And then I saw one."

"One what?" Slater asked.

Aston turned the page, fear and a stubborn refusal to accept the words he saw curdling his gut. "It was a horrific sight," he read. "A small, gray man with a large head and dark bulbous eyes. The creature brandished a spear and, without thinking, I reacted defensively. I drew my .45 caliber Colt Peacemaker, a gift from my grandfather, and emptied it in the direction of the creature. At least one bullet found its target, for the creature lay dead before me. And then from behind, I heard angry muttering and saw movement. Lots of man-sized, shining chitinous black creatures, with huge mandibles snapping like blades, stalked toward me from the shadows. I panicked, flung the revolver at them and ran blindly into the darkness, howling as I went from the pain stabbing through my knee. I felt as though the joint were disintegrating further with every agonizing step. Behind me, the mantic creatures followed, unhurried. In screaming pain, my flight slowed, but still they didn't overtake me. This is, after all, their domain, and I suppose they knew they would find me in their own time. Perhaps the hellish things even enjoyed the sport of my impotent flight.

"I made it to a large cave before my ruined knee finally gave out and refused to carry me a single step further. Almost unconscious from the pain, the fear, the weakness of hunger, I dragged myself hand over hand into the deepest shadows I could reach. I am out of options, out of luck. I believe also I am out of time. I write this entry now and I pray, and I wait."

Aston turned the page. Nothing. The rest of the journal was blank. "We know how far his prayers got him."

"I guess that would explain the stone blade in his heart," Slater said. "We found him where he wrote that last entry. But as he was killed by that blade and not chopped to pieces like Jen's colleague, do we assume another of the little gray men finished him, rather than the creatures?"

"Mantics," Aston said quietly. "That's what he called them."

"And little gray men?" Slater said. "Sounds a lot like the aliens described by modern-day UFO enthusiasts. Is this whole thing some elaborate hoax?"

"Or maybe some crazy theories are not so crazy after all," Aston said. "Except for the primitive weapons. But maybe they could be little gray men that aren't actually aliens. Just some sort of ancient race. Lee described the one he saw as brandishing a spear. He was killed with a stone dagger. Hardly the tools of an advanced alien race." Aston paused, thoughtful. Then he said, "Although this is pretty recent, so if it is an ancient race, they were still here only a hundred or so years ago. So they could still be here now, having survived for millennia!"

"Unless a UFO crashed in the Antarctic millennia ago and the survivors made their way down here and found a way to survive?" Slater said. "They may have lost their technology that way, but lived on."

Aston shrugged. "Holy hell, Jo, it's all so absurd. But so was the idea of a dinosaur surviving in a Finnish lake."

Slater managed a smile, then it faded. "I wonder if they are still alive, still here, watching us."

"People right here, right now, are dying," Aston said. "We have to assume it's all real, and that it's all still happening. So where are they? Why aren't they confronting us?"

Slater shivered again, then scooted up closer to him

and rested her head on his shoulder. Aston thrilled at the warmth of her, the closeness. "You're an ass, Sam Aston."

"I know. I'm sorry, Jo. It wasn't... personal."

"Yeah, right. And sorry isn't really good enough. You're the only person in the world who can understand what I went through. What we went through. And I couldn't talk to you about it. I had no one who believed me."

"I struggled with it, honestly I did. But I had debts..." He stopped, took a deep breath. "Nah, you're right. I was an asshole."

"Especially after we, you know, connected like we did."

Aston felt a slight flare of resentment at that. "Well, you made it pretty clear at the time that was a one-off."

"At the time. We were facing a fucking dinosaur, Sam! That's not to say we wouldn't have found time for each other again afterward. But you let me think you were dead!"

Aston huffed a genuine laugh. "I will never understand women."

"That's because you're an asshole."

"Yeah. I'm sorry. I mean that."

She pressed more comfortably into his shoulder and he puts his arm around her. "Let's just survive this one together," she said. "Once everyone is rested, we get the hell out of here, then out of Antarctica. After that, who knows, right?"

"Right."

"But you're going to have to make it up to me, asshole. I'm going to make you suffer."

He grinned. "Fair enough."

Exhaustion dragged at Aston. He rested his head against hers and shut his eyes.

CHAPTER 20

The cavern had dropped into a quiet stillness, the entire team asleep or dozing. He had no way to track the passage of time down here, but Dig O'Donnell was fairly certain it must be night in the real world above. They had been exploring, sampling, discovering, for hours. Sol Griffin was right to call a rest period, and it was the perfect opportunity for Dig. While everyone else slept, he had read key passages from *At The Mountains Of Madness* again. He was convinced these were those mountains. Lovecraft was a master storyteller, no one could argue that, but the man was a prophet, too. It took aesthetes like Dig to see that, to recognize the man's greatness and his treatises.

Dig looked around again, to ensure that everyone slept. Even Reid and his two armed cronies, Tate and Gates, sat back against the walls of the tunnels they guarded, weapons across their knees, eyes closed. He thought they were only dozing, ready to act in an instant, but if he remained quiet, they wouldn't notice. He crept unnoticed over to where Jahara Syed lay sleeping. Careful to make no noise, he looked through the biologist's samples. He found what he was looking for, holding the small jar up into the green glow of the cavern. A small fish, maybe two inches long, swam confused circles around the confined space. Its flesh was pale white, almost translucent, the bones of its tiny skeleton clearly visible. It had a semblance of eyes, that glowed softly green, and a brighter green stripe along each side of its narrow body.

He had been sure from the start that the life down here was connected with what he sought. He'd always known there was a measure of truth to the story Lovecraft penned, facts and real events underlying the fiction. And those facts further revealed by the subsequent stories of other prophets like Clark Ashton Smith and August Derleth. These men were aesthetes too, channeling cosmological truths.

Dig had seen Aston and Slater huddled together over something and had sidled into the next alcove of rock, unseen, but close enough to hear Aston's voice as the Australian quietly read aloud. And that had convinced him. That account had been the final corroboration. All the proof he needed. His fears had melted in the face of evidence. The explorer, Professor Murray Lee, had not been losing his mind. The voice he reported hearing was very real, and still here, Dig was certain of that. It was, after all, eternal. And in order to hear that voice himself, he needed to commune with the life of this magnificent place.

He licked his lips, checked around himself again. Everything still, everyone quiet in slumber. He unscrewed the lid of Syed's sample jar, took a deep steadying breath, then drank down the contents. He crunched the wriggling fish once between his teeth, tasted a jet of bitterness, then swallowed it all down with the hard, mineral-tasting water. He shuddered, whether from disgust or anticipation he couldn't honestly say, but a joy thrilled through him nonetheless. He slipped the empty jar back into Syed's bag, then sat quietly, waiting. Genesis Galicia's story about Spedding made perfect sense. That and the words of the journal had all coalesced into a solid and perfect course of action. All his frustrations slipped away, now he had finally figured out the process. He licked his lips again, still tasting the bitterness of the unfortunate fish, but anticipation made the discomfort worthwhile. He sat waiting, willing the connection to rise, the magic to happen.

Nothing. His elation began to morph into anger and frustration. Why not him? Was he not deserving?

Nonsense! Who among them could possibly be more deserving? Perhaps that Genesis Galicia, Jen, knew more than she was letting on. What about the story of her colleague had she omitted in the telling?

The woman lay alone, sleeping to one side of the large space, thankfully far from any of the dozing guards. Dig carefully crept around glowing stalagmites and crouched beside her. He would not be denied now, not when he was this close. He pressed one hand over her mouth and the other tightly around her throat. She startled awake, eyes bulging wide in shock. Dig leaned close, almost near enough to have kissed her if he wanted.

"Quiet! Don't make a sound, okay?"

Eyes still wide, tinged with panic, she nodded rapidly.

"Tell me everything you know about what lives down here! Tell me what you left out!" His voice was an urgent hiss.

Her brows scrunched together and she shook her head.

Dig lifted his hand slightly from her mouth. "Why not? Tell me!"

"There's nothing to tell," she said in a harsh whisper. "I don't understand, I told you everything."

She drew a breath, as of she were about to scream, and Dig slammed his hand back over her mouth, felt her lips grind against her teeth. She grunted in pain. "I'll kill you if you raise the alarm, you hear me?"

She nodded again, tears in her eyes.

"You must know more. Tell me."

She seemed to think for a minute, then nodded again. Dig gently lifted his hand, ready to slam it back if she screamed. He wasn't lying. He was more than prepared to kill her. A kind of ecstatic rage rushed through him, made his heart pound.

"I swear, I know nothing more about the creatures than what I already told you," she said tightly, quietly.

"But there's a shrine, with weird pictographs. Maybe you can understand that better than we could? We didn't have long to look at it before we were attacked."

"Where is it?"

Jen raised one hand, pointing across the lake to one of the tunnels on the far side of the cavern. "That passage. After a long way, maybe ten minutes walking, it forks. Take the left fork."

"You're sure?"

"Yes. I remember."

Dig smiled, a new certainty rising in him. Yes, she was right. That's what he needed, of course. He was being tested. He needed to prove himself, unravel the clues, prove himself worthy. Then another thought occurred to him as he looked down at Jen's terrified face. As soon as he moved away from her, she was certain to scream for help. He wouldn't make it more than five paces. Well, no matter, he had what he needed. Before she could react, he put one leg over her body and sat heavily on her, pinning her arms to her sides with his knees. He was twice her size, covering her easily, trapping her legs down with his feet. He leaned his weight forward, one palm over her mouth and with the other he squeezed her nose shut. Her eyes bulged further, panic in her darting eyes as muffled screams erupted from her. He lay over her more heavily, constricting movement, air, and sound alike. She thrashed against him, tried to buck, but he was twice her weight as well and, weakened as she was, she had no chance of dislodging him. Her struggles became weaker, her eyes rolled up and closed. She tried one last time, then fell still.

"Diiigbyyy..."

Dig startled, sat up, looked frantically around. But everything remained still, the team still slept. Jen was inert beneath him. The guards dozed.

"Diiiiiiigbyyyyyy..."

The voice was in his head. It was happening! He called.

Elated, dizzy, Dig rose silently and crept across the cavern on silent feet, heading for the tunnel to the shrine.

CHAPTER 21

Alex Wong was wondering if he should call another base camp staff meeting, just for something to do, when the screaming started. Still no trace of Steele, the guard now officially reported as missing. Still a massive storm coming in, getting too close for comfort. Still no report from the team down below. And now shrill screams from the front lounge. Or somewhere outside it.

He dashed from his office and before he got to the front of the building he caught sight from a side window of two large all-terrain vehicles and a swarm of soldiers. "What the hell?" he managed, staring incredulously at the heavily armed squad moving towards the base. The screaming came from Priya Yardley, a decent enough security guard in Sydney, but who clearly fell to pieces at the first hint of a real threat. Alex had no time to wonder what she was doing outside before the lead soldier whipped the butt of his assault weapon around and silenced Priya viciously. She collapsed and lay still, scarlet stark against the white snow from her nose and mouth.

"Shit!" Alex barked, and sprinted for his office. There was a contingency option to lock down the base with triggers strategically placed in various locations. The nearest was right on the desk he'd just left.

He skidded on the polished floor as he took the corner through the door at full pelt and slammed his hand down on the lockdown button. Red lights in the ceilings of all the rooms and corridors began to flash, a siren whoop-whooped from hidden speakers, and all the doors closed and locked. Wherever anybody happened to be, that's where they would stay for now.

What the hell were military types doing here? Should he call Arthur Greene? Maybe Priya Yardley and her sudden screaming had saved them after all. Those guys would have waltzed straight in unchallenged if she hadn't raised the alarm with her fear.

Alex sat at his desk and called up the base CCTV. He flicked from screen to screen, making a quick mental inventory of the whereabouts of all the staff. Bemused faces occupied most rooms, some people in angry conversation, others banging on doors in frustration. Alex keyed the public address system to try to calm everyone down.

"This is Alex Wong," he said, cursing the tremble he heard in his voice. "The base is under attack from assailants unknown and currently on lockdown. I don't know what's happening, but you're safe in here, so don't panic. Sit tight while I get some answers."

He flicked the CCTV to an outside view and watched the soldiers milling around by the main entrance. The man who appeared to be in charge gestured left and right, sending his minions jogging off. Presumably in search of another way in. But the base was secure.

Then someone else approached across the white expanse. Large, heavily-muscled in olive green combats. With a pulse of shock, Alex realized it was one of the scientists returned from below. Anders Larsen, the unlikely looking geologist. The man would meet the same bloody fate as Priya Yardley, surely? But Alex had no way to warn him.

Then Larsen approached the leader of the attackers with a broad smile and an outstretched hand. They greeted each other like old friends. What the hell was going on? Well, more fool Larsen, because Alex certainly wasn't letting him in now.

After a moment of conversation, Larsen moved

towards a small shed to the side of the main entrance. Alex knew it contained power relays, over-rides, fuse panel, and other associated paraphernalia for the maintenance of the base. It also contained a user console like the one on his desk. Alex's face sank into a frown as he watched Larsen unlock the shed with a key from his pocket, then crouch just inside the door. It was really no surprise when the sirens and lights all went still, the sudden silence sinking over the base like a cloak.

"Well, that's us screwed," Alex said with a shake of his head. He quickly rose and headed for the main staff lounge where the majority of the others were gathered. Perhaps safety lay in numbers.

"There you go," Larsen said with a smile.

Jasper Olsen slapped his shoulder. "Good work!" He barked some orders and the majority of his squad swept into the base.

"Don't hurt anyone unnecessarily," Larsen said. "Those guys are just working stiffs."

"I know. They'll only get hurt if they resist. If they co-operate we'll see them looked after until all this is dealt with."

After a few minutes, a large man with curly hair came back outside. "All secure, sir."

"Any casualties?"

"One guy tried to be a hero, but he found the floor pretty quickly. The boss in there, a guy called Wong, has told everyone to do as they're told. They're all together in the largest lounge area."

Olsen looked at Larsen and gave him a smile. "See!" He turned back to his officer and gestured to the woman lying on the snow, bleeding and crying softly. "Take her inside, fix her up, and tell Alpha Squad to regroup with me.

You take command of Beta Squad and hold the base."

"Yes, sir!"

When the man had jogged back inside, Olsen said to Larsen, "Once my men have returned, you can lead us directly into these mysterious caves, yes?"

Larsen grinned. "Of course."

CHAPTER 22

"Aston! Sam! Wake up!"

Aston blinked, dragged up from a deep, dreamless sleep. He was surprised at just how far under he had fallen. He must have been more exhausted than he realized. Slater sat beside him, head cocked to one side.

"Listen!"

He sat up straighter, wincing against stiff muscles, and strained to hear. A soft croaking sound came from the other side of a cluster of stalagmites. "That's where Jen Galicia is lying," he said, scrambling to his feet.

The croaks turned into pained coughs as Aston and Slater rounded the rocks and dropped to a crouch beside the biologist. She writhed weakly on the ground. Another commotion started on the far side of the cave, distant and muffled. Aston chose to ignore that for a moment.

"Are you okay?" Slater asked, helping Jen into a sitting position.

Jen gasped, her throat rasping. Slater grabbed a canteen and let the woman drink deeply. "O'Donnell," Jen said at last, water dribbling off her chin. "He choked me. Tried to kill me!"

Aston was bemused. "What? Dig?"

"Yes."

"Why?"

"I don't know. He wanted information about the creatures, kept saying I had to tell him everything I knew. I was scared, so I told him about the shrine and the pictographs, but he tried to kill me anyway."

"Wait," Aston interrupted. "What pictographs?"

"Something I saw not far from here. I took photos, I found the whole thing pretty fascinating, but then the attack happened and I forgot all about it. It came back to me in a panic because I was desperate to come up with something, anything to tell him. To try to distract him."

"Then what happened?" Slater asked.

"He choked me!" Tears breached her cheeks. "I thought I was going to die, I blacked out. I don't why I'm still alive."

Sol Griffin had approached from behind and made them jump when he spoke. "He'd have had to keep choking you for a good three minutes to actually kill you. Most people don't know that. First you fall unconscious, but if the person stops throttling then, your body starts to breathe again. Thankfully he didn't choke you long enough to cause brain damage, at least by the look of things."

"Well, that might be useful knowledge at some future point," Aston said sarcastically. "Meanwhile, what the hell is Dig up to?"

Sol shrugged. "Having heard this, I can only assume it was Dig who got Gates, too."

"Got?" Slater said, aghast. "Is he dead?"

"No, sorry. Not dead. But hurt. I'm guessing Gates woke as Dig tried to sneak past, but O'Donnell belted him with something, right upside the head. Gates has a hell of a bruise, probably a mild concussion."

"Do you think he'll be okay?"

"He's wobbly, but I'm sure it's not the first time he's been knocked out." Sol grimaced. "I think he'll rally soon enough, but not without a hell of a headache. He said he didn't see who hit him and we were just trying to take account of everyone. Dig is indeed missing."

"What the hell is he up to?" Aston asked again.

"Don't know and don't care," Sol said, turning back to

survey the cave. "Screw him. And screw this. We're going back now. Jen, if you're not strong enough yet to walk, we'll take turns carrying you."

Activity filled the cavern after Sol's shouted order. Packs were organized, equipment put away. A hasty meal was eaten cold and then everyone gathered by the large pool. Larsen had already gone AWOL, now Dig had become strangely violent and gone who knew where. Aston looked around the small remaining group and wondered how safe they were. He and Slater were fit and strong, as was Marla Ward, though the young woman had the look of a rabbit about her, like she might bolt on her own for safety at any moment. Sol Griffin was a bear of a man. Terry Reid and Ronda Tate were badasses, as was Mike Gates notwithstanding the slight glaze currently in his eyes. Jahara Syed looked frightened, but she was smart. He assumed she would be fit and capable too. That just left Jen Galicia, still weak and unable to stand or walk without aid. Nine of them, one pretty much an invalid. He chewed his lower lip in frustration. If it was as simple as walking back the way they had come, it shouldn't be too hard. They could take turns helping Jen and it would be a long slog, but nothing more. However, his gut told him nothing was going to be that simple.

"Before we start," Aston said. "There's something you all need to know."

Sol frowned. "Go on."

Aston pulled from his jacket the journal he and Slater had read. "I found this on the first body we encountered. You guys need to know what he reported in here."

He didn't read all the entries again, but summarized the contents to the increasingly uncomfortable group. Aston was pleased that they seemed to accept the presence of strange gray hominids, and of the creatures the Professor called mantics. Really, they didn't have much choice but to take everything on face value at this stage.

"Sounds exactly like what attacked us," Jen said quietly when he got to that bit.

"So I think we need to be prepared," Aston said. "I think we've been lucky so far that we haven't actually run into these things. Or perhaps they're watching and biding their time. But Larsen is missing, Jeff Gray is missing. We've all seen the blood, right? Let's stop pretending. We might not have faced a frontal assault, but I think we are under attack."

"Then we treat it like so," Terry Reid said. "Tate, you take point. Gates, you're dizzy, but capable. Stay with the group. I'll bring up the rear. We move as fast as we comfortably can, but we don't rush. We stay quiet. We stay alert." He looked to Sol Griffin. "All ready?"

Sol gave a nod and Ronda Tate moved ahead to take point as instructed. Her face was set in grim determination, and she had her assault rifle held loose but ready, not casually slung as it had been all along until now. Everyone was clearly on edge, not just Aston. They started to move out, heading down the long, twisting dark passage back to the next cavern, headlamps swinging left and right, striping the walls. Sol half-carried Jen, one beefy arm around her back. She walked unsteadily beside him, her face hard, eyes narrowed with the effort. Bruises were already beginning to show on her throat.

Aston ground his teeth. Damn that Digby O'Donnell. What had got into the man? Too many damned H. P. Lovecraft horror novels, no doubt. But was that really enough to send him over the edge? Aston wasn't fool enough to think that a book could drive someone to murder, but it must have triggered something that led to Dig's deadly actions. Big Terry Reid took their six, his dark face lost under the headlamp he kept dialed down low. His weapon was also held at ready, panning slowly back and forth as he moved.

Distinct tension rippled through the group. Aston couldn't tell if it were due to fear of being attacked by the creatures they'd heard about or perhaps eagerness to pay O'Donnell back. Probably a bit of both. Maybe even fear that O'Donnell may attack them again.

Aston's own tension surely included all of those things to some degree, but also more. He remained deeply concerned by what he'd learned, and what he hadn't yet had the chance to ascertain. The mysterious hominids, the glyphs, the odd plant and mineral life, it all pointed to more questions than answers. And none of that even took into account the door he had found in the pool and the new cavern that led to.

It pained him to flee without having finished the job. Irrational as it might be, he wanted answers. He supposed they would answer a few questions in the lab when they got back topside, assuming they made it safely and with their samples intact. Perhaps another team... he shook his head ruefully. How ridiculous it was that he would even consider being part of another SynGreene team after they'd hidden the story of the previous one. He'd be a fool to have anything more to do with the company, despite his aching need for answers. Perhaps he would have to learn to live with the mystery. To hell with them. He'd collect his pay and return to a somewhat normal life, the burden of his debts to Chang completely lifted.

Yes, despite everything else, having that monkey off his back would make all this worthwhile, even if he spent the rest of his life wondering about the strangeness under the ice. That was the ticket. Buoyed by this thought, he picked up the pace, moving up right behind Tate, hoping to help the whole group move more easily. She glanced back at him, about to speak when he saw something ahead. He grabbed her forearm, motioning for quiet, and then pointed.

She squinted into the darkness. "What is it?"

Aston took a deep, trembling breath, his momentary elation deflating. He whispered, so as not to panic the group. "I think I spotted one of the mantics."

CHAPTER 23

Jo Slater moved with the group, feeling like she couldn't trust a soul. Aston had managed to redeem himself somewhat in her mind, but she was still cautious of his motives, concerned about what else he may not have told her. And she hated that she had gone from grief to mistrust with nothing in between. She wanted to trust him again. She wanted her friend back. She shook her head. The man was a freaking goofball, a typical guy. In some ways she couldn't hold that genetic programming against him. At least he was trying to be a better man, however much of a terrible job he made of it. She moved beside Jen, on the other side to Sol, and offered an arm. "Can I help?"

Jen flicked her a wan smile. "I'm just so damned weak!" She leaned in, one arm over Slater's shoulders, the other over Sol's. Thankfully Slater was tall enough that the imbalance didn't make her more hindrance than help. "But I'm getting stronger," Jan said. "I can feel my strength returning with every bit of food and drink."

"We'll pause again soon, have another quick bite," Sol said. "Lots of small feeds is best for you right now."

They pushed on, silence but for their footsteps descending again after their few words. Everyone concentrated on walking carefully, making sure not to slip, trying not to make noise, to be alert like Reid had said. The passage echoed as their boots scuffed, occasional drips surprisingly loud, echoing back. The cold scent of rock and damp chilled their nostrils, despite the temperate warmth, and gave a slight cool hit to each breath. Headlamps strobed across each other like lazy swordplay as each person looked cautiously around.

Slater, breathing harder under the effort of helping Jen, glanced up from her feet just in time to avoid running into the back of Syed, who'd stopped dead. As she opened her mouth to speak, she saw past the biologist to Aston, backing up with his hand raised to halt them. He glanced back and his face betrayed a sudden fear. Adrenaline fell like a wave into Slater's gut at the same moment as Tate, up front, raised her weapon and released a deafening burst of fire. The noise wrecked their ears, muzzle-flash like orange lightning made them all blink. In seconds everyone was screaming and scrambling back.

"Go, go, go!" Tate yelled, and fired again.

Gates stumbled through, adding his gunfire to Tate's as Aston yelled, "Mantics!" He gestured frantically for them all to hurry back, then Terry Reid's weapon began to bark short bursts of ear-splitting fire in the other direction.

Slater turned on the spot. "We're trapped!" she shouted over the noise of the gunfire. "They're coming from both directions!"

The passage turned into a strobing chaos of noise and light, and Slater caught glimpses in the crazy crisscrossing beams of headlamps and flashlights, and the intermittent flashes of gunfire. Creatures, as tall as the biggest man among them, like giant black termites with shining exoskeletons like armor. Kaleidoscope eyes glittered in the light bursts, powerful mandibles like an ant's, only as long as her arms, snapped and clacked.

Sol pulled pistols from his jacket, one in each hand, and stood beside Reid, firing expertly from both simultaneously. Reid kept his fire in short controlled bursts, as did Gates and Tate at the other end. Slater felt like the meat in a very ugly sandwich and thought she would surely die here. How many of the things were there? It was hard to believe that all the stories and legends they had heard were real. It was disturbing enough to think of them in journals, but now proof positive skittered left and right before her eyes, getting closer every second despite the assault rifle fire.

Bullets pinged off the rocks of the walls and ceiling as the creatures zigzagged their way down the narrow passageways. Showers of green sparks like tiny fireworks erupted as bullets ricocheted off the mantics' heavily plated exteriors. But they didn't slow. The bullets seemed to cause no real damage.

Slater stared, horrified, and couldn't help wondering if they really were aliens wearing some strange armor, but she dismissed the thought before following it too far. Unrecorded creatures were bad enough. She didn't want to consider anything even less likely.

A burst from Ronda Tate found a gap between a mantic's body and head and neon green sprayed out. The creature let out shrieks so high pitched they were almost beyond hearing.

"Aim for the joints! They're vulnerable there!" Tate yelled, and the others took up their defense anew.

Slater huddled with the rest of the team between the two fights, hands pressed over her ears against the deafening reports. Unable to doing nothing any longer, she ran to Gates's side and pulled the sidearm from his hip holster. He made room for her and she flipped off the safety and began emptying that clip, aiming for the thin joints in the articulated limbs. It gave her pleasure to score a couple of good hits, watch legs fly apart and the giant insects fall. But others simply swarmed over them.

The creatures were almost on them, chittering and glistening in the bursts of light and noise. Slater took a step to one side and her headlamp beam struck a mantic full in one of its multi-faceted eyes. It hesitated, flinched even, and seemed to stagger back a couple of steps. Slater pumped four bullets right into that illuminated orb which burst in a spray of bright green. The mantic shrieked and fell.

"Their eyes are sensitive to the light!" she shouted. "Blind them!"

The others took her lead, aiming their headlamps for the creatures' eyes. Sol, Syed, Aston, even Jen, all pushed forward with flashlights, stunning the creatures with bright beams. A couple more mantics froze, turned their heads, but then charged again regardless, bullets pinging off of them with green flashes of sparks.

"Everybody fall back!" Reid yelled. "The way back is clearer!"

He continued to shoot behind Slater as she tried to flash her lights forward and run backward. Sol's guns still fired, too. The lead mantic in the charge toward her fell, another stooped as if to snap a bite from it, but more surged on, clambering over their fallen kin without regard. Slater's pistol clicked empty. Gates, perhaps still woozy, was left ahead of the retreating group. He fired rapidly, going from short bursts to full auto in a panic. Tate screamed something unintelligible, bullets glanced off the crown of the lead mantic's skull, but the creature moved side to side with surprising agility.

Gates was too slow to react, suddenly an island of one man as the others hurried back, and the dodging creature snatched him around the middle in its huge mandibles. He howled, trying to raise his rifle to pump rounds into the thing, but it reversed its course and dragged him away in the dark. His rifle clattered to the ground.

Aston dove forward to grab it. "Turn around!" he yelled. "Run back to the green cavern! Maybe the light there will keep them at bay!"

Claws seemed to crawl up Slater's spine as she turned away from the mantics still chasing them and ran at full speed, towards the flashes of gunfire from Reid and Sol.

With Syed's help, she almost dragged Jen along, but the exhausted woman found some reserves of energy and stumbled with more strength than she had shown before. Adrenaline, Slater thought, was a hell of a drug. As they stumbled on, Slater used the hand not holding Jen to keep firing rounds blindly behind her from her pistol. Then it clicked empty and she concentrated only on flight.

Ronda Tate stopped, still facing the horde coming the other way. "Go, go, go!" she hollered, bracing into rapid bursts of fire to hold them back.

Reid and Sol moved to support Tate as the others all ran back for the green cavern they had so recently left. The three still firing moved back as the team gained a lead and soon they were all bolting for the green glow in the distance. As she ran, Slater was sickeningly aware that they were once again moving farther from surface, back deeper underground with every step.

CHAPTER 24

Digby O'Donnell stood staring in mesmerized wonder. Galicia had not been lying about the shrine. It stood in a small cavern, gently lit by more of the glowing vines and deposits of greenium. The cavern floor was concave, gently falling to a low center, and in the middle of that space stood an arch of rock. It seemed to have been carved from the very stuff of the cavern itself. No, Dig corrected himself. Not carved. Grown. As if two stalagmites, thicker at their base than a grown man's waist, had formed straight up like normal, but had then slowly curved over to meet each other and form the arch some eight or nine feet above the ground. Was that even possible? It didn't matter, here it was. Standing under the high bow of strange rock was a pile of stones, each perfectly flat, every next one smaller than the one below, like a stack of ever-reducing pancakes. A complicated sigil of many intersecting lines was carved into the top surface of the uppermost, smallest flat stone, about the size of a dinner plate. Dig reached out one trembling hand and gently ran his fingers over the lines, felt an electric thrill that seemed more than mere excitement.

But more interesting than all of this were the pictographs carved around the arch itself, covering both back and front, a high curve of text from the ground on one side right over to the ground on the other, on both sides. He imagined the front as one long passage, then the back of the arch as another. And more than that, behind the strange monument, the entire rear wall of the cave was flattened and bore a huge body of text, hundreds of small pictographs in a square at least six feet on each side. So much information.

Was pictographs the right word, he wondered, or should he say hieroglyphics? That term was usually reserved for ancient Egyptian script, but could he be certain this wasn't from a concurrent culture? The symbology was incredibly similar, though subtly different in key ways. Might this be a dialect of ancient Egyptian? A precursor? It thrilled him to consider it might be something older. Too many questions, he simply wanted to read it. He desperately ached to glean whatever knowledge it offered. But that would normally take many hours of conscientious study.

And still that whispering voice cajoled him, sibilant in his ears, tickling his hindbrain. Visions flickered in his mind's eye, snatches of the caverns, of tunnels and caves. Some he knew, some he had never seen, and he thought perhaps he was seeing what others before him had seen down here. Or perhaps, what others were seeing now. But none of it helped him understand the knowledge written all around him. "Tell me!" Dig demanded of it. "These words, they must be the key to understanding. To understanding everything! Explain them to me!"

But no revelation came. Just the ongoing soft whispering of his name and a strange, dragging sensation exhorting him to go deeper, to keep moving. With a hiss of frustration, he pulled a small digital camera from his jacket and carefully snapped photographs. First from afar, capturing the whole arch front and back, the wall of text as a whole, then close-ups of all the pictographs, of the pancake stack of stones, of the strange design atop them.

"I'll study these," he muttered to himself. "When there's more time. I can work them out, I can learn their secrets. Time. I just need time." He giggled, tucked his camera away. For now, he could no longer resist the pull drawing him on.

He moved around the arch one more time, intending to return along the narrow passage that had led to the shrine and this time take the right fork, deeper into the caves, when he spotted something else. A small cairn stood between himself and the pictograph-covered arch, dozens of small stones piled into a fake stalagmite about two feet tall. As he leaned down for a closer look, he sensed power in there, a buzz almost like a live electricity source. He shoved at the pile with one palm and a flash of pain nearly blinded him.

He staggered back, letting out a cry of surprise and shock. He blinked, shook his head, but the light didn't go away, shining bright green. He took a deep breath, steadied himself, and looked at the mess of stones he had scattered. An idol of some kind, seemingly carved from pure, unblemished greenium, lay on its side, revealed by his push. He crouched, his eyes slowly becoming accustomed to the new brightness.

The idol was of a figure, weirdly proportioned, head too large, eyes too big. It had thin arms raised in supplication and around its body looped many coils of... something. Vines? Ropes? Dig stared in wonder, trying to understand. The figure gave the impression it was ecstatic to be so bound, not scared or restricted, like it reveled in the embrace of whatever held it. And it was beautiful, the execution of the carving exquisite. Who would bury this treasure and why? Why not display it?

Dig reached out, picked the idol up and gasped as energy rushed through him. At the same time, the skin of his hands burned like the thing was hot, but the sensation was distant, like the memory of someone else burning. His thoughts dissolved at the pure ecstasy that surged into the rest of his body and mind as he held it. He imagined the purest cocaine and thought it would not hold a candle to this rush of pure joy. And yet, below the pleasure, entwined with it like whatever arms entwined the figure of greenium, was a sensation of joyous malice, of desperate need. His own need, certainly, but also the avarice of something else. Something whose wishes he simply had to fulfill. Blurred, inconsistent visions flickered before his eyes, a rapid, detailed slide show of tunnels and caverns he had seen already and others he didn't recognize. He saw more arches, more carved doorways, more pictographs. He saw a dark place with flashes of fire and his friends screaming and running. He saw a large pool, crystal clear, and something caused the surface to boil and thrash. He saw hints of chittering mantics and slowly walking hominids with ash-gray flesh, watching, seeking, hunting.

With a sob of ecstatic need, Dig held the idol close to his chest and staggered back down the dark passage, his way lit by the glowing treasure. When he reached the fork, he turned, almost running to get deeper into the caves as quickly as he could.

CHAPTER 25

Anders Larsen led Jasper Olsen and his heavily armed squad into the caverns. Nerves clutched Larsen's muscles tight, but he felt excitement, too. Exhilaration that he had fulfilled his role as requested. That the whole thing, or at least his part of it, was almost at an end. The eight men at their back had the grim determination of experienced mercenaries. The scientists and their three security guards didn't stand a chance.

Well, Larsen corrected himself, perhaps those three— Reid, Gates, and Tate—they might put up some genuine resistance. He had told Olsen to target them and Sol Griffin first. Take them out and the rest of the team would quickly fall into line without the need for more bloodshed. Although they probably ought to kill Sam Aston, too. That man looked like he could be trouble.

He tapped Olsen and shared his musings and the big mercenary leader grinned. "We'll massacre them all if necessary. But don't you worry about it. We've got it in hand now."

Larsen nodded, smiled. He was certainly glad to be on this side of the forthcoming encounter. These guys were cold-blooded killers. He thought that maybe, once the shooting started and the engagement was underway, he might quickly run back in the other direction and wait for everyone topside. The less time he spent down here the better. He'd be happy if he never saw another cave for the rest of his life.

At the back of the marching squad, Adamsen and Jansen walked side by side. At first they had talked, pleased to finally be doing something pro-active. The long journey to the base had been boring, Jansen thought, and taking the base turned out to be nothing more than waiting outside a locked door until the local mole came and let them in. Now, finally, some action.

The scrape and scuff of their boots echoed off the curved walls of the passage, their flashlights striping the dark rock, the uneven ground. They made no effort to conceal their progress. After all, what resistance could a bunch of scientists and a couple of hired guns really offer? Jansen realized that maybe putting this expedition team under control might be as boring as taking the base and his excitement waned. He turned to Adamsen to run the thought by his friend, but the tall, blond man wasn't there.

Jansen frowned. He looked forward into the group, but everyone he expected was clear to see, except Adamsen. He glanced back, shined his light into the darkness, and no one was there either. He opened his mouth to call out his concerns when something dark flashed across his flashlight beam. Dark but shiny, the size of a large man. He had the bizarre sensation that it was a VW bug car, zooming along on its back wheels like Herbie in those crazy old films. But it had seemed to have waving limbs and glistening fangs of some kind. Surely not. He swallowed, nerves twanging taut. The squad marched on while he stood motionless, panning his light left and right. Surely he had imagined it. But where the hell was Adamsen?

"Commander!" he called out, and heard the marching boots slow, then stop. He didn't turn to see them, but imagined them all looking back, brows furrowed.

"What is it, soldier?" Olsen's voice seemed more distant then he had expected.

He opened his mouth to reply but the darkness right

beside him came alive and something ice cold and frighteningly hard closed around his neck. He tried to scream but no sound came and then there was only pain and darkness.

Larsen's guts turned to water as he, along with the rest of the squad, watched the soldier's head detach from his body. His headlamp waved hectically as the head rolled across the passage floor, repeatedly shining on bright black carapaces and multi-faceted eyes. Long, curved mandibles snapped and clicked and the passage was suddenly full of giant, swarming creatures. It was like they had stumbled into a scene out of a bad B movie.

The squad erupted into action, firing into the darkness, green flashes and sparks bursting off the creatures as they advanced.

"Fall back!" Olsen ordered, and the squad backed along the passageway, deeper into the caves, firing in controlled bursts.

Larsen hurried behind them, made sure the weapons were facing away from him and all the soldiers were between him and whatever the hell those things were. He realized, as they rushed deeper into the caverns, holding the monsters back with gunfire, that they hadn't taken the fork towards the cavern with the vines and the stream running across it. They were in uncharted territory, the snapping, glistening creatures between them and escape back to the surface, and they were being forced still deeper. He couldn't help wondering if that's exactly what these things, whatever the hell they were, desired.

CHAPTER 26

Aston tried his best to swallow down anger and frustration. And, he had to admit, no little dose of fear. Everything had turned bad so quickly, it was hard to credit, but this argument was getting them nowhere. They were back in what had become casually called the green cavern, where the greenium was brightest. Where the pool with the strange door at bottom sat placid and calm on the far side from where they stood.

Reid kept demanding that they fight their way out. Now they were aware of the enemy, of its limitations, they could concentrate bright lights to hold the chitinous creatures at bay and battle back to the surface. Sol Griffin refused to accept that. The creatures could, he assured them, easily back around like they had before and trap them, hem them in. They had done it once, though the party had no way of knowing how. They could do it again. Perhaps they were able to grab the ceiling of the tunnels like cockroaches and scuttle silently above, as Jen had suggested before. Or perhaps there were cracks and passages hidden in the darkened folds of rock that the scientists hadn't seen.

"We wait!" Sol shouted, anger tinging his loud voice more than ever.

"Wait?" Reid demanded. "For what? For a host of angels to fly down and lift us up through the rock?"

"Don't be absurd. Until someone comes. Until a rescue is effected. Thankfully those things are clearly reluctant to come in here." He looked around the cavern. "I think it's too bright for them with this much greenium glowing from the walls, and our halogens keeping it all charged. We're safe in here, so we wait."

"And how long will our batteries last on those lights?" Aston asked. "I have to agree with Reid. After all, who's coming? The remaining staff at the base are hardly trained to rescue us, and they don't have the manpower. And besides, they don't even know right now that we need rescuing. No one does!"

"Someone will come when we don't go back topside," Sol insisted. "Wong knows the team has enough supplies for a maximum of three days. If we don't return after three days, he'll know something is up and send a rescue party."

"Really? Is that pre-planned?" Aston asked. "Because it seems bloody unlikely to me. After all, no help came for the previous team, and they were down here long enough to die!"

"Not true," Sol Griffin said. "We came. We're the help."

"Oh, really?" Aston's anger was finding new heights. "You expect us to believe we're a rescue mission? We're a second effort, another team sent down here based on the assumption the first team was long dead and gone. Admit it! You expected to find bodies at best. That Jen survived is close to a miracle. We were no rescue team."

Sol remained tight-lipped, cheeks red with barely contained rage. Aston thought perhaps the man was getting close to the end of his tether, that all his preparations, all his expectations, had been blown far out of the water. After all, who could possibly have expected this turn of events?

Maybe Sol and SynGreene had thought the previous party lost, or maybe poisoned by the greenium somehow, something basically mundane. Attacked by mantics? Stories of pale-skinned hominids? Strange red knives in the chests of centuries-old corpses? Everything they had found had to be well beyond anything Sol had planned for.

"There might be another option."

They all turned to see Jen Galicia standing behind them. Standing unassisted, Aston noticed, as she ate another ration. The food and water must be finally giving her some strength. But she was still pale as milk, trembling with the effort of remaining upright.

"What option?" he asked.

"There might be a clue in the photos I took of the shrine. I need a new battery for my camera."

A battery was quickly sourced from Marla Ward and they fired up Jen's camera, huddled around to look at the small screen on the back. She flicked through pictures of a shrine, a strange, smooth arch with a stack of flat stones beneath, pictographs on its curving sides. Another shot showed a small stone cairn, and behind it rows and rows of pictographs on the wall.

"It's like someone wrote a novel," Slater said. "With the notes Professor Murray Lee made in the journal, maybe we can decode at least some of this."

Aston pulled the small book from his jacket and began flicking through the pages. He looked at Sol. "Give us some time with this first." He glanced at Reid. "Yeah? Just some time to maybe understand better what's happening?"

Reid let out a grunt of annoyance and turned away. He barked at Tate to watch the two tunnels leading away from the far side of the lake, then went to stand by the tunnel leading back.

"Looks like you've got some time," Sol said with a grim smile. "If you can figure out anything useful, we'd all be very grateful."

Aston moved with Jen to sit on a rounded rock, and Slater sat on Jen's other side.

"Let's see what we can do," Aston said, finding the first of Murray's translations and holding the book open for the others to see.

Sol Griffin had moved to guard one of the tunnels on the far sides of the lake, Ronda Tate moving to stand at the mouth of the other. Terry Reid still watched intently down the only tunnel they knew would lead them out again.

Aston, Slater, Jen, Syed, and Marla sat in a tight group near the lake's edge. The team muttered to each other, picked unenthusiastically at food and drink, biding their time, until eventually Aston, Slater, and Jen had done all they could.

"Okay," Aston called out. "I think we have all we can get."

"What does it tell us?" Sol asked.

Aston laughed darkly. "Not much and nothing good. As far as we can figure it, someone lived down here. No idea who or what they were, the pictograph in the journal is simply translated as 'people' or 'the people'. They lived beneath the earth for an indeterminate length of time. But some of these people ate the 'shining fish', which we suspect, from the context, is some kind of taboo. There are lots of sections, great chunks of text, that we can't translate. We've done our best to guess."

"How confident are you that it's right?" Sol asked.

Aston shrugged. "In broad strokes, I think we've got the gist of it. More people ate the fish and were either driven away or left on their own. Either way, they were outcasts from the people in general. Something happened, some event we can't figure out, and the outcasts... awoke, we guess, something bad. Murray translated the bad thing as 'overlord'. Murray suggested a number of different translations—Master, Ruler, Leader, and Overlord. But it's overlord that he stuck with for the rest of the text after that."

"Overlord of what?" Marla asked, looking around them. "The great lord of the dank green caverns?"

Aston smiled. "I guess so."

"And what is this overlord?" Syed asked. "What manner of creature? A person or something else?" She didn't seem too bothered by the revelation, Aston noted. If anything, she appeared eager to know more.

"No idea," Aston said. "But it seems the overlord sent its minions after the people. Again, that's the word Murray used. Minions."

"Those nasty-ass creatures that took Gates," Reid said bitterly from across the cavern.

Aston glanced over, but Reid still stared ahead, down into the blackness, keeping his distance from the group. Aston looked back to their notes. "Okay, so it seems that enemies came, who wanted to control the Overlord. They brought people with them and fed their heads to the overlord, or something like that."

"They did what?" Syed said, eyes wide. Her eagerness seemed to wane.

"That's the best we can figure," Aston said. "Those victims then became like the creatures, the mantics we guess, and fought the people. It was a kind of civil war down here. The people were driven back, and they took up shelter in new caves, where there were none of the shining fish to be found." He tapped the page with one forefinger. "This last bit is perhaps oddest of all, but our best guess is they come out from time to time to get what Lee called 'bloodstone'."

Slater held up the dagger they had taken from Murray's chest. "We think it's this stuff, the same stone as the blade that killed Lee. It's like a kind of ruddy obsidian. I don't think I've ever seen anything like it before. But I think maybe it's the only weapon that might work effectively against the mantics."

"Is that all we've learned from this?" Sol asked. "That crazy story and that our only chance might be hand to hand combat with stone age weapons? That's not much use at all."

"No, it's not," Aston said quietly.

"Too late to worry now," Reid called out. "I see mantics down this tunnel. It seems like they don't want to get too close right now, but they're getting bolder by the minute."

"The glow of the cavern hurts their eyes," Slater said. "But I guess they'll get over that soon if they want us badly enough."

Aston handed the journal to Slater, hefted Gates' rifle, and moved to join Reid. He caught glimpses of glistening black far away in the darkness.

"I've got movement too," Tate called out.

Sol turned back to his tunnel, straining to see into it. After a moment, he nodded. "Yep. Me too."

Reid turned to Aston, his eyes narrowed, haunted. "We're surrounded."

CHAPTER 27

A ston pursed his lips in thought, his mind calm despite the dire circumstances. They had an option.

"They're getting closer," Tate called from across the cavern.

"Here too," Sol said. "I think they're moving slowly and letting their sensitive eyes adjust. They know they have us trapped, so they can take as long as they like."

Aston was a little surprised by the high tremor in the otherwise unflappable man's voice.

"We don't have enough ammo for this," Reid said quietly beside him. "We know their weak points, we can more effectively defend ourselves, but it's only a matter of time. If there's enough of them, we're gonna run out of bullets before they run out of bodies."

Aston remembered Gates, screaming in the creature's mandibles as he was carried away into the darkness. "Okay," he called out, loud enough for everyone to hear. "You need to listen to me and not ask questions."

Aston walked away from him, back into the middle of the cave near the edge of the glimmering pool of clear water. Bright slashes of neon green darted around in its depths. "I didn't mention this before because as soon as I came up from the water, everything got crazy and I agree that getting out is the best option. But there is another way."

Slater walked over to him, brow furrowed. She looked from him down into the water and back again. "What's down there?"

He wasn't surprised she had immediately guessed the

truth. She was sharp that way. "When I dove earlier, I found another door at the bottom of this pool. I went through it. There's a short underwater passage, then it comes up in another cavern. I didn't check it, but there's a passage leading away from that cave."

"You're suggesting we go deeper?" Sol said.

"You think we stand a chance against those things?" Aston gestured towards the tunnels. "We know there's more than one way in and out of these caves, if the other stories we've heard are to be believed. That door and the tunnel on the other side have to go somewhere."

"Maybe just deeper in," Tate said. "It doesn't mean there's a way out."

Aston shrugged. "True. But there might be. And right now, there's definitely no way out of here."

"Getting closer!" Reid called out. "We'll have no choice soon!"

"What if the creatures are waiting on the other side when we get there?" Syed asked.

"Then we're no worse off than we are now. But they might not be."

Sol turned away from the tunnel he was guarding. "He's right. This is a nobrainer. We have to go through and take our chances."

"How far of a swim is it?" Jen asked. "I don't know how long I can hold my breath."

"Me, either," Marla said. Her face was pale. "I'm not that great a swimmer."

Aston thought for a moment, then, "Okay, it's about twenty feet down in this pool. Then you go through the door, along a short passage that then curves back up to the new cave. You'd be under a minute, tops. Sol, you had ropes in your pack, right?"

"I have one. It's thin rappelling rope, one hundred and fifty feet."

"I think that'll be enough. Quickly, pack up only the essentials, whatever each of you can carry in a small pack. Make sure most of it is food. I'll dive first and take Sol's rope through. You guys just have to pull yourselves hand over hand along the rope. It'll lead you down and back up." He looked at Marla. "Easy, right?"

She gave a weak smile and nodded.

"Okay, let's go."

Sol threw the rope to Aston while everyone else busied themselves organizing essentials to take through. Aston realized his hands were shaking as he tied one end of the rope around a sturdy stalagmite at the lake's edge. Was he leading them all to their deaths? Perhaps it would be better to die violently but quickly, swarmed by the mantics here, than risk a slow, miserable death of starvation elsewhere. But he couldn't think that way. He had to believe there was another way out, a better option than starving or becoming something else's food. He put the coil of rope over his shoulder and slipped into the strangely lukewarm water of the pool. Taking three long deep breaths, he held the last and dove. The door was still there, not the figment of his imagination he had briefly feared. He pulled himself through, feeding out the rope as he went, then up the short passage. His heart hammered as he surfaced in the pool on the other side, eyes scanning left and right in the soft green glow, expecting a swarm of mantics to descend on him. But the cave was empty, silent and calm, gloomier than the larger cave with the halogens. Easier for mantics to enter, but he decided to let that thought go for now.

He pulled himself from the water, secured the rope to the nearest strong-looking stalagmite, then dove back in. In moments he was back on the other side with the team, thankful to see the mantics hadn't braved the bright cavern yet.

"Okay, let's go. Just follow the rope."

Marla stepped quickly forward. "Can I go first? Or I'll lose my nerve."

Aston nodded and she threw herself in, face scrunched up like she was about to cry. Aston had to admire her. After all, real courage wasn't a lack of fear. Real courage was being terrified, but doing the thing anyway. "I'll help Jen through," he said. "The rest of you, go."

They found a natural order. Slater followed Marla, then Syed. Sol went next.

"Me and Tate will come last," Reid said. "You go. I'll bring the rope in case we need it again."

Aston nodded, turned to Jen Galicia. "Are you ready?"

"I guess so."

"Okay. I'm going to free dive with you. This is my job, okay? So don't worry." He slipped back into the pool. "Hold me around the neck like you're riding piggyback, hook your feet around my waist."

She did as he asked, breathing short, nervous gasps. Her body trembled against him.

He swam into the middle of the pool. "Okay, really deep breath, trust me, and try to relax. Just don't let go."

"Okay."

He felt her lungs fill against him. "Here we go."

He sucked in a breath of his own and dived down. He went as quick as he safely could, careful to get low enough that he didn't scrape her on the door or the roof of the short passage. She gasped as they surfaced in the new cave, the others watching anxiously from the edge. By the time Aston had carried Jen to the solid ground, both Tate and Reid had come through, the latter coiling the rope as he went. He untied the other end and Sol put it in his pack.

"Everybody okay?" Aston asked.

"Considering the circumstances, yeah." Slater smiled, but her eyes were pained.

He couldn't blame her. He figured everyone else must

be feeling something akin to his own fears, the foremost among those a sense of crushing claustrophobia. Had they just trapped themselves in a deep and twisting underground tomb?

"Let's just take an inventory of weapons and ammo," Reid said. "We need to start being a lot more frugal with our usage."

"I've got Gates's assault rifle with a nearly empty clip," Aston said.

Reid nodded. "Tate and I have what's left in the clip and one more each. We both have a sidearm, two clips for each."

"I've got Gates's pistol," Slater said. "But it's empty."

Reid handed over one spare clip for her. He patted the pistol at his hip. "I'm keeping what's in here."

"Fair enough."

"That it?" Reid asked.

Sol held up his own two pistols. "I switched out clips when we got to the green cavern. These are both full, but that's all I have."

"Jesus." Reid pursed his lips. "We're not in a good way here."

"But there's nothing we can do about it," Sol said. "Okay. Let's move on."

Only one passage led from the cave, and they headed for it, big Terry Reid up front. The rest followed, with Ronda Tate covering their six. The passage curved gently left and right a couple of times, then quickly opened out into a huge space. They all stopped dead in stunned surprise.

"Oh, my God," Aston said.

CHAPTER 28

Digby O'Donnell wor**ked** his way deeper into the realms of the persistent voice. He knew he was descending, and cared little for how far he might be led, as long as the mystery of the voice revealed itself in the end. He held the glowing idol close to his chest, hugged against him like he protected it, and followed its insistent pull. The skin of his hands blistered and peeled, but he paid no mind to the pain.

The whispering cajoled him, sometimes muttering his name, sometimes words of a language mysterious and barbed. He longed to understand the things that sounded like gibberish, he knew great knowledge lay in those entreaties, but they meant nothing to him. His frustration grew.

Tiredness dogged every step, sleep tugging at the edges of his consciousness. He should stop, rest. When was the last time he slept? No matter, there were more important things than sleep, even if exhaustion did make his vision blur. He staggered, tripping on the uneven ground, and went heavily onto one knee. Pain barked up his leg from the impact, but he held the idol tight. As he sucked in a breath and stood again, his mind seemed to shatter and escape his body. He cried out, sudden disorientation making him nauseated, then he saw another passage, as though looking through someone else's eyes. Or something else. The vision was clearer than any snippet he had sensed before, then it fractured into dozens of repeats, a kaleidoscopic view of swirling imagery. He drew in breath again, tried to process what he saw, and the pictures in his mind changed, then changed again, rapid variations. He saw dark tunnels, scant bits of green light, barely noticeable to human eyes, but painful to this view. More than enough for him to scurry along, trying to find the peace and comfort of darkness. He hated the light, no matter how faint, every striation of bright green like a tiny pinprick to his eyes.

Dig realized he now saw through the eyes of the creatures. The mantics. He leaped from one to the next to the next, seeing what they saw, feeling their stresses, their drives. As the realization dawned the process increased, clearer than ever, like flipping from one television channel to another, ever more rapidly. Through the eyes of one, then another, and then another, he traveled at great speed along the tunnels, even as his body stumbled and staggered along, as if of its own accord.

And then he saw a dull, green glow approaching, and realized it was himself, carrying the idol. Through numerous other eyes, he watched a kaleidoscope of Digs tripping and jogging through the darkness. As he approached himself, the brightness of the idol became too much and the creatures closed their eyelids and turned their heads away.

Dig became at once himself and the creatures, he sensed them lurking nearby, so many of them, but knew also their reluctance to draw near the idol. In snatched glimpses he watched himself pass by, protected by his treasure, and sensed himself go deeper, ever toward that other presence.

Then that presence became a pressure in his mind, a force of unknowable puissance. And he realized he only perceived the edge of it, as if just nudging the very tip of something too massive to comprehend. Yet he was also somehow a part of it. Could he share its thoughts and sensations like he shared those of the mantics all around him? Did he dare?

He reached out with his mind, seeking, and for a split second became aware of inconceivable age, of omnipresence. He was deep beneath waters of emerald green. A Jade Sea. Somehow he knew that was the proper name for the place. And then the presence turned its attention to him and he screamed. Too much, overwhelming. Howling, he felt himself falling, and everything went black.

CHAPTER 29

Aston felt a slight hint of madness tickling his mind, only just beaten out by the overpowering sense of wonder. The short low tunnels, the caverns, however large and intricate with vines and crystals, paled into insignificance against the sight before them. The passageway opened out onto a wide, slightly sloping, apron of rock. Standing with the passage at their backs, the space in front of them was gargantuan. The roof of the new cavern had to be a hundred feet above, the walls fanned out to make the place at least five hundred feet across, probably more. The walls and ceiling were bright with glowing green vines and crystals, filling the cavern with a soft glow. Stalactites dozens of feet long hung in profusion from above and filling the cavern floor was a city.

Buildings of one or two stories, some carved into the walls of the cavern, others built from quarried stone, stood in seemingly random rows and groups. In places the natural topography of the ground made the clusters of buildings closer together or further apart, most had small windows, all had low doorways, the majority without doors. Between them, stalagmites stood where trees might adorn a normal town.

"What the..?" Slater breathed, but nobody else had a voice to share.

Then Reid moved forward, pointed with his assault rifle. "Bodies. Old ones."

The group walked cautiously in amongst the buildings. Houses? Aston wondered. What else could they be? And sure enough, there were dozens of corpses lying in the streets, clearly the remains of a battle fought a long time ago. They were desiccated, mostly skeletal, but with remnants of dried and browned flesh hanging to the bones like human jerky. They still bore the ragged remains of clothing, military uniforms, and some broken weapons lay near them.

Reid went to one and crouched, looked closely at the insignia on the uniform. "Russian," he said. "I'm a bit of a military history nerd. I recognize these. Early- to mid-nineteen-fifties."

"Did they fall prey to the mantics?" Sol asked.

Aston spotted something and shook his head. "Maybe some, but not all. Look." He pulled a bloodstone knife from under one corpse, not unlike the one that had killed Professor Murray Lee.

"Knife wounds are evident in the remaining flesh of this one too," Reid said.

"And here," Syed confirmed, crouching near more bodies. "All three of these have stab marks in the skin, and scoring on the bones of their ribs." She gently moved a skull and winced. "Looks like this one was stabbed right through the left eye." Moving another, she checked the head again. "This one was bludgeoned, so not only knife attacks."

"But all pretty primitive weapons," Aston said. "They must have had a large advantage of numbers, given these soldiers were armed with guns."

He moved further along one street and spotted another bloodstone blade protruding from the rib cage of a fallen soldier. It appeared a little different from the others. Instead of a simple long, pointed oval of stone with a rounded grip, this one was carved into the shape of a long, curved dagger. The craftsmanship was magnificent, the details intricate, a cross-guard at the hilt, fine lines along the blade and a perfect, razor-sharp edge along one side. He slipped it out from between the dead man's ribs and turned it over slowly in his hands, admiring it. What was this stuff, that Lee had dubbed bloodstone? He'd never seen stone quite like it before. And why did these attackers use it? It could be simply a lack of metals in the underground catacombs that had driven whoever these people were into a kind of stone age, but why this particular stone? Was it unique to this region? And yet it was unlike all the rock they had encountered so far, so it must have been mined elsewhere. Perhaps deeper, or in some part of the underground network they had yet to see. Or perhaps brought with them from wherever they had originated. Thoughts of alien origins flickered through his mind again, but he pushed the idea aside. Regardless, he felt that he should keep at least one of these weapons close to hand. He still had the one he'd taken from Lee's chest.

Catching Slater's eye, he gestured for her to join him. She and Marla came over together, eyebrows raised. He saw fear like his own reflected in their expressions. "Hold onto this," he said, handing Slater the blade that had killed Lee. He gave Marla the one from under the corpse he had found moments before, and kept the intricately carved one for himself.

"Why?" Slater asked.

Aston shrugged. "Call it intuition. I just feel like we should hold onto them. Besides, as we recently established, we don't have many bullets left. At the very least they're a weapon that's easy to use, and knives won't run out of ammo. Better than bare fists, I guess."

Slater and Marla shared a nervous glance, then both nodded and slipped the blades into their jackets. Aston pocketed his, too.

"This is too weird," Tate said from the back of the small group.

"No shit," Marla muttered.

Tate gave a small, humorless laugh. "Well, yeah, a huge city under the Antarctic is weird, but I mean the battle. Where are the bodies of the others? Whoever was fighting the Russians? Did they kill them all with no casualties on their side? Seems unlikely."

"More likely they carried their own dead away," Reid said, standing and looking around the huge space. "To hide their losses, maybe? Or just out of respect, to conduct burial rituals or whatever."

"Yeah," Aston agreed. "And I can't help wondering if the survivors are still here."

CHAPTER 30

Consciousness crawled back into Dig O'Donnell's brain and he gagged, certain he was going to vomit. He coughed up only bitter bile, and spat it onto the cold rock. When was the last time he ate? As he sucked in his next breath, green and black visions scattered past his mind's eye, the kaleidoscopic view of a hundred mantics, still hiding in the darkness all around him, and concealed in dozens of other places throughout the network of tunnels and caves.

He tried to remember what had happened, why he had fallen. He recalled the touch of that ancient mind, that all-powerful consciousness. He recalled how it had threatened to burst his brain like a squeezed pimple. With a sob, he pushed the thoughts from his mind, staggered to his feet and stumbled in blind circles. The mantics' sight flooded him again and that sighing, whispering voice goaded him on. As if drawn by a magnet, he leaned sideways and staggered with the motion lest he fall. Before he knew it, he was running along dark passages, taking turns and forks as if a native to the way.

Diiiiigggbyyyyyyy…

Diiiiiiggggbbyyyyyyyyyy…

He kept going, down and down and down. And then he emerged into a space that was wide and cold and huge. The rock above his head curved up and away, rising to hundreds of feet above where it gave off am unearthly glow from the vine-like growths and clusters of bright green crystals. And below it, spreading as far as Dig could see, was a sea of glowing green. The Jade Sea. The water itself sparkled, illuminated from within by ethereal light.

This was the place. The presence lived here, that ecstatic being. Seeking to bask in its manifestation, Dig moved to the edge of the water and dipped his finger in. He anticipated the action would lead him to feel closer to the presence, but it didn't. Frowning, he moved forward, up to his knees in the water, the rock solid beneath his feet. It was cool, but not freezing. He sensed dozens of mantics draw up behind him, saw himself from behind through their eyes.

Then his mind and stomach lurched and he saw himself from inside the water, standing there, the idol hugged still to his chest. From directly below, he saw himself through the eyes of a fish that swam up to his feet, even as he himself watched the fish approach.

He was Digby and he was the fish. He grabbed it, or perhaps it swam into his hands, he didn't know which and the distinction was irrelevant anyway. He raised the fish, glittering and dripping from the water, and took a bite. He howled as he felt teeth tearing through him, screamed in agony and shuddered in ecstasy simultaneously as tears rolled down his face.

And then the great presence took hold of him, controlled him, and he gave himself to it willingly, gladly, with abandon. He dropped to his knees, the glittering water lapping about his waist, and received the visions of the mighty awareness.

CHAPTER 31

Larsen ran through darkness, the thunder of assault rifle fire deafening behind him. His flashlight beam danced left and right as he scanned the floor to avoid falling, bursts of light from the weapons fire occasionally reflecting off damp rock above.

He knew they were hopelessly lost. Whatever memory of the route they had taken had been abandoned in the panic. Wherever the green cavern might be, he didn't think he would ever find it again. Retracing their steps might be possible by following the trail of broken and bleeding creatures and soldiers, but that seemed incredibly unlikely as there were far more monsters than men and any chance of returning the way they had come seemed a foolish hope. Survival seemed a foolish hope.

He rounded a bend, saw another fork ahead. The gunfire stopped and he glanced back. Only Olsen and Jensen were there, and they both barreled right past him, running headlong. He caught glimpses of dozens of the giant, insect-like creatures skittering along the passage toward them. Only two fighters left, and they'd both given up. As they veered down the left fork, Larsen broke into a run and chased them.

His satchel bounced heavy against his hip, containing a possible escape, if only he had time to use it. Unbeknownst to the mercs, one of his plans was something of a final solution. If they couldn't take control of the green cavern, and all the valuable greenium it contained, he carried explosives to bring it all down, killing everyone still in it. Halvdan would be able to excavate later, assuming

Larsen led him to the collapsed cave. The greenium would survive. Or Larsen could have sold the secret to someone else, played Halvdan off against some other interest. If he was the only one left with the knowledge of the valuable stuff's location, his options were legion. But all those plans hadn't taken into account a swarm of monsters. How could anyone have considered that possibility?

Weighing his options now, he found himself in a considerably less favorable situation than any he had entertained. If he had time, just a few moments, to arm the explosives, he could blow the passageway behind them to keep the creatures at bay. He was reluctant, both because it would potentially waste the explosives and also cut off their only known means of escape. But it was completely cut off right now by hordes of creatures anyway.

They stumbled out into another cave, like the green cavern with the pool, but much smaller. Even so, the vine-like growths lit it with a soft glow. Olsen looked back and slowed, then stopped.

Larsen paused to see what had caught the mercenaries' attention. The passage behind them was empty. Olsen cautiously approached, shined his flashlight into the darkness.

"They're holding back," he said. He moved the flashlight left and right, then again, then smiled. "They don't like the light. They're avoiding this cave, and my flashlight."

"This won't buy us much time," Larsen said. "We still can't go back that way, there's too many to hold off by shining flashlights in their eyes. Eventually our batteries will die. Then we will. They live here, surely they can't avoid all the caverns with enough vines to light them?"

Olsen frowned. "They are moving slowly forward."

"Letting their eyes adjust to the change in brightness, I expect," Larsen asked. "I think maybe it just takes them a while."

"Maybe."

"Only one tunnel leading out," Jensen said. "Sir, maybe we should just keep moving for now?"

Olsen nodded and took the lead again, Jensen hot on his heels as they left the cave by the opposite side. Larsen stared down the passage with the reluctant creatures, thinking again about his explosives. Perhaps this brightness would buy them enough of a head start to survive. He'd think again if they started to catch up. But he knew he had to do something soon, else they'd all be dead.

CHAPTER 32

Aston explored the bizarre subterranean city with Slater and Marla close by him, while Sol moved with Reid and Tate. Syed sat with Jen on a kind of bench carved from the rock beside one small house.

They found the far side of the habitation, the whole place maybe five hundred feet across and perhaps a thousand feet long. Completely empty now, long abandoned, even the buildings were empty of possessions or furnishings. Other than the bodies of the Russian soldiers near the entrance, the place was devoid of any signs of life beyond its construction. Several passages led away from the city, most of them small and dark. The biggest were the one they had entered by, and another one of a similar size directly opposite, on the far side of the city. It was a kind of Russian roulette deciding which to take, Aston mused. Maybe they could cautiously explore each one for a little while, map the place out, and then decide which way to go. If nothing else, this city and the numerous exits gave him hope there would be another way to the surface, if only they could find it.

"I don't think there's anything else to discover in here," Aston said eventually. "It feels like this place was cleaned out a long time ago. Like, eons ago."

"We should rest," Sol said.

"I've lost all idea of what time of day or night it might be up there," Marla said.

Sol looked at his watch. "Well, the actual time is mid-morning. But that's a bit irrelevant now. We had our night interrupted at God knows what time. Other than a couple of hours rest before Dig attacked Jen, we've hardly slept in two days. We're all exhausted, we have shelter here, so I say we take the chance to sleep."

"Good idea," Reid said. "But we do it in shifts, always two people on watch. I'll take the first, then Tate can take the second. Who'll stay up with me?"

"I will," Marla said. "I'm too buzzed to rest right now anyway."

"I don't think we should rest in any of the dwellings though," Slater said. "Feels like too easy a place to be trapped."

Aston pointed over to their right. "There's a kind of natural clearing over there. Some rougher ground, a little raised. Gives a good view all around."

Reid nodded. "Sounds like a plan, let's go."

Before long they had established a small camp on the rocky clearing, finding places to lie that were the least uncomfortable given the circumstances. Reid sat on one side, looking back toward the tunnel they had entered by. Marla sat on the other side, her back to him, staring disconsolately off in the direction of the other largest way out.

Aston lay down with Slater close by, her back to him. He reached out, laid one hand on her shoulder. She patted his hand, but neither of them spoke. Syed and Jen settled not far away. Tate lay down right behind where Marla sat. Sol sat beside Reid, the two men talking in whispers. Aston thought how it might be nice to spend some time with Slater when they weren't in mortal danger one day. First a dinosaur, now this. He vowed that once they got out of here, he would try to take Slater somewhere nice and safe. If she'd have him. Her breathing slowed and exhaustion crept over Aston like a tide. He closed his eyes.

Sudden, ear-shattering gunfire ripped him back from sleep seemingly moments later. Tate had rolled up onto one knee and was rapid-firing bursts left and right. Reid and Sol on the other side stood back to back, firing with apparent abandon.

"The bastards are everywhere!" Tate screamed, finding her feet and pushing Marla behind her.

Aston and Slater jumped up, helped Syed and Jen to their feet. Tate wasn't lying, the entire huge cavern seemed to swarm with mantics, the soft green light reflecting off their shining carapaces. Clearly they were getting bolder in the light. Reid and Tate aimed for joints and eyes, dropping several. Sol's fire was less accurate, but he helped to hold the creatures back briefly, then looked at his empty guns in despair. He backed behind Tate as Aston took his place, pumping rounds from Gates's dropped rifle as best he could. Slater fired fast from her pistol, switched out the clip for the one Reid had given her, and emptied that. As she clicked empty, so did Aston. Panic started to thrum through him as he became convinced they were going to die here. Tate switched to her sidearm once her own rifle was spent.

"Get away from open ground!" Reid yelled. "We have to try to defend ourselves in a narrower passage, some place where they can't surround us." He ran, firing, clearing a path.

Aston questioned the wisdom of it, as they'd been surrounded in a tunnel before, but at this point anything seemed preferable to standing vulnerable in wide open ground.

As Reid moved, Sol kept pace beside him, Marla a step behind. After them came Slater and Syed. Aston helped Jen, staying close to Tate as she covered their rear, the whole group moving towards an exit tunnel on the far side. A blur of motion to their right made the group swerve like a school of frightened fish, but Sol Griffin wasn't fast enough. With a howl of panic, he fell and the mantics swarmed over him.

"Move!" Tate screamed, pushing Aston and Jen forward, Sol already forgotten.

They ducked left and right, dodging the fast-moving mantics, then realized they'd moved aside from the others up ahead.

Aston looked across the gap between them. He was nearly at the mouth of one tunnel, but a swarm of chitinous creatures was between him and Slater. As Slater, Syed, and Marla were driven sideways towards the next tunnel around, Slater realized they had been separated, reached out to Aston. In the moment of pause, she didn't see a mantic closing up behind her. Aston opened his mouth to shout, but Marla was already there. She pulled Slater violently to one side, saving her boss at the last instant, but it cost the sound engineer her life. The creature's mandibles snapped shut and Marla's head leaped from her neck, face wide in a pained expression of shock as blood fountained up below it.

"No!" Aston yelled, drowned out by Slater's own scream, then Tate was hauling him and Jen towards the tunnel mouth.

Reid stepped up and pushed Slater and Syed into their tunnel, then turned back to hold off the advancing mantics. He fired three shots, then his gun fell silent. His face turned into a grimace of pure rage as he began laying punches left and right into the creatures' multi-faceted eyes, but then they covered him and blood gouted up and sprayed the walls.

Slater and Syed were swallowed by the darkness of the passage as Tate pushed Aston into their own, screaming at them to "Run! Just fucking run!" and Aston, still hauling Jen Galicia with him, couldn't help thinking they were going to run straight into more of the bloodthirsty creatures and what was the point anyway?

In darkness, they fled, Jen's weight dragging down on Aston, but he refused to let her go. His mind was filled with images of death. Reid, Marla, Sol, all gone. Slater and Syed somewhere separated and he may never see them again.

"Jo..." he said, voice edged with the panic roiling in his gut.

He sucked in a huge breath. He'd be damned if he would collapse in the face of this, no matter how ridiculous the odds, no matter how deadly the enemy. He would go down fighting, howling his rage into the face of death. He redoubled his efforts, almost lifted Jen off her feet as he ran alongside Tate.

They came out into a large chamber and Aston actually laughed at the ridiculous lack of luck they had. At least it wasn't mantics. "Hold it!" he shouted.

Tate raised her pistol, but Aston pushed the barrel down.

"Don't bother. We're surrounded."

CHAPTER 33

Jo Slater ran alongside Jahara Syed into the darkness of the tunnel, her mind spinning in shock. Was everyone but them dead? She'd seen so many go down. The image of Marla's shocked face would haunt her forever. It seemed that whoever came to work for her met a grisly end and she wondered if maybe she was a cursed journalist.

Syed cried out as she stumbled and Slater caught her by the elbow, hauled her along. No, they couldn't all be dead. Madness snapped at the heels of her mind when she thought like that.

She had seen Aston forced into the next passage around, and Tate had been with him. And Jen too? It was hard to remember. But Aston had been alive. If nothing else, she needed to cling to that knowledge, that hope. Somehow they would have to find a way to loop around and rejoin each other. Or both escape by separate routes and meet again on the outside.

"They're coming!" Syed cried, glancing back over her shoulder.

Slater trusted the woman's word, didn't risk a fall by looking back herself.

"Let's get somewhere bright. Find another cavern with vines or something."

"That last cavern was bright with vines and crystals," Syed said, her voice trembling on the verge of open panic.

"Let's hope that once they go along dark tunnels, their eyes take a long time to adjust again to the next bright place. It's the only hope we've got. We keep moving from one to the next, no rest until we get out."

Syed nodded, brows knitted. Slater wondered if her biologist's mind was working. That was good, anything to distract her from giving in to fear.

"That could be why we keep getting reprieves," Syed said. "If we don't linger too long in any one place and they have to keep readjusting, we can maybe stay ahead of them."

"It's the best plan we've got."

"It's the only plan we've got! But do you really think we can find another way out?" Syed asked.

"We have to. There must be multiple ways in and out of a network this big. The evidence of habitation means at some point it was well populated. There's no way there would only be one entrance to a place so vast. We just have to keep moving, keep looking." Or die trying, she thought, but chose not to vocalize that addition. Syed wasn't stupid, and would be entertaining the same thoughts, she was sure.

They ran on, keeping their headlamps aimed at the ground to avoid tripping on the rocky debris strewn everywhere. Finally, Slater noticed a soft luminescence ahead. The by now familiar green tinge was like a breath of fresh air. "Come on!"

They redoubled their speed and burst out into a cavern that was long and low, but had a fissure all up one of its long walls from which bright green vines snaked out like veins, lighting the place. As they skidded to a stop, Slater rejoiced at the sight of three other people already there. Her mouth started to form Aston's name, but her relief was short lived. Anders Larsen and two mean-looking mercenaries she had never seen before turned in surprise and brought their weapons to bear.

Slater threw her hands up. "Don't shoot! We're unarmed." She still had the pistol jammed into the back of her pants, but it was useless without ammo. She knew Syed didn't even have a knife, but her bloodstone dagger was tucked safely in her jacket.

"Jo Slater and Jahara Syed," Anders Larsen said. "Well, well, some of you still live after all. Just you two?"

"Yes," Slater said quickly, before Syed could answer. "Everyone else is dead. We need to get out." She couldn't articulate exactly why, but she felt pretty certain Larsen was not their friend. If he thought Aston, Tate, and Jen were dead, as the others really were, perhaps she would buy them a chance to escape.

"Well, that's okay," Larsen said.

Slater was stunned. She was definitely correct that he was not their friend. "Okay? Everyone's dead, Larsen! How is that okay?"

He grinned. "Because you're still alive and we only need one guide."

"To where?"

"Back to the big cavern, with the lake and all the greenium crystals. We got lost in these damned tunnels. We need to get back. So you'll show us the way."

"But we..." Syed started.

But Slater spoke quickly over the biologist. "Yeah, sure, okay. We'll do that, if you use those guns to protect us." She knew they had little chance, unarmed as they were. At least Larsen and his angry-looking friends had weapons. Perhaps she could use them as much as they used her. "But we can't go back that way, it's swarming with mantics. And they're catching up."

Two tunnels led from the far side of the long cave in which they stood. Larsen gestured to the one on the left. "Well, we can't go that way for the same reason."

Slater forced a smile, hoping to project a confidence she didn't feel. "Not a problem." She pointed to the other tunnel. "We can go that way." It was a ploy to keep moving at least. Syed looked at her, but Slater refused to meet the woman's eye. "Let's move," she said. "The quicker the better." She hoped Aston was having better luck.

CHAPTER 34

Aston stared in resigned astonishment at the second underground city they had discovered. Like the first one in pretty much every way, except this one was clearly inhabited. Dozens of creatures stood all around him, Ronda Tate and Jen Galicia, with bloodstone knives and spears all pointed menacingly.

His initial thought had immediately gone to aliens, the "grays" so commonly referred to in popular culture and conspiracy theories. But after a moment it became clear they were something different. Almost certainly not aliens, he decided, but hominids who had evolved and adapted to their subterranean surroundings. Where they may have originated, why they had been here, were questions he thought may perhaps never be answered, unless they could communicate. Even then, how much of their own history would they know? The habitation, the simplicity of the city, pointed to a largely undeveloped society, not unlike he imagined the Neanderthals of history to have been. But these creatures bore no resemblance to heavy-browed, hairy, dark-skinned cavemen he'd seen in displays at museums.

Small of stature, these people had pale, almost bone white, skin, and lean, spindly muscles stretched along fine limbs. Their skinny bodies made their heads appear overlarge. Their eyes were even larger than their heads should have allowed, with huge pupils, which Aston presumed were for drinking in maximum light. They had very little body hair, and what did cover their heads was wispy, nearly transparent. Their spear shafts were made of all manner of improvised tools, most clearly scavenged from other people like himself who had intruded into their domain. Among the weapons he saw shafts of ski poles, old-fashioned backpack frames, even rifles, with the sharpened bloodstone jammed into the end of now useless barrels.

"What the hell is this?" Tate whispered, her pistol hanging forgotten beside her thigh.

"It's the answer to why we've seen signs of civilization that clearly wasn't the work of the mantics," Jen said. "Let's assume they might be friendly."

"What if they plan to eat us?" Tate asked.

"There's too many of them to fight," Aston said. "Let me try to talk to them." He stepped slightly forward of the two women, then immediately stopped when the crowd of pale folk bristled, brandishing their weapons. "Okay, okay!" He raised his hands, palms out, tried to force a smile, though he felt nothing but fear. And a mild sense of wonder. Perhaps he needed to focus on that. He pointed at his chest. "I'm Sam Aston." They tilted their heads at his words, clearly more curious than aggressive at this point. He tried again, tapped his chest. "Aston."

One of the creatures lowered its spear and pointed to itself. "An-na-ki," it said, in a high, breathy voice. Immediately many others became animated, started chattering in a series of rapid clicks and chirps interspersed with vaguely recognizable syllables of speech more akin to known language. Regardless, it was all far too fast and garbled for Aston to follow. The one who had spoken rounded on the others, its voice sharp, angry. They settled slightly and it turned back to Aston, gestured to itself again and made the same sounds. "An-na-ki."

Aston pointed toward it. "You're Annaki?"

The creature pointed to itself, then the two either side of it. "Annaki. Annaki." It gestured to take in the crowd of gathered pale folk. "Annaki."

"They're all Annaki," Jen said. "They have a collective name for themselves."

"It's a start," Aston said. He smiled at the one who had spoken and gave a small bow. "Annaki," he said. "Hello. It's nice to meet you."

The group chattered rapidly again, their tensions easing.

Aston pointed to himself again, said, "Aston." He gestured to the others. "Galicia. Tate."

The first creature bobbed excitedly. "Annaki-Akan!" it said, pointing to itself. It gestured left. "Annaki-Innka." Then to the right. "Annaki-Oto."

Aston grinned. "Now we're getting somewhere. Hello, Akan!"

The creature gave a throaty cough that might have been a laugh. It pointed to its mouth and made chewing motions with its small, pale teeth.

"It's offering us food," Jen said.

"Hell, no." Tate's brows creased in a frown. "I ain't eating anything from this crazy place."

"They must live on something," Aston said. "If it's glowing green, we don't eat it, though." He nodded to Akan. "Okay."

There was clearly still some dissension among the population, but on the whole the Annaki seemed to have relaxed. Aston and his friends were led to one of the larger dwellings and guided inside. He wondered how they remained safe from the mantics. Were they in league with the creatures? Or did they have better defenses? This cavern, like so many others, had webs of glowing vines crawling from fissures in the walls and ceiling, the enormous place lit in the gentle green glow they had become used to. Deposits of greenium glittered here and there, the dark curling ferns growing in fissures all around the walls and floor. But the mantics could clearly grow used to the brightness in time, as the recent attack had proven. They had hardly rested at all before they were overrun. And that cavern had been no different to this one, only perhaps it was a little smaller. Had the Annaki relocated to a bigger home cave? Regardless, they seemed to exist here quite comfortably, so they obviously had some way of controlling or holding back the mantics. He realized every weapon, from spears to knives to sword-like machetes, had been made of the strange rock Murray Lee had dubbed bloodstone. Was that the answer? If so, what was it about bloodstone that did more damage than bullets? And where did they get it?

He and his friends were led to a smooth rock being used as a table. On it were piles of mushroom-like fungi, pale and smooth, and dried out cockroach-like bugs. Neither had the bright green glow of the vines or the fish they had seen. Annaki-Akan pointed to the food, then his mouth. Aston's reluctance must have been clear on his face, for Akan moved forward, took one bug and a pinch of fungus and ate both together with relish. He nodded, stepped back, gestured again.

"I am starving," Jen said. "And still weak as a baby."

"We'll need energy," Aston agreed. "Beggars can't be choosers."

"Holy hell," Tate said. "I feel like that chick from the Indiana Jones movie. The one they tried to feed eyeball soup."

Aston managed a grin."

The three of them took some of the fungus and tentatively ate it. Aston found it dry, dusty, spongy in texture with a subtle savory flavor, but it wasn't too unpleasant. He tried a little more. "It's okay," he said.

Tate and Jen both chewed, faces twisted in mild concern. Or perhaps disgust.

"Well, in for a quarter, in for a buck," Aston said, and threw one of the dried bugs into his mouth. It was crunchy and rich, with a nutty taste that he found strong and slightly unnerving. After a few chews he grew used to it. "Actually not bad," he said with a smile.

Jen and Tate gave identical shrugs and the three of them ate their fill of small mushrooms and beetles. Some of the Annaki joined them, clearly some hierarchy at play where a handful of the pale creatures ate while the rest filed out and went about their business.

Aston hadn't realized how hungry he was and felt strength and clarity of thought return as he ate. He didn't like to guess at the actual nutritional value of the stuff. Looking at the Annaki, he didn't fancy living on a diet of it for long, but in the short term, it was a valuable feed.

As they had their fill, Aston tried to communicate again. "We need to find our friends," he said.

Akan looked quizzical, tipped its head.

"Our friends," Aston said. He pointed to himself, then Tate, then Jen, then pointed to three fingers on his left hand. He did it again, then held up the last two fingers of that hand, pointed to them and shrugged. Akan was clearly confused. He repeated the gestures, then swept his arm around to encompass the cavern they were in and beyond. "We have two more friends," he said, despairing and frustrated. "We need to find them."

"I don't think he gets it, man," Tate said. "I say we let them take their chances and convince these guys to show us the way out. They must know one, right?"

"No way!" Aston said. "I'm not leaving Jo down here. And Syed was with her."

"They're probably dead already. If not, they probably will be soon."

"We can't know that," Jen said. "And we can't just give up on them. We have to try to find them."

Tate laughed, but it had little humor in it. "Do we have to? Really? I'm thinking all I have to do is get the hell out of here."

"You're not a bad person, Ronda," Aston said. "You really going to be selfish now? We can ask these guys to help us find Slater and Syed, and then show us all the way out. They've survived for who knows how long down here, so they can obviously avoid the mantics. We'll be safe with them if we befriend them."

Tate pursed her lips, shook her head. After a moment, she looked down, but said no more. Aston had to hope she'd stick with them. He turned his attention back to Akan. "Our friends." He stopped, thinking. Then he pulled the bloodstone dagger from his jacket. Akan made positive noises, pointed to the weapon and moved his arms like mantic mandibles. "These work against the mantics?" Aston asked.

Akan tilted his head, confused again. Aston shook it off. He needed to focus. He used the point of the dagger to scratch crude drawings in the loose grit of the cave floor. He made five stick figures. He pointed to the first, then at himself, and said, "Me. Aston." Then he pointed at the next one and then to Tate. Then to the third one, then to Jen. Akan frowned, then nodded. It pointed to the other two stick figures and looked around.

"Yes, exactly!" Aston said. He gestured widely once more. "Where? Where are our two friends?"

Akan paused, seemingly in thought. Then it took out a bloodstone dagger of its own and sketched a rough map in the dirt. He marked several passages, then drew a huge circle. He added ripple marks, making the circle look like a body of water. He tapped at it, as if to say 'Try here'.

When the other Annaki who had remained with them realized what Akan had drawn, they set up a clamor, jabbering and clicking. Akan argued back. The conversation grew heated, adversarial.

"They sure don't like his suggestion," Aston said to Tate and Jen.

Akan argued some more, then barked a couple of short, sharp phrases. He seemed to have some authority and the others reluctantly quieted down. Akan stood and motioned for Aston to follow.

He saw it was trembling, nervous even in its conviction. "We'll come with you," he said, hurrying Tate and Jen along. But he wondered if it was a mistake.

Akan and two other Annaki led the way, the two clearly reluctant but doing as they were told. None of them seemed happy.

"Where is it taking us, do you think?" Tate asked.

"I don't know," Aston said. "But wherever it is, I think this little guy is scared shitless of what's waiting there."

CHAPTER 35

Slater led the way through dark tunnels, shining her headlamp before her. Syed walked at her side, the biologist's face set and determined, but fear was obvious in her eyes. Slater hoped her pounding heart couldn't be heard over the scuff and scrape of their footsteps. She had to think of something, because if she continued to lead them blindly along dark passages, eventually they would tire of humoring her. And then, she thought, they would almost certainly shoot her.

She clenched her teeth, literally biting down on the panic that threatened to rise and take her sanity away. The pressure of these dark tubes of rock had started to become a palpable force, the claustrophobia repeatedly stripping her breath, forcing her to gasp great lungfuls of frightened breath. She didn't want to die down here, by any means. Not at the snapping mandibles of the mantics, though at least that would be quick. She didn't want to be shot either, even if that was equally swift. But most of all, she didn't want to wander lost and frightened, only to get weaker and weaker until she eventually starved to death in the dark, with no light, no food or water, no friends. No hope. She suppressed a sob, thoughts of Aston coming back to her. He had to be alive. If recent events had taught her anything, it was that Aston was hard to kill and the bastard had a habit of popping up again. She had to hold onto that hope. If she considered him already dead, the insanity would leap from the base of her gut where it swirled and throttle her mind in an instant.

Keep moving, find Sam, get out. Keep moving, find Sam, get out. It became a mantra as she walked.

"Seems like we're getting nowhere," Larsen barked from behind her.

Her back arched from the jab of his pistol barrel. She staggered forward a couple of extra paces away from it. "Just be patient," she said, cursing the high note of fear in her voice. "We have to go a long way around, because we couldn't go back the way we came."

"We will shoot you and scavenge your supplies if you don't help us," he said. "You know that, right?"

Slater laughed in spite of herself. "You're a really great motivator, Anders. I bet you'd quickly rise to the very top of middle management if you took an office job."

To her surprise, Olsen, the merc leader, laughed out loud. But when he came up alongside her, his face was scarily hard. "He is less than a leader," Olsen said, his voice heavily accented Scandinavian. "But his point is true. We won't carry baggage. Where are you leading us?"

"Back to the green cavern, just like you asked. Only it's a circuitous route, that's all." She realized the slight glitter of nascent vines that seemed to thread a lot of the tunnels between larger caves, appeared to be brighter. She grabbed onto that small detail. "See how these are glowing more? That means we're getting closer."

Olsen's eyes narrowed. Clearly he didn't believe her, but he dropped back a pace or two again. Although she couldn't feel its touch, she strongly sensed the presence of his assault rifle inches from her back.

Syed glanced over, a question in her eyes. Slater gave the tiniest shrug. Maybe there was something to it. The tiny filaments of vine did appear to be increasing. They trudged on, leaving a little more hope behind with each step. Syed's headlamp flickered and dimmed a little, then came back. Her hand rose to it, panic in her eyes.

"Turn it off for now," Slater said. "Save your battery.

We can manage with mine."

Olsen said something in rapid Norwegian from behind them, then Jensen and Larsen's lights clicked off. Slater allowed herself a small smile. It was some comfort, at least, that even the big tough mercs were as concerned about survival as she was. Even if they did end up shooting her and Jahara, it gave her some melancholic pleasure to know they'd probably still die here, too.

With the sudden reduction in light around them, Slater noticed a soft glow far ahead. She allowed herself a moment of hope. The smear of green luminescence along the walls was definitely more than the simple hints of tunnel growth. Had she, through dumb luck, actually managed to guide them back to the green cavern after all?

She thought about saying something flippant like, Here we are then! but decided against it. No point in tempting fate. They had seen other brightly illuminated caverns, had nearly died in one despite the safety they thought it offered. Several of them had, in fact, died there. She drew another deep, nervous breath and pushed on.

"Is this it?" Larsen said from behind as the brightness grew. The relief was apparent in his voice.

But they stepped out into something none of them could have anticipated. The passage opened into an impossibly huge space. The walls and ceiling disappeared into infinity, lost away and above in the distance to clouds of swirling, pale green mist. To their right, the ground rose to a high ledge of rock, the wall rising above it to be lost in fog. To their left, the rocky ground curved slowly away into fog-shrouded distance. Several more tunnels emerged at various places along both sides. But in front of them, shimmering and gently lapping, was water that could only be described as an ocean. It glimmered with its own green phosphorescence, sparkling in tiny wavelets that rose and fell. The edge lapped softly at the rock, in a gentle mesmerizing rhythm that left pale deposits of brightness behind that slowly dimmed, only to be replaced with the next gentle wave. Mist swirled over the surface of the water that seemed to stretch away from them forever.

Slater's breath was trapped in her chest with wonder, but Larsen managed to find his voice.

"What the hell is this?"

CHAPTER 36

Digby O'Donnell let the sentience of a thousand beings thrum through his mind. The sensation was agony and ecstasy. It was transcendental and destructive. It was more than he could ever have imagined.

He knelt in water that lapped, glittering, around his hips, his mind far from his own. Things moved in the sea all around him, bright darts of fish, slowly pulsing clouds of microscopic luminescence, occasionally even a gently pulsing, glassy jellyfish. They seemed to come to him in worship, in deference, drawn by his connection to everything in the writhing network of caves and tunnels, but more importantly, his connection to what lay beneath, out there. And no doubt, his connection was evident in the brightly glowing idol he held in blistered hands. The idol that grew brighter by the moment.

The Jade Sea was immense. Even if it had some boundaries in this world, its reach was eternal, through other worlds, other dimensions, glory without end, and Digby's mind stretched and warped through them all.

The waters began to roil, as if something gargantuan stirred deep, deep under the soft rise and fall of the surface. Bubbles rose, the lapping waves increased. The mist, writhing like lazy ghosts across the surface of the sea, began to thicken. Its activity increased, as though it were alive, and excited. More clouds built up in the distance and rolled toward the shore as if with purpose.

Digby's connection to the strange life underneath increased too, clarity coming ever more quickly. He knew the mind of the Master. The Overlord of All. He knew its corrupted desires, its need. It wanted to consume, to feed on the conscious life of anything that moved in the many realms. It starved. It wanted to devour the minds of individuality wherever it found them. Digby shivered with the deep vibrations of its malevolence, its darkness, its hatred. It yearned for dominion, for control, everything that could ever be under its command, for no reason beyond the removal of agency from everything else. The Overlord simply wanted to be lord over all without any challenge, without any contest. It required the deep, total peace of utter control. And Digby would facilitate that. He would usher that forward. It began here, but it wouldn't end here. This was only the germination of the seed of the end of everything.

Digby laughed maniacally, thrilled and horrified. Tears streamed down his face, falling into the Jade Sea with small sparks of green brilliance, his grief and ecstasy becoming part of that great body that stretched beyond worlds.

The idol grew hotter in his hands, painfully so, threatening to strip the skin and flesh from his bones, but he couldn't let go. His fingers could no more release the idol than his neck could voluntarily release his head. He raised the idol high, his hands as though on fire, pain radiating down his arms, and he howled. The waters surged and bright green arcs in the sea and sky flashed like lightning.

CHAPTER 37

Annaki-Akan and his two reluctant companions guided Aston, Tate and Galicia down twisting passages. They seemed to travel for a long time, Akan's friends regularly chittering at their leader only to be shouted down. The tension rose among them, obvious in their movements, and that only made Aston more nervous.

"Where are they taking us?" Tate asked suddenly, as if reading his mind.

"I don't know."

"I don't trust them. We don't know they're our allies just because they let us eat some of their mushrooms."

Aston sighed. He couldn't argue with that assessment. "I'm with you, really. We have no idea what's going on. But look at our options. We couldn't go back the way we came, because the tunnels were swarming with mantics. We have no idea where to go if we strike out on our own. So what's left? I say we let these guys show us whatever it is they want to show us."

"What if they control the mantics?" Tate asked. "What if they've used them to herd us and now they're taking us to some ritual cavern to lay us on a slab and carve out our hearts like ancient Mayans or something?"

Aston laughed. "Well, I guess that's much the same in the long run as being decapitated by mantics, but we wouldn't go down without a fight. I reckon we can take these three little guys, don't you?"

"Sure. But not if they're leading us to a cave full of mantics. Or something worse."

"However you look at it, we're no worse off than

running for our lives, being chased by mantics. Especially given we have close to no ammo left. What do you have there?"

Tate lifted the pistol in her hand, looking at it with distaste. "One full clip, but it's my last. After this, we're back to the stone age."

Aston still had his bloodstone dagger. The three Annaki leading them each carried a bloodstone spear. Stone age indeed. "Well, I guess you treat that last clip like gold and save it as long as you can."

"I might save it for myself," Tate said bitterly. "If we get surrounded by those monsters again, I'm not getting eaten."

"I don't even have a club," Jen said quietly. "Even if I had the strength to use one."

"Here," Tate said, and handed Jen a bloodstone knife.

Jen smiled. "Thanks. That actually makes me feel a little better."

"Always better to be armed with something."

"Where did you get that?" Aston asked.

Tate grinned. "I lifted it from the Annaki city back there." She opened her jacket to reveal another tucked into her waistband. "I got two in fact, but you're not getting your hands on this one. That's for when my pistol becomes useless."

"That's okay," Aston said. "I still have one of my own. So at least we all have a knife."

Tate laughed, shook her head. "Jesus fucking Christ. We're bringing knives to a bug fight. We're no better off than them!" She nodded towards the three Annaki ahead of them.

"Well, they've survived this long," Aston said, though he didn't fill himself with much hope by the observation. Not knowing how they had survived so gave him a menacing sense of dread.

Up ahead he saw a greenish glow, softly pulsing against the tunnel walls. The Annaki began to chirrup and chatter again, obviously getting more nervous by the step.

"Here we go," Aston said. "Be ready."

"For what?" Jen asked.

"I have no idea," Aston admitted. He wondered if they had managed to finally come around full circle and were back at the green cavern. He hoped they were, as he was tempted to immediately club the three Annaki and make a bolt for freedom once he knew where he was again. But then thoughts of Slater came back to his mind and he knew he couldn't leave without trying to find her. He had to believe she was still alive. "Just be ready for anything, Sam," he whispered to himself.

As they moved closer to the brightness, he saw something strange happening to the bloodstone tips of the spears the Annaki carried. He pulled out his own dagger and the phenomenon was repeated there. The strange stone seemed to emanate a dark aura, like shadow growing out from it in a thin shroud, as if the bloodstone deflected the green light like oil pushed aside by water. It was simultaneously beautiful and deeply disturbing. He glanced over at Jen and Tate and they had noticed too, their brows cinched in frowns of concern.

They pushed on, rounded a slight curve in the tunnel, and saw the mouth of rock open out. Whatever Aston had thought they ought to make ready for, the sight that greeted them stopped him dead. He was most certainly not ready for this. They emerged onto a wide ledge of rock in an inconceivably large space. They had to be out in the open, but that was impossible, because Aston knew they were hundreds of feet under the Antarctic. A storm whipped the air, bright green flashes in swirling clouds above an impossible glittering green sea.

"What the actual fuck?" Tate shouted, dropping into a

defensive crouch, though what she planned to fight was a mystery.

The three Annaki seemed equally surprised, the two subordinates making furious motions toward the water, shouting and screeching at their leader. Annaki-Akan looked left and right, then up into the writhing sky. His eyes were wider than ever, fear evident on his pale face. Aston thought that perhaps they had anticipated the giant sea, but not the furious conditions. The other two barked seemingly final words at Akan and then turned to flee. As they tried to push back past Aston, Jen, and Tate, Aston realized they might need all the weaponry they could get. He slammed a palm into the chest of one and wrested the bloodstone spear free of its grasp. The other looked left and right, then dropped its own spear at Tate's feet and they both bolted back down the tunnel. Akan shrilled something high and panicked, but Aston, clutching the stolen spear, paid him no further attention. He had been distracted by figures moving in the distance, down near the shore.

He pointed. "There's Slater and Syed!" They were under guard, three armed men and, if he wasn't mistaken, one of them was Anders Larsen. He had never trusted that muscular so-called geologist.

Annaki-Akan forgotten, he took off at a sprint, Tate running along beside him, and Jen dragging on what reserves of energy she had left to follow them.

CHAPTER 38

Slater tried to process what she saw, the impossible sea stretching seemingly forever, but she retained enough self-awareness to keep an eye on Larsen and the others too. Larsen himself apparently verged on panic, eyes darting in every direction as he stepped randomly from foot to foot like a child in desperate need of a bathroom. Olsen and Jensen stood stoic, faces creased in frowns, waiting for something to happen, or someone to issue an order. It seemed their military mindset had locked them into a mental holding pattern. She didn't think the inertia would last long.

Larsen turned suddenly to her and closed the distance between them in two fast strides. "Show us the way back to the green cavern! Now!"

Slater shook her head, tried to work some saliva into her dry mouth. "I can't. I... I think I must have made a wrong turn. I got lost. Sorry, I have no idea where we are." Her mind worked quickly, appalled with herself that she was admitting to this truth, but the sight before them had stripped her of the ability for artifice. Would he kill them now, out of fear if nothing else? She had no idea how to process any of this and every new revelation added to the insanity instead of helping to explain it.

Mist over the ocean thickened, began to creep forward as if grasping for them. Cloudy tentacles wound across the rock, growing stronger, darker, almost as if they had a physical form beyond simple vapor. Slater noticed Olsen had seen them, too. He stared in consternation then half-heartedly swung one booted foot through one questing tendril. He seemed slightly unsatisfied when it broke apart and swirled away like smoke. It seemed to behave differently to how he'd expected. And how Slater herself had expected, for that matter.

"Where are we?" Larsen shouted at her. "What the hell is happening here?" Without waiting for an answer, he turned away from her, raised questioning hands at Olsen and Jensen.

"You think I know?" Olsen said. "There is nothing natural about any of this and the sooner we get out the better."

"I don't know the way!" Larsen's voice was cracked, his mind close to snapping right behind it.

Olsen gestured towards Slater. "So get back to convincing her. She's the only one who knows. Or claims to know, at least."

"We don't know!" Syed said, pushing up close to Slater. "But maybe together we can find our way." She looked Slater. "I don't think we should stay here, at least. This place can't be safe."

Slater was inclined to agree with that, then something caught her eye. In the distance, waist deep in the shallows of the impossibly glittering sea, she saw a figure. He was holding aloft something that shined a brighter green than anything else around him.

"Who's that?" she called out, pointing.

The others squinted into the distance, shielding their eyes against mist and the brightness emanating from whatever was being held up.

"Is that O'Donnell?" Larsen asked.

The mist grew thicker, obscuring the figure. Writhing closer and higher, like a thing with a conscious will. As it began to obscure anything in the distance, including the man in the water, Slater looked back the other way, towards the high ledge of rock. She startled, realized someone was dashing toward them. No, more than someone. Three people, two in front, one lagging a little behind. They seemed to be carrying spears. But a grin split her face at the first bit of good news in a long time. It was Aston and Tate in front, Jen Galicia, face set in grim determination, following doggedly behind. Her heart lurched, she raised a hand to acknowledge them, but the mist thickened more than ever and obscured them all. Surely they had seen her, they must have. They were running right towards her.

But that meant they were running right at the armed mercs too. She turned back and realized the fog had become so thick she could barely see Larsen only a few feet from her. He and the other mercs still seemed to stare off towards Digby O'Donnell, all three taking a step toward the man as the mist closed around them, hiding everything from view. She grabbed Syed by the wrist, whispered, "Come on!" and took off at a run toward Aston.

CHAPTER 39

Alex Wong sat with his staff, lamenting his life choices. Whatever had led to all this, he questioned if it was worth the paycheck. But, he consoled himself, these burly, heavily armed mercenaries had assured him and his staff that as long as they all sat quietly, no harm would come to them. He had to believe that. They would apparently be shipped off Antarctica and back to civilization soon if they behaved themselves. So far, the mercs had done nothing to dissuade him of the truth of it. So they just had to wait. He could do that.

Priya Yardley lay on one couch, sleeping fitfully, her face swollen and bruised. On the next couch lay a man called Tom Shelton, his cheek split open and patched now with a band-aid. Apparently he had tried to act like a hero when the mercs had swept in and one had floored him with the butt of a rifle. At least the fool hero hadn't been shot. Tom's boyfriend sat on the floor beside the couch where Tom lay, one hand gently stroking the injured man's hair. On the plus side, between them Priya and Tom presented an ever-present warning that these guys weren't mucking around. Quick and dangerous violence lay in wait for anyone stupid enough to try to stand up to them now. Perhaps a few hours of boredom wasn't so bad. All the time things were dull, it meant no one was getting hurt. Alex knew well the old curse, May you live in interesting times. He had had more than enough of interesting and longed for the tedious monotony of base life again.

Just a few hours, they had promised. Or would it be longer? Alex thought about the first team that had gone down and never come back. Then the second team had been sent and no word had come from them until these mercenaries arrived. Were they lost too? Although Anders Larsen had come back then returned underground with the other squad of mercs. So perhaps it wasn't that people were lost down there, but detained for some other reason. He didn't like to consider what that reason might be. Maybe now they were all gone, dead somehow, and only the people in this room were left alive anywhere in the region. If Larsen and the other mercs didn't come back up, how long would they wait here before deciding it was time to go?

"Hey," he said, addressing a curly-haired merc called Hagen who seemed to be in charge of the other two soldiers left behind.

"What?"

"How long are you going to wait? Like, what are your orders if they don't come back?"

Hagen frowned, a slow, dull thing. "Why wouldn't they come back?"

Alex smiled inwardly, but kept his face neutral. "You haven't heard?"

"About what?"

"An entire scientific expedition was lost in those caverns. They went down and never came back. This team is the second, sent down to find them."

"What?"

The three newcomers exchanged nervous looks. Alex couldn't help easing his boredom by playing with them like this, but his question was genuine. "So do you have orders for if they don't return?"

Hagen shook his head. "No. We're expecting them back any time now."

"And if they're not?"

A new tension had risen in the room, boredom turned

OVERLORD | 223

to frightened attention.

Hagen started to speak again, but was interrupted by one of his squad. "Sir, what was that?"

Hagen turned. "What was what?"

"I heard something." The man, tall and angular with ash blond hair, moved nearer to the wall at the end of the lounge room where he had been leaning against a table.

"What did you hear?"

"Kind of a thump, against the wall here." The tall man leaned close, then jumped back as another thump, this one distinct, sounded through the prefab wall.

"The hell is that?" someone asked in a querulous voice. "Everyone is here."

Hagen turned back to Alex. "What's back there? Could the team come back that way?"

Alex frowned, picturing the base layout in his mind. "Nothing's back there really," he said. "That's just an internal wall, a corridor outside it and the kitchens on the other side. But all the staff are here, so there's no one in the kitchen. If anyone came in the back way, they might pass through there, but we'd have seen them going past these windows, I think."

He gestured outside at the uniform whiteness, the scattering of sheds and equipment. The elevator entrance to the caverns was a good hundred yards beyond the base in the opposite direction. The thump came again, louder this time, followed quickly by two or three others, spread along the wall, then scratches and scrapes.

"It moved!" the tall man said, bringing his assault rifle up to bear.

"What did?" Hagen demanded.

"The wall! The fucking wall flexed!"

More rapid thumps and knocks sounded, then more scratching and scrabbling noises. "Sounds like a pack of dogs trying to get in," Hagen said, moving a few steps nearer.

Alex moved back in the other direction, subtly indicating to his staff to join him in moving as far away from that wall as the room would allow. Gathered by the windows, they watched the three mercenaries line themselves up a few feet apart all facing the wall as it flexed again and the noises, more insistent than before, continued.

Alex opened his mouth, about to suggest they all decamp to another part of the base, maybe even his office, where they could see what was back there on the CCTV monitors. But the words froze in his throat when a large, zigzagging crack split the wall from floor to ceiling. Shocked barks of surprise and a couple of screams filled the air, then the wall burst open.

Beyond the split, the dark corridor could be seen, and it writhed with movement. Alex frowned, trying to make sense of the shadows, then needed no more time when they spilled into the room. Huge black, shining creatures, giant armored bugs with glistening carapaces and snapping mandibles, each at least the size of a grown man, fell into the lounge like maggots pouring through the split skin of a corpse. Bizarrely, their faces, including their large-looking eyes, were covered with ragged strips of cloth, seemingly taken from a wide variety of sources. Jackets, pants, even the acrylic lining of tents, all torn into strips and tied in place.

The room filled with thunder as the mercenaries staggered back, firing staccato bursts from their assault rifles. Bright green sparks flashed and spat as the bullets bounced off the shining shells. The tall blond man had been nearest to where the wall had burst open and the creatures fell upon him first. His screams were high-pitched and unreal as blood sprayed the walls and floor, his body parts quickly scattering as his screams were shut off. But the thunderous gunfire continued, people ran randomly, screaming and crying, with nowhere to go. Having backed up to the windows, the creatures now blocked the path to the only door out of the room.

The creatures, blind by the coverings, turned quickly left and right responding to wherever they perceived sound to come from. They snapped and tore and pulled limbs from sockets. And despite occasional success from the remaining two mercenaries shooting them down, more and more came. The corridor behind the burst open wall was thick with them.

Alex Wong, pressed into one corner with the wet, warm sensation of urine soaking through his pants, found himself wishing more than ever that he was bored again.

CHAPTER 40

Aston couldn't believe the speed with which the mist had encroached and smothered everything. He had definitely seen Slater and Syed, with Larsen and two other armed men. As he ran toward them, he had caught a glimpse of something, of someone, in the edge of the water, holding up a kind of small statue that shone a bright green. He was quickly becoming sick of anything green. He would kill for a chance to gaze once again upon a blue sky. And he had a feeling he would have to kill to do so. He was fine with that.

Another thing he had seen as he ran towards them was Slater glance in his direction, her face splitting in a grin of recognition just before the mist had swallowed her up. He had to keep going in that direction, he couldn't lose her again now, not this close.

The fog was cold against any exposed skin, its touch like frozen silken fingers brushing him. He blinked in surprise as rain spattered his face, momentarily confused by it, then it came again. Not rain, he realized, but spray from the water that had begun to roil. He heard it now, churning and splashing, repeatedly sending up the spray that rained over them all.

"What's happening?" Tate yelled.

"I don't know, and I don't care. Let's get to Slater and Syed and then get the hell out of here."

He caught hints of movement in the rolling mist, then jumped as bursts of gunfire popped and barked, bright orange bursts of muzzle flash briefly penetrating the green-tinged whiteness. He crunched in on himself as he ran, trying to cower and move at the same time, hoping no stray bullets came his way. What the hell were they shooting at? He hoped it wasn't Slater and Syed.

"Look!" Jen called out from a few paces behind.

He turned to see where she pointed and saw bigger shapes scurrying, half-shrouded in the fog. "Damn!" he hissed, watching the unmistakable outline of mantics swarming past. He heard a scream, both high-pitched and muffled by the fog at the same time. It was impossible to tell if it was male or female, and he desperately hoped it wasn't a friend.

A mantic burst out of the fog right in front of him and he cried out, automatically bringing up the bloodstone spear he carried. He put his weight behind it and drove it at the creature's face. He had a moment of elation watching darkness burst out as it sank into the mantic's eye, but flinched away as the thing's head exploded in a blinding flash of bright green surrounded by black shadow. Messy, but damned effective, he thought.

Then he realized that the spear's shaft had broken, the bloodstone point lost somewhere among the mantic's remains. It was good the bloodstone worked against them, but not if it only worked once like that. There were far too many to make it a viable defense. He drew the bloodstone dagger from inside his jacket, thinking he would be better able to keep hold of it than rely on shafts of who knew what scavenged junk. Tate stood beside him, a dagger in one hand, her spear in the other. Jen stood on his other side, her own bloodstone dagger held out in front of her, the three of them isolated in the fog as screams and gunfire and mantic shrieks echoed around them.

Another shadow approached, and Aston crouched, ready to fight. Then he realized the shape was human. He wondered if it might be Slater or Larsen, but as the figure appeared out of the gloom he was astounded to see it was

Sol, battered but very much alive.

"Is it good to see you!" Sol said.

"How the hell did you survive?"

"Honestly, more by luck than anything. I fell into a crevice in the rock which bought me a few seconds and I somehow managed to crawl aside of the bastards that knocked me down. They couldn't get to me, too big to fit. Then I managed to escape into a tunnel. Not without a souvenir, though." He turned one leg to show them the back of his thigh where an ugly gash soaked his pants in scarlet. "I've lost rather a lot of blood. Feeling a bit weak, if I'm honest."

Aston was amazed at the man's resilience, but he'd take all the help he could get right now. "How did you get here?"

"I don't know. I was just trying to stay ahead of the mantics, then I heard noise and came in this direction. What's in here? Seems like a big cavern. Why all the mist?"

Aston barked a short laugh. "Mate, you have no idea."

Another burst of gunfire ripped through the air, and then they heard the high-pitched keening that told them one of the mantics had gone down.

"Larsen is back," Aston said. "He's got some armed goons in tow. He's also got Slater and Syed. We need to find them."

Before he could say more, something burst from the fog and slammed into him, sending him crashing to the ground. He brought his dagger half up before spotting the swish of long dark hair and realized it was Slater sitting awkwardly on top of him where they'd fallen.

"Thank God!" she gasped and planted a kiss on his lips. His eyes widened in surprise and she quickly broke away, realizing what she'd done. He didn't mind at all.

She rolled off him and stood, and he rose quickly behind. Despite her embarrassment, he pulled her into a hug. "I'm so glad you're okay."

She returned the embrace, her face pressed into his shoulder. "Me too. But what the hell is going on?"

Syed was with her, the six of them huddled together in the swirling fog.

"Something significant is happening," Syed said. "But I have no idea what!"

"No shit," Sol said. "But I think I saw somebody sitting in the water, holding up something that shone like an emerald flame. You think he's the one stirring all this up?"

"That's Digby O'Donnell," Slater said.

Aston turned to her, stunned. "You're sure?"

"Pretty sure, yeah. We got a good look right before this thicker fog swept in."

More gunfire popped and muzzles flashed, thankfully moving a little further away from them, but other shadows still moved in the clouds that swirled close like curtains, chilling their skin.

"What the hell is he doing?" Aston asked.

"Who cares?" Sol said, wincing as he pressed a hand to his wounded leg. Blood oozed between his fingers. "All I care about is getting out of here. If he–"

Sol Griffin didn't finish his sentence as a massive, writhing black tentacle whipped out of the mist, coiled around him, and swiftly carried him away. The others stood stunned, watching as the large man was lifted high into the air, roaring in defiance. After a couple more seconds his roar turned to a scream that died wetly. Presumably, Sol Griffin had died too.

"What the fuck was that?" Tate said, eyes wide as full moons.

Another tentacle appeared, slick and black, most definitely solid, and thicker around than Aston's waist, lined with suckers the size of teacups. This one writhed behind them, feeling its way around in the fog. Reflexively,

Jen Galicia, standing nearest to it, swept her bloodstone dagger across the top of its slick black surface. Dark shadow burst up from the point of impact, then a bright green ichor pulsed up and the tentacle drew back. Aston was pleased to see the dagger hadn't been destroyed by the act.

"I think we should all run!" he shouted, and as one they took off into the mist, staying close together and putting the horrendous ocean behind them.

CHAPTER 41

Slater, Aston, and company ran through the fog, staying close together so they didn't lose each other. All Slater wanted was the safety of a dark tunnel, hopefully free of mantics. A tunnel that would lead them back to the green cavern would be ideal, but at this stage she would take anything that wasn't this mayhem and whatever those writhing black tentacles belonged to. She remembered them diving through the underwater door, traveling through the strange city, running blindly from one cave to the next. How could they possibly find their way out? Maybe with enough time and supplies, and without mantics attacking them, they could eventually retrace their route. She hoped with all her heart that's what would happen. Or if not, that they could find any other way out. Just to be back above ground, fresh air and open skies. She would gladly welcome the endless white expanse of surface Antarctica in place of the dark tunnels and green glows of subterranean Antarctica.

Fatigue turned her muscles to water. Her lungs burned with each inhale and exhale. She wondered if she had enough left in her to make it back to safety.

Please, she begged silently to herself. I just want to get out. Let us escape!

Then they burst into a clearing in the fog and her stomach sank, her mouth fell open in shock.

"How the hell did we get turned around?" Aston said, spinning on the spot, staring into the swirling whiteness.

They stood at the edge of the glimmering green sea, the mist a wall around them, seemingly held back by Digby

O'Donnell, kneeling in the water not ten feet away. He still held aloft the glowing green thing. From close up, Slater saw it was an idol of some kind, but its glow must have provided heat as well as light, and a lot of it. Dig's hand holding it was red, almost fleshless in places where the skin and meat had been burned away. His other hand repeatedly dipped into the ocean and came back up to splash his face.

O'Donnell cried out, a wail of pained ecstasy, and Slater realized he wasn't washing his face. Blood and fish scales dripped from his cheeks, as tears poured from his eyes. Even his tears glittered greenly. All around him, fish and other creatures swarmed as if drawn to him. Flaccid jellyfish and pulsing shrimp, wriggling worms and fanning stars, and dozens of fish of all sizes, all glowing from the inside out with that incessant green light. And Dig repeatedly scooped up whatever his hand found and crammed it into his mouth, chewing manically, his cheeks bulging, the green brightness showing through the stretched skin, ichor running over his chin..

"He's eating them all," Aston said in disgust. "He's not right in the head."

Slater wondered if there had ever been a greater understatement.

"Dig!" she shouted. She moved a little closer, brushing off Aston's hand as he plucked at her arm. "Digby! You have to stop whatever it is you're doing!"

He made no sign that he'd heard her, just gathered more glowing creatures and crammed them into his packed mouth. He crunched and chewed, as much of the masticated mess falling back into the ocean as whatever he managed to swallow. The other things swimming around him were in a frenzy, snapping it up, eating their unfortunate fellows only to be grabbed and bitten by Digby themselves.

Aston came to stand next to Slater. "What are you doing?" He waded knee-deep into the water and reached out to slap Digby's shoulder. "Dig, what's going on?"

Finally, the man turned. His eyes glowed bright green. "Yog-Sothoth!" he cried. "Through all time and space, he comes!"

"What the hell is he saying?" Tate demanded.

Aston looked back to her, refusing to believe Digby could be this delusional. "Yog-Sothoth. The man is obsessed with *At the Mountains of Madness*. It's a story by H.P. Lovecraft about…"

Tate scowled. "I don't give a rat's ass what it's about! I'm putting an end to this." She raised her pistol and took aim at the back of Dig's head.

Slater opened her mouth to protest. She couldn't allow cold-blooded murder, could she? But then surely Digby was beyond redemption, beyond saving. His mind had surely snapped and who knew what would happen to his body after the amount of infected sea life he had consumed began to spread through his cells. But her unspoken protest was unnecessary.

Before Tate could squeeze the trigger, a thick, shining black tentacle snaked out from the wall of mist in front of them and grabbed her. Her body arched, mouth agape in shock, as she was wrenched away, back into the fog, so quickly her cry of alarm was whipped from her throat as she went.

Slater screamed out the mercenary's name, finding herself knee deep in the water next to Aston as she staggered forward in some pointless attempt to follow the woman. There were two quick gunshots, then a blood-curdling scream that stopped midway. For a moment there was silence but for the roiling sea and Digby's maniac giggling and chewing, then Tate's body came flying back through the air. It landed with a slap on the ground at the ocean's edge. The top of her skull was gone, as if bitten off, her brain nowhere to be seen.

"Oh, God," Slater said. "That's what the journal meant by eating people's heads? It eats their brains?"

More gunfire sounded through the thick fog behind them. Slater looked that way, wondering how many of the three mercenaries remained alive. All of them? Was Larsen dead? Were they shooting at mantics or the black tentacles that so easily plucked people from the shore?

O'Donnell was laughing again, high-pitched and crazed. "We join, we commune, through Yog-Sothoth we see all," he said in a screeching, inhuman voice. "All will come to him. All will serve him."

"Digby, please!" Slater said. "You have got to stop this!" She began to wonder if Tate had had the right idea, and fingered the bloodstone knife in her jacket pocket. Was she capable of murder? Of plunging it between Digby O'Donnell's shoulder blades? Would it even help now?

"We just have to get away," Aston said, pulling at her sleeve. "Try to run again, put this water at our backs and find the cavern wall. Follow it until we find a passage away from... this!"

Slater looked from Digby to Aston and back again, her brain spinning in neutral. Any second she expected a thick tentacle to snatch her up and part of her almost welcomed it, an end to this insanity. But no, she wanted to survive. They all needed to live, no more death.

"You don't understand," Digby said, turning to face them at last. He no longer seemed so dazed, his eyes still bright, unnatural, incandescent green, but focused. "I can see it all."

"What do you mean?" Aston asked. "What can you see?"

"I see what he sees. I see everything that Yog-Sothoth observes. I see wherever his minions look, every one of them at once. My mind is legion."

"You can see through their eyes?" Aston asked. "All of them? The mantics?"

Digby grinned, nodding. "That's how I found this!" He hefted the idol in his burned, mutilated hand. "And how I found this!" He used the idol to gesture out around them, taking in the whole infinite cavern, the shining sea, the creatures it contained. "I am one with all of them. Every fish, every mantic, every living thing that has ever eaten and joined, I see through them and they through me." He shrilled crazed laughter. "Every single thing. I see the caverns, the passageways, the door in the lake, the lift to the surface. I see you, us through so many different sets of eyes right now. From the beasts, too!" He made another sweeping motion, this time behind them.

Slater and Aston spun around, saw a crowd of mantics standing behind Jen and Syed where they trembled on the shore. The creatures swayed gently, otherwise immobile, watching them, but blocking their retreat.

Slater startled at the sight of them, Aston raised his dagger.

"Could he be telling the truth?" Slater asked.

"Maybe. I don't know. There's a fungus that turns ants into zombie drones. It's essentially a natural form of mind control. Fungal cells inside the ant's head release chemicals that essentially take command of the insect's central nervous system."

"All right. I don't need a lecture right now. All I wanted to know was is it possible?"

Aston shook his head. "It shouldn't be. This is a far cry from zombie ants. But he does seem to have control of the mantics."

"Don't worry," O'Donnell said. "They won't harm us here, not now. Through him, through my connection, they do my bidding. I am with them. I am them."

"If that's the case," Aston said, "you can have them show us the way out. Let's all get out of here!"

O'Donnell laughed again. "There's no need! Soon we will all be one with him!"

"Digby, it's not a god!" Aston yelled at the man. "I don't know what it is, but what you believe is a fiction. That thing, that monster out there, is some mutant, yes, but it's no god. Some kind of cephalopod, a giant octopus, some presumed extinct mega-fauna, that's all. But whatever it is, it doesn't have some greater plan. It's just another predator and it wants to eat us!"

"Yes!" O'Donnell agreed. "Eat us! But it is a god, Sam. Oh, in fact, it's more than a god. And it will make us all one with its glory."

Slater felt faint. "Sam," she said. "You were right. Let's just go!"

"But how will we find our way?" Jen Galicia said.

Aston shook his head, squared his shoulders. "If Dig here is telling the truth about seeing through their eyes, I can only think of one way."

Slater looked over at him, read his expression and intent. "Sam, no!"

CHAPTER 42

Aston swallowed hard, a little appalled at the course of action he was considering. But he could think of nothing else. They would almost certainly die down here, one way or another. Lost and starving, or killed by mantics. Or even killed by the Annaki. He wasn't sure if the Annaki had led them here to show them a possible answer to questions or to sacrifice them to this creature, but either way, he had lost all trust for the strange, pale race. He couldn't help feeling a little like a cow led to slaughter. But if they were going to survive, they needed to be proactive. Running blindly along the dark passages wasn't the kind of proactive they needed. They could go in circles for days, and then starve. Assuming they avoided all the other kind of deaths in the meantime. The chance of finding another way out was surely lowest on the list of possibilities. After all, how far had they come? How deep had they gone?

He looked back over his shoulder, thinking of all they had been through to get here. They could retrace their steps, possibly. But that would mean returning through the Annaki city. It would mean risking tunnels they knew were swarming with mantics. And even then, he would have to remember every twist and turn, every choice of route they had made, and he would need to remember it all in reverse. He didn't think he could do that.

So it left only one option. There had to be some kind of hive mentality happening with these creatures. Some chemical connection that was triggered by the consumption of whatever the glowing green substance was that affected them all, some by-product of the vines or the greenium. Or both. Either way, if O'Donnell was telling the truth, it would allow Aston to see a way out. And if Digby was lying or simply delusional, well, they were as good as dead already anyway. And if the green stuff poisoned him, the same conclusion applied. He had to take a chance. It was the only chance he could think of.

Refusing to consider it any more deeply, he waded out next to O'Donnell and looked down into the water.

"Sam, no," Slater said again, but he ignored her.

Aquatic life gathered around O'Donnell, some gently milling and floating as if in a trance, others feeding off the scraps that fell from Digby's mouth. Every creature seemed to face the man, like they were somehow in obeisance to him. Or perhaps the man was irrelevant and they faced the burning idol. Fish, crustaceans, jellyfish, even a massive, albino tortoise with glowing green eyes, its shell as long as Aston was tall. They all watched O'Donnell like a dog watches its master.

Aston took a deep breath and ducked a hand into the water. He scooped up a fish about the size of his middle finger. Slater's voice was panicked, screaming at him, trying to stop him, telling him he had no idea what he was doing, or what it would do to him. Syed joined in, and Jen Galicia too, all begging him not to do it.

"Let's just go!" Slater yelled.

"We have to know where to go!" Aston said, and shoved the wriggling fish into his mouth. He bit down, chewed hard and fast. The flesh was ice cold and bitter. He felt the thing burst, tasted salt with the bitterness, and swallowed it all down as quickly as he could, suppressing the urge to gag. The others around him fell silent. He realized he heard no more gunfire either, and hadn't been for a while. No shouting, no scrabbling of mantics. Were Larsen and his friends dead? All he heard was the lap of the shining sea, the bubbling further out.

He felt nothing else.

Digby O'Donnell stared up at him and Aston met the man's eyes, saw madness there. *What have I done?* he wondered. Perhaps he hadn't done anything at all. Would he simply go crazy like Dig?

Heat began to swell inside his gut. A strange dizziness swept over him, making him stagger, and for a moment he leaned forward, convinced he was going to vomit the half-chewed fish back into the ocean. He gasped a breath.

"Sam? Are you okay?" Slater's hand on his arm was heavy, her grip trembling.

"I'm okay," he managed, but he wasn't certain.

He straightened, heard a soft chuckling laugh. Dig had his head tipped to one side and Aston looked into the man's eyes again, saw the green brightness in them, the glowing idol held almost as if forgotten in Digby's ruined hand. A slow smile spread across Dig's face and Aston saw a frown overlaid on it. As if Digby were grinning and concerned at the same time. Then, with a shudder, Aston's perception caught up with the simple view and he realized he was seeing two things at once. Both his view of Digby O'Donnell and Dig's view of him, blurred together in his mind.

"The edibles are kicking in?" Slater forced a faint smile.

Aston couldn't answer. He staggered, cried out in disorientation, as visions flooded through him. He saw the ocean from a dozen different viewpoints, he saw dark tunnels and glittering caverns, he saw the Annaki city and the lift to the surface. He even saw glimpses of the base, too bright to really determine clearly and he cried out. He didn't want to be blinded like that. The images snapped away. He thought of his friends, and saw them from numerous points of view, through the eyes of the mantics nearby, and through Digby's eyes. He saw them shimmering through a greenish haze and realized it was the view of every creature that drifted at his knees.

He sobbed out a noise of confusion, nearly fell, overwhelmed by the mass of sensory input. No wonder Digby had gone mad. How could he do anything but follow the man into insanity? No brain could process this. What had he done?

Dizziness became too much and he fell suddenly sideways. He heard Slater cry out, then ice cold seawater closed over him. He couldn't suppress a gasp of surprise and sucked in icy brine, started coughing and gagging. Hands grabbed at him and hauled him from the water, dragged him to the stony shore. But the icy shock had been a benefit, helped him to find a center and push away the vast majority of input he was receiving.

As he sat coughing on the shore, he tried to think only of the route to the surface and a series of images flickered through his mind. Then again, and again, like a loop of film on repeat. From one mantic's view to another, he saw the way out. Was he just remembering now, or was this truly a shared intelligence? A hive mind of incredible complexity? He felt the intent of the awful, chitinous creatures, and realized their malice was gone. He remembered Digby saying how they wouldn't attack now, how they were one, he and the creatures. And now Aston was one with them too. Whatever impossible biological connection he had made, it gave him that power, and it was a valuable one. He knew the way out and he could protect his friends. How it had happened he might never truly know, but it had happened and he wasn't going to waste the opportunity. Even if it drove him mad, it was worth it to get the others out, to save Jo Slater. He owed her that.

He looked up into her concerned eyes and smiled. "I know the way," he said. At the same moment, he became aware of another consciousness, a deep, dark, unfathomable mind. It ached of eons and hunger, of isolation and loss. The giant creature in the sea, the overlord, whatever it was. He imagined the noxious Yog-Sothoth, the thing Lovecraft had imagined, and saw how Digby's obsession would easily overlay that fantastic fiction on whatever this animal was. But it was no god, that he knew. Like he had told Dig, it had to be some giant, previously unknown cephalopod, a monstrous octopus or squid from some age before modern humans, long since considered over. But this one animal remained, alone and constantly close to starving. Better there was no life here at all, Aston thought, and this thing would die. But instead, it found sustenance in the inhabitants of the caverns, the offerings of the Annaki to appease it. And it lived on in terrible ravenous loneliness. It felt him, too. He sensed its attention boring down on his thoughts.

Then something seemed to crush his waist. Confused, he looked down just as Slater screamed and saw a slick black tentacle wrapped tight around him. He managed an "Oh!" of surprise and then he was snatched up, rising quickly out over the glittering sea. The speed of the abduction was enough to make his spine pop, his head spin. He was instantly high over the water, and saw a giant writhing black shape just beneath the glittering surface.

CHAPTER 43

High above the water, Aston tried desperately to control the flood of sensory input and the fear that threatened to snap his mind. Held fast by the slick tentacle, he hung in the air, disoriented by the wavering motion and the sight of himself from numerous angles. Yet despite the fear, he experienced a surge of elation too. Surely this was what had driven Digby on, this sensation of happiness, of gladly becoming a part of the whole.

The biologist in him quickly assessed the emotion and he realized it was a kind of mental anesthetic, a chemical design to make any creature more willingly a part of the hive, of the gestalt mind. He resisted it, refused to give up his individual thought. "I will use you!" he yelled out. "I won't become you!"

But his voice was weak and thin, his body shivering with the need to join the horde. He tried to ignore all the other visual input he was receiving, but one signal was too strong. As he looked down on the shadow in the water, that entity looked back up at him and he saw what it saw, witnessed his tiny, insignificant body thrashing high above, weak and useless.

The creature drew him down, drew him in toward it and at the same time it rose to the glimmering surface. He watched himself go down from above even as he saw himself drawn low from below. Was he going to experience himself having his brain eaten?

He heard distant screams from the shore, Slater yelling his name over and over again. His awareness flipped and he saw his predicament from the perspective of the other creatures, saw his friends' distress from Digby O'Donnell's crazed eyes. He watched himself from the myriad aquatic creatures moving lazily around the giant creature in worship. It was dizzying, sickening, but one thought remained strong despite the confusion. He was keenly aware that he had only seconds to live.

The ocean's surface broke and poured off the giant slick bulk of the creature. Its body rose, squid-like, one giant eye glowing so brightly green that he had to look away. And in redirecting his gaze he spotted its gaping maw, with rows and rows of sharp, scintillating teeth. As the beast drew him closer, a bizarre, tentacle-like tongue extended from the mouth, as thick around as his body, questing upwards. At the tip, opening and closing with a wet smacking sound, was a suction cup-like appendage, ringed with more, tiny razor-sharp teeth.

This is how it bites off the skull, Aston thought. And then it sucks the brain out.

He wondered what bizarre biological imperative had driven it to consume brains. Was it driven to eat anything else? Surely something this size would require a lot more sustenance than that, even to exist in this famished state. Was the desire for brains some by-product of the green deposits in the other creatures that otherwise sustained this beast more than simple meat might? He shook his head, trying to free his thoughts of science and concentrate only on survival. Did he have any chance at all?

Bloodstone. He remembered Jen cutting the tentacle with her dagger and that tentacle swiftly retreating. Could that be the answer? He scrabbled in his jacket and pulled free his own intricately carved dagger. With a yell of effort, he swept it down and gouged it into the shining wet flesh of the tentacle that encircled him. He saw a dark burst of shadow like he had seen before, a spurt of bright green ichor. A deep, resonant rumble of pain thrummed out from the creature, that grew into a shriek that he heard in his mind, but not his ears. Through his oneness with O'Donnell and all the other creatures, he knew they felt it, too. He gasped at the sharp blaze of agony in his mind as he felt it with them.

He sensed O'Donnell flinch in pain and surprise and the man dropped the idol into the churning sea. Aston felt a surge of hope as the overlord paused, stunned by the unexpected hurt and somehow partially disconnected now from all it knew of the cavern, all its sensation of feeding. The idol, in the hands of a living being, obviously amplified the beast's attraction, drew it forth. With that connection severed, the idol in the water untouched, the Overlord began to sink back into the water, its grip on Aston loosening.

As a grin of triumph spread across his face, Aston saw through O'Donnell's eyes as the madman scrabbled into the water and gathered up the idol again. As he recovered it, the connection between them all returned, strong and clear, and the coil about Aston tightened crushingly again.

CHAPTER 44

Slater ran back and forth along a short stretch of the shore, trying desperately to see through the thick curtain of fog. He couldn't be gone, not after all this. To be snatched up and carried away like that, she refused to allow that to be her last memory of Sam Aston. But she couldn't put the image of Tate's desecrated body slapping back onto the stone from her mind.

"Jo, I think we need to go!" Syed said, grabbing hold of her sleeve.

"No!" she shouted.

"There's nothing we can do. We'll be next. Let's take our chances in the tunnels, find a way out."

Jen Galicia stepped up, a bloodstone spear held in a white-knuckled grip. "I think she's right, Slater. We have to go."

"I won't leave him!"

"You saw what it did to Tate!" Syed said, her voice tight with the effort not to cry.

"Look out!" Jen yelled, and the three of them ducked as another jet black, dripping tentacle whipped past them.

"We have to go!" Syed said.

They moved away from the water, ducking as the tentacle quested across the rock for them. Then a sudden, bass rumble made the ocean shiver and Digby O'Donnell cried out, as if in pain. Slater looked over and saw he had dropped the idol into the roiling sea. The tentacle reaching for them stilled for a moment, then slowly withdrew.

She frowned, looking from the retreating tentacle to Digby and back again. Then Dig was face down in the water, his back moving up and down as he thrashed around. He rose, triumphant, the glowing idol held aloft once more. Two more tentacles whipped back through the swirling mist, reaching for them.

"Get down!" Slater yelled, and all three of them dropped to the hard, cold stone as the tentacles crossed in the air above them, seeking and writhing. Slater understood. The idol was the key. Not just in terms of symbolism, but it somehow called the overlord. Directed the giant, instinct-driven animal mind of the thing. She had no idea how, but it seemed too evident to ignore.

Before the tentacles could loop back around again, she dashed forward and tried to wrest the strange statuette free of Digby's grip. It was hot, searing her skin. She cried out, dropped back and scrabbled in her pockets for gloves. Warm sheepskin, the outer layer thick leather, she hoped they would be enough. She pulled them on and began to wrestle with Dig again. He cried out nonsensical babble, pulling the idol close to his body and trying to move deeper into the ocean, pulling her with him.

Slater was in good shape, but O'Donnell showed surprising strength. He let go with one hand and elbowed her in the mouth. She grunted in pain, staggered backward as she tasted blood, and sat heavily into the water. It swept up over her shoulders, splashed coldly into her face, but that had the advantage of clearing her head from the ringing of the blow.

"Fuck you, Digby!" she growled, and hauled herself back up, her clothes heavy from being sodden.

Another tentacle reached past, then she heard a grunt of effort and another bass moan as Jen Galicia slashed at the shining black flesh with her bloodstone spear. Digby cried out in pain along with the beast and Slater took her chance. She drove herself forward, chest deep in the cold sea, and swung a punch at Digby's jaw. She connected with a satisfying crunch, made him grunt in pain, but he stayed up and didn't release the idol.

Jen continued to slash and stab at the tentacles with her spear, trying to buy them time. Syed waded out into the sea, heading for Slater. She welcomed any help she could get against the crazed O'Donnell, but then screamed wordlessly as another thick tentacle snaked out of the mist and plucked Syed up and away.

Tears in her eyes, Slater turned her attention back to Digby, trying to catch up to him, but wading through the shoulder deep water was too hard. He was taller, stronger, able to keep his distance from her, grinning as he held the glowing idol above his head.

Slater growled, tried to push faster and saw Jen coming in from the other side, heading for Digby's back. But did the woman have the strength to carry on? Her face was pale, darkness ringed her eyes. And was Aston still even alive? She had to believe he was, but even then, she was failing.

Through O'Donnell's eyes, Aston witnessed Slater's pain and struggle. He tried to take control of O'Donnell's thoughts, tried to make the man drop the idol again, but ironically, it was the idol that seemed to make the man invulnerable to him. And once again, the creature's awareness was back on the present and Aston was drawn in again. That thick tongue-like appendage with its slavering, teeth-filled sucker, reached up for him once more.

A sudden thought occurred to Aston, a memory of something O'Donnell had said. They do my bidding. He had been talking about the mantics, about how the group was safe from them if O'Donnell willed it. If he couldn't convince Digby to do his bidding, maybe he could get the mantics to respond.

Several of them still milled around in the mist on the shore, confused by the complicated and contradictory thoughts of all those sharing the hive mind. Too much free will was being exerted on something that should work as one unit. Aston forced his attention to a small group of three of them near the struggle between Slater and O'Donnell. He put thoughts of threat and danger into their minds. Then he directed that thought at Digby O'Donnell, forced the mantics to see Digby as the danger, as the source of the confusion. "Finish him!" Aston shouted, with his voice and his mind. "Take him out!"

The three simple-minded creatures turned and waded out into the water as Aston felt the touch of cold, black slime on his face. He snapped back to his own present and realized the tooth-filled sucker was about to clamp over the top of his head. With a shriek of panic, he slashed at it with his dagger.

The overlord bellowed in pain, quickly retracted a few feet, then immediately came for him again. Using all his strength, Aston drew back his arm and flung the dagger directly into the approaching, slavering maw.

CHAPTER 45

Slater struggled with O'Donnell, coughing as the sea splashed into her face. But he was too strong, wouldn't give up his grip on the idol, and only moved deeper into the water. Jen Galicia was halfway to reaching them when another tentacle swept by and drove her back. She slashed at it with her spear, and another deep groan came from beneath the waves. Then another one, louder and more pained than ever, even though Jen hadn't struck the creature a second time.

Slater pulled back one hand and punched Digby in the face again. He laughed at her, spat out blood and a tooth, but still would not relinquish his grip on the idol.

Then Jen was screaming from near the shore. "Jo, look out! They're coming!"

Slater turned, wondering who the hell they were, and her stomach dropped as she saw three mantics, surprisingly fast in the water, heading straight for her. She quickly stepped back, raising her hands to try to ward them off, but they all headed straight for Digby.

She barely had time to flinch away before they fell on the man. He cried out, "No!" in pain and disbelief, and then they were tearing him apart, his blood spreading in rapid clouds through the green water. The idol tumbled from his hands, splashed into the sea and began to sink.

Ducking a sweeping mantic forearm, Slater dove under, snatched the idol up, and quickly waded away. As she searched the shore, she turned to see Digby gone and the mantics floating further out, directionless.

"What are you going to do?" Jen asked.

"I don't know! But this is the key, I'm sure of it." Slater stared, wondering if she should hold it up like O'Donnell had done and try to will the beast away. But she hadn't communed, she hadn't eaten of the green stuff like Digby had. Like Aston had.

"How did Digby control it?" she asked.

Jen gave a humorless laugh. "That lunatic didn't seem like he was in control of anything really," she said. "More like he was just stirring it up."

Slater remembered when O'Donnell had dropped the idol, how things had calmed momentarily before he had recovered it. There were no tentacles reaching for them now. Maybe the overlord was already going away. She needed to ensure that continued. She looked around, saw the fog seemed to be thinning, the waters less disturbed. She called Aston's name, but got no reply.

"I don't know how to end this!" she said, but fury, exhaustion, fear, all took hold and she wanted only to smash everything. She raised the idol high and smashed it into the ground. It thunked but didn't shatter. It didn't even appear to have a chip in it. Nothing seemed to change.

They both turned at the sound of a cry in the distance. "Aston?" Slater screamed.

She saw the bloodstone spear Jen still held, remembered its powerful effect against the beast. "Give me that," she said, and Jen handed it over.

Slater took it in a two-handed grip and stabbed it into the idol. A blinding flash burned her eyes, and the statuette exploded. Her howl of shock and pain mingled with Jen's as they were sent flying, shards of stone slicing into any exposed flesh. But with their cries, a deafening shriek filled the air, so loud Slater thought her ears would burst. The very ground shuddered and giant stalactites fell from high above, somewhere lost in mist, and splashed into the sea, or crashed and shattered onto the rocky ground all around them. As Slater and Jen grabbed hold of each other in an attempt to steady their stumbling on the heaving ground, a massive wave crashed into them. It lifted them high and fast. Slater had a moment to notice the cavern wall rushing toward her. Sharp pain blossomed in her head, a hollow thud rang in her ears, and everything went black.

CHAPTER 46

Aston had watched with grim satisfaction as the dagger had slammed into the Overlord's mouth and flash with darkness and green ichor. The creature bellowed, clearly hurt, and then Aston had seen through Digby's eyes as the three mantics fell on the man. Everything became lost in a confusion of sights and sounds, he tasted O'Donnell's flesh and blood even as the mantics tasted it, he felt the agony in the creature's maw, he experienced Digby's pain as he was torn apart. It all combined into a maelstrom of emotion that Aston was incapable of processing, that threatened to shut his mind off like a light switch, and some deep part of him welcomed that. Some part of him even desired it. Then through it all, he realized O'Donnell had dropped the icon. His connection dimmed, the thrumming, vibrating sensations lessened. The Overlord, lamenting its pain, began to sink back below the waves.

Aston opened his eyes, saw the scorched and damaged mouthpiece retract into a black and bony beak deep within the thick roots of the writhing tentacles. He allowed himself a smile, struggled to break free of the coils about him, but the Overlord would not let him go. Yet still it withdrew.

After all that, it's going to drown me, Aston thought, incredulous. An incongruous, unlamented death. Unless Slater lived to remember him. Perhaps that would be enough.

He suppressed a gasp as the tentacle slipped beneath the surface and he was plunged into the icy water. Green luminescence flickered all around him and he was pulled deeper. He struggled, wished he still had the dagger to stab and slash at the limb that bound him, but he was useless in its grasp. He thought of Jo Slater and briefly, through the eyes of a mantic, caught sight of her and Jen Galicia, stumbling from the water onto the rocky shore. He saw her raise a spear, as the pressure built and his mind began to black out. At least she was still alive, he thought. And still fighting. About to stab something. He smiled. Fight on, Jo, he thought. Don't ever quit.

A blinding flash seared his mind, pain arced through every nerve he had. A great, rumbling vibration rose up from the gargantuan beast as it sank below him and he was tumbled over in the churning, bubbling water. Turned over! His hands went to his body and he found it free of the restricting tentacle. The Overlord had released him, whether by design or by accident, maybe it had simply forgotten what it held. Regardless, he was free.

He swam upwards, following the rising bubbles, his lungs screaming for air, blackness encroaching on the edges of his vision. He broke the surface and gasped air in, coughed and spluttered, gasped again. But his clothes were heavy with water and dragged him back down. He fought once more to the surface, sucked in desperate air, then the waves closed over him once more.

He sensed the retreating presence of the Overlord as it sank back down to whatever stygian depths in which it dwelled, lonely, hungry, desolate. His heart ached for the thing. It had an intelligence that caused it pain. Like all cephalopods, it was smart, curious, playful, inquisitive. But it lived alone in the dark and it knew its fate, was driven mad by its isolation. There was nothing Aston could do for it. His struggling mind pictured it out in the open ocean. He imagined some underwater channel, like the one in Lake Kaarme that had allowed that prehistoric anachronism to travel between the lake and the open sea.

Would people ever be able to somehow drill something similar to allow this leviathan to escape? Was such an enormous feat of engineering even possible? People would need to know about it first, at the very least. Or perhaps, with the idol destroyed, it would finally be called no longer, and starve. A slow and agonizing, but welcome death. And, as he sank back down again, Aston felt a sadness rise that he would never be able to tell anyone about it. Would Slater? Did she even know the half of it?

He gave up the struggle of trying to reach the surface, the muscles of his arms like jelly, unable any more to pull him through the sparkling sea. He reached out with his consciousness, trying to see through the eyes of anything still on the ocean shore. He found one mantic, realized the Overlord's swift retreat back beneath the surface had caused a giant wave to smash the shore. Everything was dead up there, this one mantic the only thing he could connect with other than the sea life that swarmed everywhere underneath.

He shook his head. After all that, even Slater hadn't managed to survive. This foolish endeavor had killed them all. Then the mantic's gaze fell upon a sodden lump up against the cavern wall, dark hair stuck wet across the back of the jacket. Slater's body, face down. Grief swallowed his heart.

And then she stirred. Joy pushed the grief aside and Aston watched Jo Slater raise her head and look groggily around herself, eyes cinched narrow in pain. But she lived! What he would give for just one more kiss with her.

He bumped into something hard. Looking down, as the blackness began to close his vision to pinpoints, he saw the curving white shell of the huge turtle. Its green eyes met his and he saw himself, slack-faced. "Take me to the surface!" he begged with his mind, imagining himself laying across its back as it swam to the shore. Some sensation of acquiescence came from the creature and it rose up beneath him. He was lifted swiftly through the water, his lungs burning again. And then the sea sluiced off him and he gasped in air. The majestic creature bore him slowly to the shore and tipped him into the shallows. With the last of his strength, he crawled to the water's edge and rolled onto his back before passing out.

CHAPTER 47

Aston was shivering so much, his teeth rattled together. At least, he thought, that means I'm still alive. Unless it finally is a cold day in Hell.

"Sam!" Someone was calling him from very far away, their voice muffled by distance. And another sound insisted on his hearing, a repetitive thump-thump.

He sucked in a deep breath, wincing at the pain it caused in his chest.

"Oh, Sam! You're alive!"

The voice wasn't nearly as distant this time, much closer in fact. Somewhere right nearby. And the thumping sound was his own heart, his pulse a rapid pressure in his ears. Memories came flooding back, the giant cephalopod, the crazed attacks on shore, the dark flash of the bloodstone dagger hitting that terrible mouth, Slater's spear shattering the idol.

His mind stuttered and, though his eyes were still closed, he saw a glimpse of a body lying on the shore, two people crouched over it. The clothing was familiar. One crouching person had long dark hair, hanging in wet ropes about her face. Slater! She was alive. But his eyes weren't open. He sensed the chittering mind of a mantic and his awareness flipped back to his own eyes as they opened and he saw Slater leaning over him, her face split in a smile. The mantic that had been watching him lying on the rock squatted nearby, lost and directionless. On his other side was Jen Galicia, also alive, though battered looking. Her eyes had dark rings around them, the skin of her face drawn tight.

Then Jen's face was obscured as Slater leaned in and planted a hot kiss on him. Her lips against his was the best sensation he could ever remember feeling and he reached up to her cheek. She sat back and scowled. "You're such an idiot, Sam Aston!"

He managed a laugh. "What?"

"What were you thinking, eating that stuff? Are you okay? Is the... whatever it is dead?"

Aston pulled himself up to a sitting position, his heavy wet clothes squelching around him. "I think I'm mostly fine. And no, it's not dead, but it has retreated. The idol Digby had seems to summon it somehow."

"How?" Jen asked.

He looked over at her, shrugged. "I don't know."

"Well, it's destroyed now," Slater said. "So I guess the creature won't be coming back again."

A wave of sadness passed through Aston as he considered that again. It was possible that it would remember to come this way without being called, but seemed unlikely, given what little he had discerned about it. It could no doubt feed elsewhere, might live on in its ravenous loneliness. How far did this vast underground sea extend anyway? Maybe, if they could escape, he might be able to find out, to send a survey team. But all that depended on them getting out and that had to be his only concern now. With a start, he realized that his connection to the hive mind, amplified as it had been before, had now weakened to almost nothing. He couldn't see nearly so many points of view. He couldn't remember the way out.

He sensed movement and Slater scrambled to her feet, looking around for a weapon.

"No more, please!" she said.

Aston staggered to his feet next to her, one last chance presenting itself. "It's okay. I've got this," he said. Though the connection was weak, he still sensed this one mantic nearby, still saw faint images of it looking back at them. If he was quick, maybe he could still trigger one last action in the creature.

The mantic moved cautiously towards them and Aston reached out for it with his mind. The link was weak, muted, but he held onto it like a lifeline. He thought of the green cavern, knowing they could easily find their way back from there. "Take us there," he said aloud even as he thought the same words and pictured every detail of the cavern he could remember. The shape of it, the pool, their halogen lights. "Take us there," he said again.

Slater and Jen watched closely, desperation in their eyes, not daring to interrupt.

The mantic turned and moved away along the shore, scurrying in the direction of a tunnel mouth some hundred yards away. As their connection faded even further, Aston sensed its intent. Felt its acquiescence to the request.

He let out a held breath. "He'll lead us back," Aston said.

"Seriously? And there won't be more to attack us?"

"Not now. At least, not for the moment." Aston hoped he wouldn't have to consume more of the glowing green substance to ensure that remained true. Whatever it was, it facilitated a connection to the hive mind, but it was not good for him, that much was certain. No way could anything so potent be anything but damaging to a biological system not designed for it, or evolved for it. A biological system like Sam Aston.

Exhausted as they all were, the trek was slow going, but the mantic seemed to know a shortcut. It made confident turns, always finding a passage that seemed to slope upwards. At one point it stepped into a narrow fissure in the rock and Aston, Slater, and Jen cautiously followed, anticipating a trap. But inside were roughly carved steps, almost an uneven, undulating ladder that went up and up, and opened eventually into a small cavern. They continued on.

It took a few hours, but finally Aston saw something familiar, and before long they saw a glow up ahead. The mantic paused, moving more slowly than ever, tipping its head aside.

"It's hurt by the brightness," Aston said. "Give it time."

The creature went forward a few paces and stopped again.

"We could just go on," Jen said.

"We don't know if that's where we want to be though," Aston said.

"You can't ask it?"

"No," he had to admit. "My connection with it has faded. I can't be certain of its intent anymore, but I'm pretty sure it's still doing the last thing I asked of it. Let's be patient."

Step by tentative step they kept moving, the mantic clearly reluctant, but doing as it was bid nonetheless. Eventually they emerged into the huge, glittering cavern where the vast majority of the greenium was deposited. The lake with the strange door at the bottom reflected the light, made patterns dance across the ceiling. Their halogens still lit, though fading. The mantic hung back in the remaining darkness of the passage.

"Well, I don't think we'd ever have found the way here on our own," Aston said. "But I've never been more pleased to see a place."

Slater had a wide smile on her face. Even Jen seemed illuminated somehow from her previously withered state, far beyond what the light should have shown.

"Let's get the hell out of here," Slater said.

Aston turned to the mantic, gave a nod of thanks. He was about to suggest it go on about its way when a dark shadow loomed up behind it. He opened his mouth to shout a warning, one hand flying out uselessly, but Anders Larsen, from directly behind the creature, slammed a bloodstone knife down into its skull. Darkness and green blood spattered up as the mantic shrieked in agony. Aston winced, went down involuntarily to one knee as a sharp bolt of pain punched through his brain, his connection apparently not entirely worn off yet, then the mantic died and the connection was severed.

Larsen stood there, grinning, the mantic's blood dripping from the knife. "I don't need that thing or you lot any longer," he said. "I can find my own way back from here."

"You followed us all this way?"

"I woke up after being washed onto that stone ledge back there and saw you three being led away by the bug. I guessed it was my best chance to get out, but thought I'd better keep my presence to myself."

"Just who the hell are you, mate?" Aston said. "What are you doing?"

"Right now? I'm tying up loose ends. Then I'll head back up and be the hero." He raised the knife in front of his face and dropped into a fighting stance.

Aston glanced back at Slater and Jen. "Go! No questions! Get out of here and I'll follow."

He saw doubt sweep across Slater's face, but didn't have time to convince her as Larsen closed the distance. The last thing he saw was Jen drag at Slater's sleeve and he could only hope they had both run for their lives.

He sucked in a breath and tried to steady himself. He was too tired for this, too over it all. Now this big, muscular, so-called geologist wanted to stick him with a blade right as they had finally found their way out. The thought infuriated him. Well, he thought, I guess I'll use that anger as fuel. He ducked forward and rushed Larsen, the man's eyes widening in surprise.

Aston timed his move just right, slapped the knife aside and drove a punch up into Larsen's jaw. The man tried to dodge, made it halfway, and the blow glanced along his cheek. The impact was satisfying nonetheless and Larsen staggered backward. Aston jumped aside as the geologist brought the dagger sweeping across the gap between them, parting the front of Aston's jacket.

That was too close. He needed to finish this. Unarmed against a knife was never good odds. As Larsen swept the dagger back again, trying to gut him like a fish, Aston grabbed the man's thick wrist and whipped his other elbow into the side of Larsen's head. Larsen grunted in pain, staggered, but somehow kept his feet. The guy was one tough son of a bitch, Aston realized, and his own strength was failing. Then something else moved in the periphery of his vision and Aston instinctively ducked aside.

Slater brought a large chunk of rock swinging overhead like she was pitching a baseball, and cracked it into the top of Larsen's skull. The man staggered and went down.

"I told you to run!" Aston said.

"Yeah, well it's just as well I didn't. Looks like you needed the help."

Larsen groaned on the rocky floor of the cavern, a rivulet of blood running from his head down over one cheek and ear. Then a grin spread across his face. He pulled open his jacket to reveal a thick belt of explosives strapped around his middle.

"If I can't have this place," he said, his voice slurred by Slater's blow to the head. "Then no one will."

"Oh shit," Aston said, and he and Slater both turned and ran.

They pounded across the cavern. He saw Jen Galicia waiting wide-eyed in the mouth of the tunnel leading out, then everything vanished in a cacophony of noise and light and he felt his feet leave the ground before everything went dark.

CHAPTER 48

Aston came around to the sounds of someone making a lot of effort, grunting and swearing. A sharp pain shot through his shoulder. He groaned and looked up, saw Jen Galicia dragging him and Slater along, holding one arm of each and jerking them back in fits and starts. Tears rolled down Jen's cheeks, but judging by her expression they were tears of frustration more than anything else. The woman's strength and determination was awe-inspiring.

She saw him look up and relief washed over her. "Quickly! Help me!"

A deep, sonorous crack split the air and then a booming of rocks tumbling reverberated through the cavern.

"Hurry!" Jen shouted. "The whole place is coming down!"

Aston staggered to his feet and took Slater's other arm. Between them, one arm each, they dragged her along as rocks pounded into the passageway right behind them. Dust and speckles of glittering green swirled in the air and then the only light was Jen's weak headlamp striping the walls as she moved. Aston stopped, gathered Slater up in a proper carry, and they hurried along again. As they passed through the cavern where they had first seen the vines, the whole cave still lit by their spooky green glow, more deep cracks and creaks sounded through the rock. One dark line snaked alarmingly across the ceiling right above them, dust and stones raining down.

"Hurry," Jen said again, but it was advice Aston didn't need.

"One more cavern after this one," he said. "Then we'll be through that original door and back into the cave with the elevator, right?"

"I think so."

Jen yelled out in surprise and danced aside as a huge stalactite detached from the ceiling and shattered right where she had been heading. More groans and cracks echoed as they zigzagged to avoid the deluge of falling pointed rock, the shower of smaller stones and dust. The cavern floor heaved slightly beneath their feet, a crack racing open along their left-hand side. Head down, arms burning with the weight of Slater, Aston powered on, Jen beside him. He held Slater tight against him, relieved to feel her chest rising and falling. She might be hurt, but she wasn't dead.

As they stumbled along the last tunnel, she stirred and moaned. "Aston?"

"Nearly there," he told her.

"Put me down, I can run."

He didn't need telling twice, his arms jelly, his legs like lead. As she landed on her feet, Slater staggered a little, pressing one hand to the side of her head, and Aston and Jen reached out to steady her.

"I'm okay," she said, and the three of them pushed on, the staggering, foot-dragging run of the exhausted but determined.

"Nearly there," Aston kept repeating like a mantra, to drive them all on. "Nearly there."

The wall of the tunnel cracked like a gunshot and a spider web of dark lines spread across it. More rocks and debris rained down. Then they saw light ahead, and the perfectly rectangular outline of the doorway. Growling in determination, they drove themselves on as it suddenly tilted and tipped in on itself. Yelling a refusal to be caught now, they dove through and into the bright, artificial light of the placed halogens. The ground shook, the caverns moaned.

Thankfully the elevator car was at the bottom, waiting for them. They piled in and pounded on the button to go up. The car jerked and rattled and began to rise. A wide split arced up through the rock above the sharp edges of the door in the opposite wall and the neat stones of its construction tipped and fell into the bright cavern. The wall above it slumped, the rock crashing and booming as it splintered and fell. Aston hoped the engineering of the elevator and its shaft would hold as dust clouds billowed up from below and enveloped them, made them cough and cover their faces. The whole shaft trembled, all three of them crying out in fear, but the elevator kept moving.

It seemed to take an age, but the vibration through the rocks continued, growing ever more distant, and the air chilled as they reached the surface. The three of them turned to stare out, squinting against the incredible white brightness of the Antarctic day. Aston had never been more happy to see the sun, low on the horizon. They hurried from the elevator shaft and rumblings and groans echoed up from it. The caging and shed surrounding the mechanism shifted, then, with a screeching tearing of metal, the whole thing folded up on itself and disappeared into the ground as though it had been swallowed. The ground under them tipped as if to follow it and they ran, slipping and sliding on the ice, putting as much distance between them and the sinkhole as they could. Then everything fell still.

Aston collapsed to his knees, pressed his hands into the snow and brought some up to rub onto his face. He ate a handful, grateful for its icy freshness. Slater and Jen knelt next to him and the three of them fell into a group hug, laughing at the absurdity of it all, elated with the adrenaline of survival. Eventually, they rose and trudged across the snow, heavy-footed with tiredness, heading for the base. The front doors were open, a low drift of snow gathered inside the first corridor.

"Is it abandoned?" Slater asked.

Aston had a feeling it was rather more sinister than abandonment. "Something happened here. Something to do with Larsen and those mercenaries, I'm guessing."

As they moved cautiously deeper into the base, Slater said, "Do you think Larsen was working with someone else to scoop SynGreene's discovery?"

"Seems most likely," Aston said. "The insane greed of people messing everything up once again. People suck."

"And you think those same people came here?" Slater asked. "Cleared everyone out?"

"Maybe. If we run into more armed goons after all this, I think I'll lose my mind."

Slater paused, and Aston stopped with her. She looked meaningfully at him.

"What?" He felt uncomfortable under the intensity of her gaze.

"Well, you said about losing your mind. How... how are you?"

Aston smiled despite his discomfort. "After eating the fish? You wondering if I'm going to go Digby O'Donnell mad on you?"

Slater shrugged, eyes concerned.

"Honestly, I feel fine."

"Oh." Jen's voice was small, constricted, from a few yards ahead. "Oh no."

Aston and Slater turned to see what had caught her attention and saw her looking into the main lounge of the complex, one hand covering her mouth.

They joined her and saw the cause of her shock. The room was littered with body parts, and soaked in blood. A huge hole gaped in the far wall, and several streaks of blood went through it like bodies had been dragged that way.

Aston pointed. "More uniforms and weapons. Some more of Larsen's cohorts, I expect."

Slater nodded. "Looks like it. Three maybe? I don't know, I never was a fan of jigsaw puzzles."

Aston laughed, grateful for the break in tension. "Me either. Looks like the entire base staff are in here, too. I guess the mantics came topside for a while."

"I guess that's proof they can tolerate any brightness with enough time," Jen said.

"I guess so. Let's just hope they won't be coming back again. Hopefully, everything down there had been shut off by the caverns collapsing."

"Let's call for help quickly though," Slater said. "And wait somewhere far from here."

"How do we explain all this?" Jen asked.

Aston pursed his lips, thinking about that. "I think it's best if we don't try to. We got lost down there, separated from the others. We heard sounds of fighting, but couldn't find anyone. When we finally got back to the surface, we found all this. We have no idea what happened."

"They won't be happy with an answer like that."

Aston shrugged.

They found an office and a control center and got a distress call out to SynGreene. Arthur Greene himself, after the most cursory of explanations, promised to airlift them within hours. "Maybe it's best," he said, voice heavy with resignation, "if we abandon the entire project. At least for now. Who the bloody hell sabotaged my expedition? Don't worry, I'll find out and there'll be hell to pay! Meanwhile, I'll get you back to civilization and you'll be paid. I'm so sorry for what's happened. Can I rely on your... discretion?"

"Sure," Aston said. "You pay us well enough and we'll

pretend none of this ever happened."

"Thank you."

All three were relieved, though guilty to some degree.

"I have to explain the deaths of Jeff and Marla," Slater said, her expression pained. "I can't just ignore it all."

"I know," Aston said. "But I wanted to make sure Arthur had no qualms about getting us out. Once we're back in the civilized world we'll demand his help in dealing with all the fallout."

"If nothing else, I want him to pay some compensation to their families."

"Fair enough."

They decamped to another lounge area, far from the carnage they had discovered, and found supplies. Real food, ice cold sodas, fresh fruit. It was like a cornucopia from heaven.

While they ate, Aston described his experiences. The result of eating the fish and what had happened out over the Jade Sea.

Once he'd finished, Slater said, "So you're really okay?"

"I'm not suffering any ill effects from the connection to the Overlord, if that's what you mean," Aston said. "At least, none I'm aware of. But I really don't understand exactly what happened."

"I have a theory," Jen said, chewing thoughtfully on an apple. "It's akin to the hive minds you see in nature. In bees, for example."

"I was thinking of something similar," Aston said. "Zombie ants. But this thing is so complex, so powerful."

"It can't be that simple," Slater objected. "What Aston described sounds more like telepathy or something."

"All brain activity is a combination of chemical reactions and electrical impulses," Jen said. "What we really know about that stuff is incredibly limited. Perhaps the Overlord exudes energy on a wavelength the greenium allows people to receive? Once it's in the blood, therefore in the brain, it acts as a biological transmitter and receiver." She gave a crooked grin, shrugged. "It's just a theory. Whatever the phenomenon, it's clearly very real."

Slater shook her head, not happy with the explanations but not offering any alternatives. Aston thought Jen Galicia's ideas were as good as any. But it didn't really matter. The overriding memory he had of the whole thing was the Overlord's powerful, all-encompassing loneliness. It tore at him. Hopefully the collapse of everything down there would be an end to it. In the long run, he thought that was maybe for the best. All things should eventually die.

"Anyway," Slater said. "As long as you're okay."

"I think the effect must wear off. Perhaps you need to keep consuming it to stay attached? Long-term effects would be bad, I think. But I'm fine."

"Makes sense," Jen said. "I guess your body has processed it out by now."

Slater leaned over and kissed his cheek. "Well, with any luck it's all over. Help should be here in a few hours. Let's try to sleep in the meantime. I feel like I haven't slept for a week."

"Should we take watches?"

Aston looked around the small lounge room they were in. "Only one way in," he said, pointing at the door. He dragged a small table over to block it, then put a few water glasses and jugs on top. "We'll hear it if that goes over."

They each stretched out on a sofa, the comfort incredible after so long with nothing but cold rock beneath them.

"I'm glad it's all finally over," Slater said.

"Yeah. I need a holiday," Aston agreed. "No more adventures for a while."

They fell quiet, Jen and Slater quickly dropping into

deep sleep. Aston lay there thinking about the Overlord, wondering how long it had existed. What it really was. If it was finally over. As he drifted off, blackness stealing in from the edges of his mind, he heard a distant whispered word in his mind.

"Asssttoooooonnnn…"

THE END

BOOKS BY DAVID WOOD

The Dane Maddock Adventures
Dourado
Cibola
Quest
Icefall
Buccaneer
Atlantis
Ark
Xibalba
Loch
Solomon Key

Dane and Bones Origins
Freedom
Hell Ship
Splashdown
Dead Ice
Liberty
Electra
Amber
Justice
Treasure of the Dead

Jade Ihara Adventures (with Sean Ellis)
Oracle
Changeling
Exile

Bones Bonebrake Adventures
Primitive
The Book of Bones

Jake Crowley Adventures (with Alan Baxter)
Blood Codex
Anubis Key

Brock Stone Adventures
Arena of Souls
Track of the Beast (forthcoming)

Myrmidon Files (with Sean Ellis)
Destiny
Mystic

Sam Aston Investigations (with Alan Baxter)
Primordial
Overlord

Stand-Alone Novels
Into the Woods (with David S. Wood)
Callsign: Queen (with Jeremy Robinson)
Dark Rite (with Alan Baxter)

David Wood writing as David Debord

The Absent Gods Trilogy
The Silver Serpent
Keeper of the Mists
The Gates of Iron

The Impostor Prince (with Ryan A. Span)
Neptune's Key
The Zombie-Driven Life
You Suck

BOOKS BY ALAN BAXTER

The Alex Caine Series
Bound
Obsidian
Abduction

The Balance
RealmShift
MageSign
Omnibus Edition

The Jake Crowley Adventures
Blood Codex
Anubis Key

Sam Aston Investigations
Primordial
Overlord

Other Works
Manifest Recall
Hidden City
Crow Shine
The Book Club
Dark Rite
Ghost of the Black
The Darkest Shade of Grey
Write the Fight Right

ABOUT THE AUTHORS

David Wood is the USA Today bestselling author of the action-adventure series, The Dane Maddock Adventures, and many other works. He also writes fantasy under his David Debord pen name. When not writing, he hosts the Wood on Words podcast. David and his family live in Santa Fe, New Mexico. Visit him online at www.davidwoodweb.com.

Alan Baxter is an award-winning British-Australian author who writes dark fantasy, horror and sci-fi, rides a motorcycle and loves his dogs. He also teaches kung fu. He lives among dairy paddocks on the beautiful south coast of NSW, Australia, with his wife, son, dogs and cat. Alan has been a four-time finalist in the Aurealis Awards, a five-time finalist in the Australian Shadows Awards and a six-time finalist in the Ditmar Awards. He won the 2015 Australian Shadows Award for Best Short Story ("Shadows of the Lonely Dead"), the 2016 Australian Shadows Paul Haines Award For Long Fiction ("In Vaulted Halls Entombed"), and the 2017 Australian Shadows Award for Best Collection (Crow Shine), and is a past winner of the AHWA Short Story Competition ("It's Always the Children Who Suffer"). Read extracts from his novels, a novella and short stories at his website –www.warriorscribe.com– or find him on Twitter @AlanBaxter and Facebook, and feel free to tell him what you think. About anything.

Made in the USA
San Bernardino, CA
27 January 2019